# Dark Masterpiece

Book Three in the Serendipity Series

## Brieanna Robertson

Whimsical Publications, LLC

Florida

Published in the United States by
Whimsical Publications, LLC
Florida

www.whimsicalpublications.com

Cover art by Traci Markou

ISBN-13: 978-1-936167-03-6

Printed in the United States of America

## "I am doing this out of obligation," Traevyn finished, "not by choice."

Evie stared at him, dumbfounded. He moved quickly, making her jump, and motioned her inside. She hurried to obey, grasping Seth's wrist and hauling him in after her.

"Follow," Traevyn commanded, shutting the door.

Evie trailed behind him up a staircase, her hands shaking horribly. The entire house was full of mahogany, black leather furniture, and wrought iron. She could even see a few tapestries on the walls, but her chance to take a look was limited as she hurried after Traevyn.

He led them down a hallway to a door, which he opened. "This will be your room," he stated. "The boy can have the one across the hall. You will find it slightly less prepared as I was not expecting him." He fixed his eyes on Seth.

Seth retreated behind Evie.

"The kitchen is downstairs and the guest bathroom is at the end of the hall. If you have a problem that you can't seem to solve on your own, my room is at the far end of the *other* hall, if you make a left at the top of the stairs instead of a right. When I feel like teaching, I will find you. Otherwise, please do your best to stay out of my way." He turned and strode back down the hall, disappearing around a corner.

Evie stared, acutely aware of her own heartbeat drumming in her ears. She swallowed, her mouth dry.

"Evie!" Seth hissed. "Dude, I told you!"

She blinked and looked at him. "That was not what I expected." She poked her head in her room and turned on the light. There was a queen-sized bed with a headboard and footboard of rich oak, and a vanity made of the same. The curtains were a deep purple, as was the bedspread. On one wall hung a thick tapestry of a Celtic pattern in black and gray. "I feel like I walked into a Bronte sister novel," she whispered.

"That guy is freaky," Seth muttered.

"Seth, go get our bags," Evie demanded as she fingered the tapestry.

His eyes bulged. "Are you out of your mind? That guy probably has a dungeon and a torture chamber. If I get in his way, he'll do awful things to me!"

Evie scowled at him. "Then don't get in his way!" she muttered through clenched teeth. "Just go, Seth! I'm not going back home! This is an opportunity for my future. I don't care how much of an ogre that man is, I'm staying. Now go!"

Seth threw his hands up in the air and started to grumble incoherently as he made his way back down the hall.

Evie heaved a sigh and flopped down on the bed. Her hands were still shaking. She was good at putting on a front for Seth that she didn't care how evil Traevyn Whitelaw was, but the truth was, after that display, she had no idea how she was going to survive the next three months. This was not at all what she had expected. She'd pictured Traevyn Whitelaw as this insanely passionate, yet somehow normal man who would be patient, show her his technique, and share his life experiences with her. She had not expected a devastatingly handsome Heathcliff with no desire to have her in his home at all. The way he had spoken to her, like she was an intruder in his entire universe, made her uneasy. How was she supposed to learn anything when her teacher didn't even want her there?

Barrett deBoer's insensitive words flooded her mind and made her frown. Maybe she could just get by on her intelligence, but she doubted it. This man seemed much worse than Barrett, if that was possible. Maybe if she was some gorgeous supermodel he would have reacted differently to her presence.

She all but groaned aloud. What she had imagined was going to be an amazing experience, she was now convinced was going to suck horribly.

It was going to be a long summer.

# ACKNOWLEDGEMENTS

To those in my field who took a chance on me, encouraged me, and helped me realize my greatest dreams:
Rene Walden, JT Schultz, Traci Markou, Janet Durbin, Yvette Lynn, and Dahlia Rose.

Thanks again to "My Team," Jimmy and Phil, for providing me with such great material for Traevyn's poetry.

*Also by*
*Brieanna Robertson*

## Serendipity Series

Road Less Traveled
Better Than Chocolate
Dark Masterpiece
Paladin
Stage Presents

# Chapter One

Bullets whizzed past her head as she ran, dodging the dead Confederate soldiers and evading the cannon fire. She had to make it to the shadowy figure on the hill! It was a matter of life or death! She had to give him her art portfolio or else her cat would die of starvation and Darth Vader would force her to eat nacho cheese chips! Then she would never be able to help Luke destroy the Death Star! She ran faster. She had to make it to the shadow on the hill! *DING!*

What was that?

*DING!*

Impending doom!

"Evie!"

Evie jerked her head up from where it had been lying on the table, her study guide stuck to her cheek. "The Union slaughtered the rebels at the Battle of Gettysburg right after Traevyn Whitelaw sold his first painting to San Francisco's Museum of Modern Art, where he promptly died of the Spanish Influenza," she rattled off.

Evie's beautiful, blonde friend Meg arched an eyebrow and she reached out to pull the paper off of her face. "Is that right?"

She blinked the remaining sleep out of her eyes and touched her cheek where the drool was still cemented. She made a face and tried to wipe it off. "Man, what time is it?" she grumbled.

"It's seven-thirty. We have to be to class in a half hour. I rang your bell twice, but you weren't answering, so I just used my key," Meg replied.

Evie groaned and put her head in her hands. "Crap! I

didn't get to study for Western Traditions! I was writing my stupid Art History paper all night long!"

Meg shrugged her slender shoulders and sat down across from Evie. "You'll survive."

"No, seriously." She met Meg's eyes. "Like, I didn't study *at all*. I fell asleep right before I could."

"You know you were muttering 'Luke, I am your father' when I came in?" Meg smirked.

"I was having the weirdest dream. I was half watching *Star Wars* last night while I studied for US History. I think there was something in my dream about Vader torturing me by force-feeding me nacho cheese chips."

Meg pointed to a bag of half-eaten chips on the table. "Could these have had something to do with it?"

Evie giggled and stood, stretching out her stiff back and groaning. "I'm gonna take a quick shower. I promise to be fast." She headed toward her bedroom.

"What was your Art History paper on?" Meg called.

"I had to pick an artist and write a biography on him."

"You picked Traevyn Whitelaw, I assume?" Her voice was laden with teasing.

"Of course." Evie came back out into the living room, carrying her clean clothes. "It was ridiculous. I couldn't find anything on the guy. I couldn't even find a picture. All I found was that he lives somewhere off the coast of California and that he used to be married with a daughter, but his wife left and his daughter died in some kind of accident. So, yeah, I had to try and write a five page report on that amount of information. Luckily, I was able to find his career history, but a lot of good that did me. Thank goodness for friggin' double spaced formatting or I'd really be screwed."

"Must be a private guy."

"That's all well and good for him, but not for my Art History grade," Evie snorted.

"Hey, you're still going to that thing for my brother tonight, right?"

"Like I would miss anything that your brother was at."

Meg shook her head and rolled her eyes. "You're the only girl on the planet who has a crush on Maxim. Most girls, at least normal ones, go for Jeff."

Evie smiled as she thought of Meg's charming older brother. "Jeff's my second choice."

Meg giggled. "Get in the shower. We're going to be late."

Evie turned and headed back down the hall, nearly stumbling over her fat, gray tabby cat. He meowed promptly. She frowned. "Did I ever feed you?" He meowed again. "Meg, could you feed Leo? I think I forgot him last night." After receiving an affirmative reply from her friend, she continued on into the bathroom.

She took a fast shower and threw on a green shirt and black Capri's. She didn't have time to blow dry her blonde-streaked, brown hair so she just put it in pigtails. Then it would be wavy for later. She smiled. She had met Meg their freshman year in college, and ever since, Evie had wanted to be part of her family. She had three brothers and two of them were the closest thing to perfection Evie had ever seen. Jeff was the oldest, and he was very good-looking. He was also charming and charismatic. She liked Jeff a lot, but she had always preferred Maxim. He was quiet, shy, and intellectual, but always seemed so gentle. He was also married...which sucked, but she could still dream. Her entire life was based on dreams. Besides, she still had Jeff she could go after.

Meg's other brother, Barrett, was the only one she would not consider going after. He was also, ironically, the only one who wanted to date her. Barrett was cold and rude and not her type. As much as Evie wanted to marry into Meg's family, she would not stoop to the level of Barrett.

After donning her black-framed cat glasses, she ran back out into the living room and shoved the necessary books in her backpack.

"Ready to face the firing squad?" Meg yawned.

Evie rolled her eyes and led the way out of her apartment. It would be a miracle if she made it through the day.

* * *

By the time Evie was heading to Meg's apartment, she was exhausted. Finals had nearly done her in, and she had spent the few precious hours between class and Meg's brother's BBQ cramming for the next day's exams. It was all she could do to drag herself up the steps and knock on the door.

Meg opened the door, looking perky, as always, which Evie could never understand. She had rarely seen her friend look disheveled. Her hair was always in place, her skin always immaculate, and her blue eyes always bright. It made Evie sick. Meg was a physics major, for crying out loud. She was supposed to look nerdy and unattractive.

Meg's eyes filled with mirth as she looked at Evie, who was wearing a white sundress with pink flowers on it. Her hair was down and fell in thick waves around her shoulders. "Decided to go all out, did you?" she teased.

"Shut up. I feel like a tired old hag next to you."

Meg glanced down at her attire. "I'm wearing blue jeans. Besides, with a rack like yours, I'm sure you'll be getting more looks than me."

Evie frowned and covered her breasts self-consciously. "I would hope you wouldn't be getting looks from your brothers in the first place."

Meg laughed, grabbed her purse, and the two of them headed through the town of Ashland, Oregon to where Jeff lived. He was an attorney and, therefore, had the nicest house Evie had ever seen. Not a mansion by any standard, but next to Evie's tiny one-bedroom, it looked like a castle.

They were having the BBQ in his spacious backyard, celebrating Maxim's first published novel making the best-seller list.

Maxim deBoer. Even his name seemed magical to Evie. He was nothing short of a creative genius having just published his debut novel several months ago. She had read it, of course. It was a romance. To her, any man able to write a romance novel was amazing. This just further proved her original theory that Maxim was perfect. There was no other logical explanation.

Jeff answered the door all smiles wearing an obnoxious Hawaiian print shirt that only he could get away with. He embraced his sister, then pulled Evie in for a hug also. "Evie, I haven't seen you in forever!" he exclaimed. "How are you?"

She smiled and relished being in his arms for a moment. He felt so solid and firm, all athletic muscle, and she really liked the smell of his cologne. Yes, Jeff was definitely the next best choice. He was always so vibrant and full of exuberance. She imagined life would never be boring with him. "I'm good," she replied. "Tired from finals, but alive."

He flashed his beautiful grin and took her hand in his, bringing it up to his lips. "Well, you look ravishing." He kissed her fingers, which brought a flush to her cheeks. He winked at her. "Everyone else is in the back. Can I get you anything to drink?"

She shook her head and gave a coy smile, making her way toward the sliding glass back door. Meg was already out there talking to Barrett, who looked put out, as always. She scanned the yard and saw Maxim sitting in a deck chair over by the volleyball net. He was playing with his wife's hair as she sat next to him while they conversed with a friend. Evie heaved a sigh. Alyxandra deBoer. She wished she could hate her, but she couldn't. Alyx was gorgeous with thick, black hair and huge green eyes. She was tall and slender and full of that lithe muscle that dancers had. She also happened to be the nicest woman Evie had ever met.

As if on cue, Alyx suddenly caught sight of Evie and waved her over with a warm smile. Maxim looked over at her also and grinned, making her blush all the way to her toes. Most women would find Maxim somewhat nerdy at first glance. He had brown hair that always seemed to stick up in all directions, and he wore black-framed glasses that some-how looked stylish on him when they would look ridiculous on anyone else. Evie touched her own glasses and smiled to herself. That was something they had always had in com-mon—nearsightedness.

She let her eyes sweep appraisingly over the object of her affection as she approached and couldn't understand how anyone could see him as less than beautiful. He was just as good-looking as his flamboyant brother; he just didn't flaunt it like Jeff did.

"How are you, Evie?" Alyx asked with a smile. She stood and gave her a hug. "It's so nice you could come celebrate with all of us!"

"I wouldn't have missed it," Evie said. "Having your first novel make the best-seller list is quite an accomplishment."

Maxim gave a shy smile and waved it away as if it wasn't important.

Alyx rolled her eyes. "He's too modest. Evie, have you met our friend Javan?" She indicated the blond man she had been talking to.

"Once, I think." She shook his hand and he flashed her a bright grin. She sighed and lapsed into thought as she took a seat in one of the deck chairs. She had always adored Meg's family and the circle they ran in. Everyone was always so nice and accepting, artsy and interesting. She felt warm every time she was around them, like she belonged somewhere, not like the square peg in the round hole she felt like everywhere else.

"How has college been treating you, Evie?" Maxim's soft voice asked.

Her stomach flipped, and she turned to meet his gaze. "Good...running me ragged. You know, the usual."

"You're an art major, right?"

She nodded, impressed that he had remembered.

"You should let us see your new work sometime," Alyx said. "Maybe you could sell some paintings to my brother and spice up his boring house."

Evie grinned and glanced over to where Alyx's brother was talking to Jeff at the barbeque. They seemed to be having an argument over something that suddenly resulted in an enormous amount of flame spiraling up from the barbeque, which sent Jeff running. After a moment, he approached the grill, stunned. He glanced inside, then scowled at Alyx's brother, who was laughing. He promptly started to beat him with the spatula.

Evie laughed. Alexi Oncidezzerro—Jeff's law partner and quite a stud himself. She gave a thoughtful frown. He was tall, muscled, and handsome in a very refined sort of way... She could always go after him.

Evie had always been a geek in school, and had been made fun of and teased until college. She had never been one of those slender, blonde goddesses that all the guys went after. She was petite and voluptuous. Her waist was thin and she was not overweight, but her curves would put an hourglass to shame. Her hair was thick and dark and she liked to highlight it with blonde; she was generally pretty pleased with her hair. She imagined she was attractive, but not amazingly so. She was one of those girls everyone classified as "cute." Not beautiful, not stunning. Just "cute." She was the perfect little sister, best friend type, not the hot, steamy sex type. She had accepted this long ago, but somehow, when she was with the deBoers and their friends, she felt beautiful. And they validated her passion for art, which was something she rarely got.

Anyone pursuing the arts for a career was always looked

down upon by those pursuing *normal* careers—med students, accountants, business majors. But Maxim was a novelist and Alyx and Javan were actors for the Oregon Shakespeare Company. The arts were recognized and accepted among the deBoers.

"Evelina."

Evie bristled and was brought out of her thoughts by the cold, dead, irritating voice of Barrett deBoer. He was the only one who ever insisted on calling her by her full name. She grudgingly looked up at him and sighed. "Barrett."

He smiled as much as Barrett could smile, which actually made him look as if his face might crack at any given moment. He sat down next to her. "You haven't been to my store lately," he said. "It hurts my feelings."

She forced a smile. "Well, Barrett, I've been busy." He managed a bookstore downtown, which she avoided at all costs. Barrett was not like his fantastic family. He barely smiled and, when he did, it mostly always resembled a slithering smirk. He was cynical and cold and... Well, he was a jerk. There was no other way to put it.

"Meg has time to come in and see me," he continued, "and she's a physics major. You're just an art major and you have no time for me?"

She scowled. "Surprisingly, I have a lot that keeps me busy. Even with me being a mere, lowly art major. Besides, Meg is your sister. She's family. She has to put up with you. I, however, don't."

"Hey! Food's ready!" Jeff shouted. "Everyone come and get it!"

"Yeah, if anyone finds hair in their meat it's just Jeff's eyebrows that he singed off!" Alexi called. Laughter followed.

Evie took the opportunity given and fled, seeking refuge at the picnic table where Javan, Meg, and Alexi were already sitting. She took a seat next to Meg and did her best to flash an alluring smile at Javan and Alexi. Alexi smiled back, but Javan seemed preoccupied with heaping food onto his plate. The others started to file over and Evie realized in sudden horror that the seat on the other side of her was still empty. She met Jeff's eyes as he set the plate of hamburgers down on the table and tried to gesture for him to come and sit next to her, hoping to convey the desperation she felt.

Jeff frowned in confusion and mouthed, "What?" to her.

She tried to point to the seat next to her again without having to actually stand up and flail her arms like a flight attendant. Unfortunately, she was unsuccessful. Barrett took a seat right beside her. She heaved a sigh and flashed Jeff a disgruntled look.

Jeff finally understood what she'd been trying to say. He winced and put his hand over his heart. "Sorry," he muttered.

Evie started to serve herself, engaging Meg in conversation so she wouldn't have to talk to Barrett. Soon everyone was sitting down and laughing, sharing stories and pleasant conversation. Jeff gave a speech about Maxim's book and how proud he was of his brother, causing Maxim to turn several shades of red.

Evie listened to Javan and Alyx talk about the new play they were working on, and Jeff related embarrassing stories of Maxim. Alyx and Javan recalled humorous stories of a trip they had taken with Maxim a few years ago. These stories were classics. They were always told. Evie had heard them several times before, but she never grew tired of them. It was her greatest dream, next to being an artist, to have a close-knit group of family and friends.

Her family had never really been close. Her parents were always away on business, and she and her younger brother really had no relationship at all. Her parents had always provided for them, but they had never really been close. Not like Meg's.

"So, Evie, tell us about your painting," Jeff said suddenly. "How is it coming? Sell anything yet?"

She smiled and felt her cheeks burn with a blush. "Oh gosh, no. I'm just trying to make it through school alive. Besides, I do mostly sketches anyway."

"You're going to try and sell your things after you graduate, aren't you?" Alyx asked. "You're so talented."

Evie gave a shy smile. "I would like to make a living out of my artwork, yes."

Barrett snorted. "There is no future in being a starving artist," he muttered.

"Well Evie won't be starving," Alyx retorted. "She is much too talented to be overlooked. She'll be making millions and living in Paris while you are still scraping by on your used paperbacks."

Barrett scowled at Alyx, but Evie grinned.

"Still," Barrett said, "life shouldn't be all about work." He turned to fix his gaze on Evie. "You should get out once in awhile, have some fun." He raised a suggestive eyebrow at her.

She sighed. "I have plenty of fun, thanks."

Jeff rolled his eyes. "Barrett, why do you insist on trying to pick up on Evie? It's apparent she is not interested. Why do you continue to harass her?"

Barrett looked at Evie again and smiled. "Well, because. She's intelligent." He gave an indifferent shrug. "I mean, she's no perfect ten to look at, but her mind makes up for any physical imperfections."

Evie blinked and the table went silent.

"Barrett, you just hit your all time low," Meg muttered, flinging her fork down onto her plate in irritation.

He drew his dark brows together in a frown. "What? I think brains are much better than beauty. That was a compliment."

Evie stood and turned to look at Barrett. She smiled sweetly. "Barrett, thank you for complimenting me on my intelligence. It will make the sting of rejection easier for you to bear knowing that I used my superb judgment in doing this." She picked up her half full glass of lemonade and flung it at him. She then turned and strode away, furious tears burning behind her eyes. Javan had burst into uproarious laughter behind her over the sticky liquid dripping from Barrett's dark hair and undoubtedly bewildered face. She ignored it and continued toward the house.

"Evie!" Maxim's voice called after her. "Evie, hold on a minute."

She stopped on the deck and folded her arms as he caught up to her. She turned just enough to see Meg apparently ripping Barrett another one.

"Evie, I'm sorry about my brother," Maxim said. "He's an idiot."

She looked up into Maxim's gentle eyes and sighed. "It's all right."

"No, it's not. Look, Evie, you're beautiful. Don't let anyone ever try to tell you otherwise." His smile was soft.

Evie's heart turned over and gave a small smile. "Thanks, Maxim." She wished she could stay a little longer, but she was sick of Barrett, and she didn't feel like fighting him off all night long. Besides, she knew Maxim was only saying those things because he was nice. "Hey, I'm really tired," she said. "I think I'm going to go home."

"Please don't leave because of Barrett. He really is a complete imbecile."

A pang shot through her heart. Maxim was so sweet. Alyx was such a lucky woman. "No, I have to study for my finals tomorrow."

"Okay, well, thanks for coming."

"Of course! Congratulations on your book! Tell Meg I'll see her tomorrow. One of you can give her a lift home, right?"

He nodded and smiled as she departed.

Evie made her way through the house and to her car. She knew Barrett was a jerk, but he had still managed to destroy her evening. She knew she wasn't beautiful, but she didn't need it pointed out in front of all the people she admired the most. It was humiliating. He had embarrassed her completely. Especially since she'd been trying to flirt with basically every other single guy there.

"Ugh," she muttered to herself. "How stupid can you be, Evie? None of those guys wanted you. They've known you for years. One of them probably would have made a move by now. Such an idiot. You probably made a fool out of yourself. Get a grip."

She got in her car and started toward home. She wondered if anyone would ever think she was beautiful. She doubted it. She supposed she would have to get by on her brains and her talent... Since that was apparently all she had going for her.

# Chapter Two

Evie had never been more relieved to end a semester in all her life. She headed for the main entrance of the building the way a prisoner being set free might head for the prison exit. It had been a rough, rigorous semester and she was all too happy to put it behind her.

She stopped in the foyer and admired the huge oil painting decorating the wall. It was a Traevyn Whitelaw original. He had graduated from Southern Oregon University, and many of his paintings adorned the walls. This one was, by far, her favorite. It was entitled *Innerworkings of a Creative Soul* and it was basically an abstract of blues, purples, and black all swirling in a cauldron of chaos. Everyone interpreted it as the artist's passion, that the painting was how the artist viewed his own creativity and drive. Basically, he had so much swirling around inside of him that it was an unorganized and chaotic chasm of beauty.

Evie had always thought differently. When she looked hard at the painting, she noticed that the black shades and dark purples seemed to form abstract and contorted shapes that reminded her of a man screaming. Everyone said the painting was a reflection of passion and creation. Evie had always felt it was a reflection of the deepest kind of sorrow. She had no foundation on which to base her theory. It had always just been a feeling.

"Evie!" a jolly voice called suddenly. "Oh, I'm so glad I found you!"

She turned to see her Art History and Painting professor hurrying toward her. He had a wide grin on his round face.

"Evie," he said, "I read your paper on Traevyn Whitelaw."

Evie groaned. Great. She'd probably failed miserably.

Her professor chuckled. "No, no, it was quite good. Actually, you scored the highest grade in the class. Traevyn Whitelaw is an elusive artist to write a paper on. I was very impressed."

She arched an eyebrow. "Are you serious?"

He nodded, still grinning. "Evie, you are my most promising student. Your love for art is apparent in everything you do. As you know, I myself taught Mr. Whitelaw when he attended SOU. We have kept in touch over the years."

Evie smiled, wondering what this really had to do with anything. It was fascinating, but the thought of falling onto her bed and not moving for the next hundred years seemed much more appealing to her at the moment.

"I spoke with him at the beginning of the semester about perhaps taking one of my students over the summer as an apprentice," her professor continued. "He agreed, and I have been carefully monitoring everyone since then." He put his palms together. "I have decided it should be you, Evie."

Her eyes bulged and she was sure her jaw dropped clear to the floor. "W—what?" she squeaked.

"You have the highest grade in class, work the hardest, and it is apparent that you admire Mr. Whitelaw's work very much."

Admired? She practically worshipped the man. She had prints of his paintings everywhere in her apartment and the collector's edition of his coffee table art book. She was obsessed with him. His work was beautiful and vibrant, full of deep meaning and symbolism. In her opinion, he was the greatest artist of all time, hands down. She blinked slowly, having trouble comprehending what Professor Roth had just said. "Y—you want me to be his...apprentice?"

He nodded. "You would live with him for the summer and learn from the master himself."

She could barely breathe. Her? Live with and learn from Traevyn Whitelaw all summer? Just the thought made her dizzy. She shook her head. "Professor, I—I don't know what to say."

"Say you'll go," he urged.

She nodded vigorously. Like she would ever pass up that opportunity!

"Excellent. You leave in two weeks. I will be contacting

you with directions and a list of things you'll need to take with you. Congratulations, Evie, you deserve it."

With that, he turned and left her standing there, still completely dazed. It would take her awhile to wrap her mind around this one. Traevyn Whitelaw...

A slow smile spread across her lips. She bet he was magnificent, full of life and beauty. She turned and all but fled out the door, wanting to go tell Meg as soon as possible. Starving artist her butt. Barret could stick this in his pipe and choke on it.

* * *

*Two weeks later*

Evie was beyond irritated. She had been driving for hours, gotten lost three times and, to top it all off, she had her annoying seventeen-year-old brother popping gum in the passenger's seat. She scowled at nothing as her fingers gripped the wheel tighter.

Her brother heaved a dramatic sigh. "Seriously, Evie, just let me go back home. Why do I have to come on this lame trip with you?"

"For the last time, Seth, Mom and Dad are going to be gone all summer and there's no one to watch you."

"I'm seventeen!" he cried. "I don't need a friggin' babysitter! Why couldn't you just leave me at home?"

Evie met his eyes for a moment. "Need I remind you of the last time you were left alone? Mom and Dad came back early and found two of your friends having sex in their bed while another lit up a joint in the bathroom!"

Seth huffed. "Is that going to be held against me forever? At least I wasn't doing that stuff!"

She rolled her eyes. "No, you were drunk and passed out on the sofa. Look, I'm not too thrilled about having to tote you around either. This is my chance to work with the greatest artist of all time, and I have to bring my little brother along! I'm not jumping for joy here, but Mom and Dad had no one else. I called my professor and he said it should be fine if you come with me. I have no other option and neither do you so shut up and help me look for this turnoff."

Seth sat back with an agitated scowl. Evie sighed. She

was not happy about her parents dumping her brother on her at the last minute. This was the chance of a lifetime. The last thing she needed was Seth hanging around all the time. He was a moody teenager. He would just be an annoyance. She glanced at him with his bleach-blond hair and leather jacket. He looked like Billy Idol. She was sure that would make a great impression. *"Please, Evie, you're our only hope."* Why did she always fall for that? She was sure there had to be somebody, *anybody else* who could have taken Seth. Yet, here she was, stuck with him all summer. It figured.

She guided her car down the winding coastal highway and turned onto the remote dirt road that was practically non-existent. They were somewhere in Big Sur, hours and hours away from Ashland. She felt like she had been driving for eons and the last portion of it had been on Highway 1, which was only a two-lane highway right next to the ocean that twisted and curved for miles. She had been battling Seth for control of the radio for half the journey, and he had appealed to her about five times to let him go back home. She just wanted to get where she needed to go so she could be away from her brother and away from the road.

The road took her down toward the cliffs overlooking the ocean, and the trees began to get denser and more foreboding-looking, their thick branches jutting out in awkward positions that looked like gnarled fingers. Wisps of fog slithered through the branches like serpents and Evie suddenly felt like she had ventured into a horror movie. She continued to drive, the fog getting thicker as she went along.

"Dude, Evie, this is kind of creeping me out," Seth muttered.

Evie rolled her eyes. "It's just fog." But she did have to admit, everything felt dark and ominous.

Without warning, the road widened out and an enormous, Gothic-looking house came into view. Evie gasped in surprise and slowed the car to a stop as she stared at the structure. It was nestled in a grove of eucalyptus trees, sitting like a lonely sentinel. The architecture much resembled that of a sixteenth-century manor and she briefly felt like she'd traveled through time.

"Holy crap," Seth said. "What kind of guy is this? A friggin' warlock or something?"

Evie shook her head to regain her senses and unbuckled her seatbelt. "Come on, he's an artist. It makes sense that his home would be artistic." But she couldn't shake the feeling that there was something horribly lonely and tormented emanating from the dark edifice.

She got out of the car and started toward the front door, shivering as the eerie ocean breeze blew gently across her skin. She heard the forlorn cry of a seagull as she approached and, behind it, the rhythmic pounding of the ocean waves. The breeze rustled through the leaves of the eucalyptus grove. Evie had to take a deep breath to calm her nerves before she knocked on the heavy oak door.

"Seriously, Evie, let me go home," Seth whispered, stuffing his hands in his jacket pockets. "I can hitchhike, or take a bus, or something. If you want to stay here in Edgar Alan Poe land, that's cool, but I'd rather not if you don't mind."

Evie scowled and shushed him just as the door swung open. She raised herself taller and prepared a smile, but it promptly faded upon seeing the man in front of her.

He was very tall and had thick, black hair that fell in shining strands all the way to his waist. His hair alone made her stop and marvel. She had never seen such long hair on a man. At least not on a man who wasn't a sleazy old biker, or a Native American. Then again, maybe he was Native American... She wouldn't know... And his hair wasn't frizzy and scary like those eighties rockers. It was shining ebony that looked like silk.

"Can I help you?" he queried.

Evie opened her mouth, but nothing came out. He was absolutely breathtakingly...beautiful. Beautiful like art, like the covers of fantasy books with the rugged, manly, yet gorgeous hero. His features were harsh, all hard lines and sharp angles, undeniably masculine, but there was a strange, elegant beauty around his sensual lips and light green eyes that made Evie feel like she was looking at a living masterpiece.

Seth cleared his throat discreetly, which brought Evie out of her stupor, and she gave a nervous cough. "Excuse me, I am looking for Traevyn Whitelaw," she murmured.

His facial expression remained impassive, and he merely shifted his weight in a lazy manner. It was a languid movement, like a jungle cat stretching. He sighed. "And you are?"

"Um...I—I'm Evelina Austin," she stammered. "I'm—uh—

supposed to be studying with Mr. Whitelaw for the summer...
As his apprentice."

His pale eyes seemed to look her over for a moment before they fixed on her own. "I am Traevyn Whitelaw," he stated.

She swallowed.

"Who is your companion?"

"Oh, this is my brother, Seth." She flashed a nervous smile. "My parents dumped him on me last minute. There was no one else to watch him all summer. I called Professor Roth and he told me it should be okay if I brought him with me."

His dark eyebrows drew together and he stood up straight. "Oh he did, did he?"

It was almost a snarl. Evie retreated a step as his presence seemed to suddenly fill the entire world.

"It is most certainly *not* okay," he spat, his voice a menacing growl. "Let me make one thing perfectly clear to you, Miss Austin. This apprenticeship program was not my idea or my doing. Professor Roth approached me with it, and it was out of respect and gratitude for him that I reluctantly accepted. If not for him, I would never have made it to where I am now. So, yes, you will be my apprentice. I will teach; you will learn what you will. What you do with that knowledge is entirely up to you. It is not any fault of mine if you fall flat on your face in your desired career. Professor Roth recommended you, so you must have some talent, but I want to get one thing straight, Miss Austin. I have better things to do than entertain a starry-eyed college student and her delinquent brother."

Seth frowned. "Hey," he protested.

"I am doing this out of obligation," Traevyn finished, "not by choice."

Evie stared at him, dumbfounded. He moved quickly, making her jump, and motioned her inside. She hurried to obey, grasping Seth's wrist and hauling him in after her.

"Follow," Traevyn commanded, shutting the door.

Evie trailed behind him up a staircase, her hands shaking horribly. The entire house was full of mahogany, black leather furniture, and wrought iron. She could even see a few tapestries on the walls, but her chance to take a look was limited as she hurried after Traevyn.

He led them down a hallway to a door, which he opened. "This will be your room," he stated. "The boy can have the one across the hall. You will find it slightly less prepared as I was not expecting him." He fixed his eyes on Seth.

Seth retreated behind Evie.

"The kitchen is downstairs and the guest bathroom is at the end of the hall. If you have a problem that you can't seem to solve on your own, my room is at the far end of the *other* hall, if you make a left at the top of the stairs instead of a right. When I feel like teaching, I will find you. Otherwise, please do your best to stay out of my way." He turned and strode back down the hall, disappearing around a corner.

Evie stared, acutely aware of her own heartbeat drumming in her ears. She swallowed, her mouth dry.

"Evie!" Seth hissed. "Dude, I told you!"

She blinked and looked at him. "That was not what I expected." She poked her head in her room and turned on the light. There was a queen-sized bed with a headboard and footboard of rich oak, and a vanity made of the same. The curtains were a deep purple, as was the bedspread. On one wall hung a thick tapestry of a Celtic pattern in black and gray. "I feel like I walked into a Bronte sister novel," she whispered.

"That guy is freaky," Seth muttered.

"Seth, go get our bags," Evie demanded as she fingered the tapestry.

His eyes bulged. "Are you out of your mind? That guy probably has a dungeon and a torture chamber. If I get in his way, he'll do awful things to me!"

Evie scowled at him. "Then don't get in his way!" she muttered through clenched teeth. "Just go, Seth! I'm not going back home! This is an opportunity for my future. I don't care how much of an ogre that man is, I'm staying. Now go!"

Seth threw his hands up in the air and started to grumble incoherently as he made his way back down the hall.

Evie heaved a sigh and flopped down on the bed. Her hands were still shaking. She was good at putting on a front for Seth that she didn't care how evil Traevyn Whitelaw was, but the truth was, after that display, she had no idea how she was going to survive the next three months. This was not at all what she had expected. She'd pictured Traevyn Whitelaw as this insanely passionate, yet somehow normal man who would be patient, show her his technique, and share his life experiences with her. She had not expected a devastatingly handsome Heathcliff with no desire to have her in his home at all. The way he had spoken to her, like she was an intruder in his entire universe, made her uneasy. How was she supposed to learn anything when her teacher didn't even want her there?

Barrett deBoer's insensitive words flooded her mind and made her frown. Maybe she could just get by on her intelligence, but she doubted it. This man seemed much worse than Barrett, if that was possible. Maybe if she was some gorgeous supermodel he would have reacted differently to her presence.

She all but groaned aloud. What she had imagined was going to be an amazing experience, she was now convinced was going to suck horribly.

It was going to be a long summer.

# Chapter Three

Evie had never in her whole life felt a week drag on long-er than the past one had. She had barely even glimpsed Traevyn Whitelaw since their first rather brutal meeting. When she had, he had only offered a curt nod. It was getting old. She and Seth had driven thirty minutes every night to eat at the same pizza parlor in Monterey because they were afraid to even venture into the kitchen. The rest of the time they had been living off of snack cakes and toaster pastries. Not once had Traevyn come to see if they were all right, needed anything, or if they were even still there.

There was never any noise in the house. It was so silent it was eerie, and the chilling fog that encompassed it in the morning and evening made everything seem gloomy. All of the floors on the upper story were hardwood, which made everything colder when the fog came in. Half the time Evie was sitting in bed, huddled under a pile of blankets. No one could have convinced her that it was summer if she hadn't known any better. She felt more like she was in a prison than in a famous artist's home.

A knock sounded on Evie's door as she attempted to sketch something and she called for Seth to come in. She knew it was him. Who else would it be? He opened the door, then shut it with a note of irritation. Evie looked up to see him standing there with a withered expression on his face.

"This sucks," he announced.

She arched an eyebrow.

"Seriously, I have watched so many dumb reality shows on MTV and so many re-runs of *Full House* that I think my head is going to explode. I go to sleep at night and have dreams of Uncle Jesse."

Evie smiled as her brother came to sit on the end of her bed. Considering they had not had any other human contact for the past week, they were getting along rather well. Most of the time they watched television in Seth's room. When they couldn't take any more of that, they usually resorted to playing card games and *I Spy*. It had gotten that bad. "Hey, at least you have a TV," she reminded him. "When I can't stand your company anymore I have to come in here and stare at the walls."

He rolled his eyes.

Evie giggled.

"Why are we even still here?" he asked. "It's obvious that guy doesn't give a crap whether we're here or not. Come on, Evie, we're going to die of starvation soon. I am sick of eating pizza. We've been eating it every night for seven straight days because it's all we can afford. Sooner or later, our money is going to run out and then we won't even be able to get home! I mean, has he even come to talk about painting?"

She sighed. "No. The most I've received is a Neanderthal-like grunt."

Seth sighed as well and ran his fingers through his short hair. "Please, Evie, let's just go home. This sucks so major."

She thought for a moment. Seth had a point. It was apparent that Traevyn had no intention of ever even acknowledging their presence. It irritated her. She'd had to quit her job to come on this trip. Meg was taking care of her cat, and her parents were paying her rent—paybacks for springing Seth on her at the last minute. She should at least be getting money for being there if she wasn't getting anything else. What Seth said about running out of funds was true. If they kept going at the rate they were, they wouldn't only be broke, but fat and pimply and probably sweating pizza sauce.

She smiled. "I have an idea."

He frowned.

"This will either give us some money, or change his attitude." She stood with a smirk and headed for the door. "Either way, it'll improve our current situation. I'm going to go find our dungeon master."

Seth snorted. "Good luck. If you die, I get your car."

Evie strode down the dark hall with its wrought iron candle sconces and made her way to where the staircase met the top floor. Branching off the other direction from it was another hallway, *his* hallway. She squared her shoulders, raised her chin in a determined fashion and plunged ahead, wondering where in the heck she was even going to find him. His house was only about the size of a small country.

She opened the first door that she came across, which was an office filled with so many books that she had to stop and stare. She stepped forward with caution, forgetting her purpose. She was drawn to the many works before her. Charles Dickens, Victor Hugo, John Steinbeck, and so many others. She ran her finger gently along a row of them. Well, he was a well-read ogre. Too bad he didn't have a book on manners somewhere. Her fingers grazed the spine of a book that was worn and frayed. She frowned and peered at the title. *Shakespeare's Sonnets*. She smiled and pulled it out, flipping through some of the pages. Many were dog-eared. This book had apparently been read many times.

"Taking up snooping, are we?"

Evie jumped and whirled, dropping the book.

Traevyn stood in the doorway, regarding her with his piercing green eyes. He strode forward and picked up the book. He snapped it shut with a scowl and placed it back in the shelf, trailing his fingers across the spine in almost a caress.

She took a deep breath and tried to calm the pounding of her heart that his unexpected entrance had caused. "Mr. Whitelaw," she began, sounding much braver than she currently felt. "I have a proposition for you."

He turned with a frown and folded his arms. "Do you?"

She nodded. "I want to clean your house."

He blinked, his frown growing deeper. "You want to clean my house?"

She nodded again. "I had to quit my job to come here and my funds are limited, being as I am a 'starry-eyed college student.' My brother and I have been living off of pizza, oatmeal pies, and cream cakes for the past seven days. If we are to continue in this fine fashion, I will need compensation."

His expression never changed. He just stared at her. "And how much do you charge for your services?" he asked, his voice laced with edgy mockery.

She ignored his tone and folded her arms, mirroring his posture. "Twenty an hour, once a week."

He arched an eyebrow. "Twenty an hour, you say?"

She crossed her arms over her chest. "Perhaps that's too steep for a famous artist living in a Gothic mansion. What do you think?"

His eyes narrowed. "I think you have a lot of nerve coming in here, looking through my things, and running your mouth." His voice resembled the warning growl of a large animal.

She met his unrelenting gaze. Her apprehension of him was quickly dissipating and turning into great irritation. "That's funny. I think you have a lot of nerve treating me and my brother the way you have. Did you think if you ignored us we would just go away?"

His shrug was flippant. "I was hoping."

She shook her head, not believing what she was hearing. "Then why did you even say yes to Professor Roth when he asked you to do this? Did he hold a gun to your head? The last time I checked, we lived in America where we had free will and the power to say no."

He heaved a sigh, as if it was taking great patience just to talk to her. "I am doing this as a favor to Professor Roth. Out of gratitude."

"You're saying thank you by being an ass? Wow, I guess my parents were sick the day they were supposed to teach me that life lesson. I mean, correct me if I'm wrong here, but that entire thing just seems slightly contradictory to me."

He shrugged again with indifference. "No one asked you what you thought."

She stared at him for a minute. The rage she had felt at Barrett right before she had drenched him in lemonade rose inside of her like magma. "You know something?" she said through clenched teeth. "I was so excited when Professor Roth told me about this trip. I thought that meeting you would be such an amazing experience, but I don't even care anymore. As far as I'm concerned, you can take your bad attitude and your sullenness and shove it where the sun doesn't shine!" She put her hands on her hips, her blood feeling like it was boiling in her veins. "I am sure my brother has better things he could be doing than watching TV in his prison cell, and I *know* I have better things to do. So, thank you, Mr. Whitelaw. It's been *so* invigorating." She turned to leave.

"You mean you don't want me to teach you your craft?"

he drawled after her.

She spun, and glared at him with defiance. "I don't need you to teach me my craft. I *know* my craft. I'll be an artist with or without your help. Besides, I don't see a whole lot of teaching going on around here anyway. Unless, of course, you're trying to teach me how to be a Grade A prick, because, in that case, you're doing wonderfully!" She blazed down the hall, fuming. The nerve. The outright gall of that arrogant, no-good— "Seth!" she shouted, barreling into her room. "Come on! Pack your stuff! I am not staying here one more second!"

Seth's eyes brightened and he leapt off Evie's bed. "Seriously? Alright! Finally!" He ran out of the room and back into his own.

Evie threw her suitcase on the bed and started to shove random stuff into it. She couldn't believe the audacity of that man. To act like she was the one to blame for all this! Like she forced her way into his home and took over or something! It was ridiculous. She let out a frustrated growl as she remembered the way his light green eyes had regarded her. As if she was inferior. Screw that. Apparently, her admiration for him stopped at his paintings. "What a friggin' turd!" she exclaimed.

With a scowl, she turned to search for her sketchpad. She screamed when she saw Traevyn's figure looming in the doorway. Good lord! Where had he even come from? She put her hand over her wildly pounding heart. "What, are you a ninja or something?" she cried. "Make some noise the next time you decide to sneak around!" Her eyes narrowed. "I'm leaving, all right? You don't have to stand guard."

He sighed and clasped his hands behind his back. "Twenty an hour, once a week," he stated. When she paused from her erratic slinging of clothing into her suitcase, he met her eyes. "Twenty-five if you can figure out what to do with the items in my refrigerator every evening."

She stared at him, raising herself to her full height in an attempt to make herself feel as less like a midget as possible next to his towering frame. She regarded him for a moment. His face was impassive. He waited for her answer patiently, and she noticed something in his eyes as he stood there. Something sad. Something lonely... It did a funny thing to her heart, and she felt her anger melt. She nodded slowly.

"Deal."

He gave a curt nod. "Bring your portfolio to me later tonight. I'd like to look at it." He turned abruptly on his heel and strode from the room.

Evie sighed and slumped down on the foot of her bed. Her head started to hurt. What was that? What had she seen buried so deep within his eyes? It troubled her and she had no idea why. She let out an irritated snort and shook her head. "Seth!" she shouted. "Never mind! We're staying!"

"What?" he screeched from the other room. "Oh, no way!"

She lay back on the bed and stared up at the ceiling. Well, at least she had access to the kitchen now. That was a definite plus.

"Evie!" Seth cried, flying into the room. "Come on!"

She sat up with a triumphant grin. "Fear not, little brother. I just got me a job. Our dungeon master is paying me twenty-five dollars an hour to clean his house once a week and make dinner every night."

Seth frowned and folded his arms. "You come on this trip to be an apprentice painter and end up being a housekeeper? That's degrading, Evie."

Her eyes widened. "Excuse me? Do I see you rolling in the Benjamins right now? You want to keep eating cold toaster pastries? 'Cause I sure don't."

"Fine, but still. I mean, what gives him the right to treat you like a servant when he's the one who volunteered to take on an apprentice in the first place?"

She shrugged. "Who cares? Don't worry about staying out of his way either. You want to watch TV in the living room? Go for it. You want to play your guitar? Do it. You can sit in the middle of the hall and holler like Tarzan for all I care. If we have to live here for three months, you can bet we're not going to do it like captives. He knew what he was signing on for. Let him deal with it."

Seth smiled. "No more *Full House*?"

"Not unless you *want* to keep having dreams about Uncle Jesse."

"Well, he is a hottie."

Evie laughed.

Seth chuckled and sat down on the bed next to her. "What if he gets all bent out of shape and yells at me or something?"

She snorted. "He'd better not even try it." She grabbed her portfolio and started to sift through her sketches, trying to decide which ones she should show the Master of the House later that night.

* * *

Her pictures never changed. Pictures never did. They were meant to capture the feelings and sights of a specific event or time. They remained unchanging, locked within their perfection. And, try as he might, he could not help but lapse back into the emotions of old every time he looked at them. He didn't know why he tortured himself so much. He was a masochist.

With a heavy, weary sigh, he set the pictures aside and went to the French doors in his office. He could see the ocean crashing against the nearby cliffs and wanted suddenly, more than anything, to hear the thunderous sound. He pushed open the doors and stepped out onto the terrace, embracing the evening fog as it coiled around him. He closed his eyes and listened to the pounding waves, surging forward like the emotions in his soul and crashing against the cliffs in a violent crescendo. A fleeting moment of peace stole into his heart, and he wrapped his fingers around the cold, black iron of the railing. He relished the brief moment of tranquility and the sound of the sea.

It was the only thing that ever brought him solace.

Traevyn's chaotic thoughts briefly touched on the young artist in his guest room and the way she had spoken to him earlier. He had to admit, it had come as a surprise, the way she had lashed out at him. She was so small and looked so studious. He had not expected her to hold a powder keg within her. Especially since she had barely made a peep all week.

He sighed, cursing himself yet again for allowing Professor Roth to talk him into this whole foolish apprenticeship idea. He had been a recluse for the past two years, unwilling and not desiring to share the company of others. Now he was thrown a fire-breathing art student and an added teenage boy and was expected to act as a perfect host? He had to have been out of his mind to agree to this. And it would have been nice if Professor Roth had asked *him* first before he'd told Evelina that it was all right for her to bring her brother along.

It was true that he didn't want them there. He had grown to not care for people and to hate intrusion. He felt as if they were invading his privacy, his way of life. However, as much as he hated to admit it, she'd had a point. He had been the one to accept the position. It was his own fault they were there. She was not the one to blame. She was a stranger. She didn't know him at all. She had not expected any of this.

He shoved a hand through his hair in agitation. Had he really lost all traces of humanity? What was he turning into? The troll on the bridge? Was he going to start eating goats soon? He sighed again and turned to go back inside. Well, if nothing else, he would get dinner out of the whole deal. That was the only advantage as far as he could see.

# Chapter Four

Evie's stomach rumbled at the smell of her own supper. She hadn't had much to work with, but she had found enough ingredients to make spaghetti. It wasn't gourmet cuisine by any standards, but it was better than pizza and cream cakes.

Seth wandered into the kitchen and grinned at her. "It smells so good in here." He groaned. "It's killing me."

She smiled in return and began to set the table. "It's a miracle I was able to make anything at all. I'm thinking this guy must eat bugs and rats or something because this kitchen is barren. The Sahara Desert has more food than this man does." She set the spaghetti noodles, sauce, and garlic bread in the middle of the table and brushed off her hands.

It was a beautiful kitchen, now that she'd had time to actually look at it. It was large with plenty of counter space and an island for added room. All of the counter tops were black marble, and the dining room was off to the left in front of a large window draped in heavy burgundy curtains. Evie imagined she probably could have put at least three fourths of her apartment in the kitchen alone.

"Seth, go find him," she commanded.

Seth's eyebrows shot up in the air. "Are you completely out of your mind?"

She shook her head. "No, we have to let him know dinner's ready somehow."

He snorted and sat back in his chair. "You go find him. There is no way I'm wandering around this freaky house trying to find that freaky guy. It's just not happening."

Evie heaved a sigh and put her hands on her hips.

"Seth—"

"No way!" he cried. "It's not happening! There's a Chinese gong in the corner of the living room. Why don't you use that?"

She frowned, then a slow smile spread across her lips. She felt a devilish glint come to light in her eyes. "While I think having a Chinese gong hanging out in your living room is rather strange, it could be used to our advantage." She strode with purpose toward the living room.

Seth almost fell out of his chair trying to jump up and run after her. "Evie!" he exclaimed. "You're not serious! Are you trying to piss this guy off?"

Evie located the gong. She picked up the mallet and flashed Seth an evil grin.

"Holy crap," he pleaded, looking genuinely pained. "Seriously, don't."

She pulled her arm back, then let it fly. Seth clapped his hands over his ears as the sound reverberated through the silent house so loud that the walls seemed to shake.

"Dinner's ready!" Evie shouted at the top of her lungs.

Seth winced. "You're going to get us killed," he grumbled.

She snorted. "Whatever. If that windbag thinks I'm going to make this easy on him, he's got another thing coming." She turned and headed back into the kitchen where she sat down and started dishing up her own plate.

Within seconds, Traevyn strode into the kitchen, a black scowl darkening his handsome face. He opened his mouth to speak, but Evie stood and shoved a plate in his hands. "I need you to give me money to go grocery shopping tomorrow unless you plan on me making something out of the moldy cheese. I will also need access to a computer so I can find out where the nearest grocery store is. I'm sure there's one in Monterey, but I'm not sure where as Seth and I have only ever seen the pizza parlor. Whether you wish to eat at the table with Seth and me is completely up to you, but we will not dine in the basement like common servants, if that was your idea. You can choose our company or not. It really doesn't matter to me."

He stared at her for a moment, saying nothing.

"Dinner will be served at seven o'clock every night. If you're not here, I will continue to use the gong method. If the gong method irritates you, I would suggest being here on time." She sat down and continued to eat without pause, as if she was a teacher instructing her hundredth student.

He stared at her for a moment longer, his scowl even blacker than before. After a few moments of her being almost positive that he was going to slay her with his eyes alone, he disappeared into the living room briefly, reappeared, threw two one hundred dollar bills on the table, loaded up his plate, and left.

Evie frowned as he walked away. "Well you're welcome!" she shouted after him. She took the money and shoved it in her pocket. "Jerk."

Seth started to chuckle and Evie couldn't help but grin. She had pulled that off better than she ever would have given herself credit for.

"You've got more balls than any guy I've ever met," Seth said.

She laughed and ate the rest of her meal in silence, thinking about and dreading how she had to take her portfolio to Traevyn later for his inspection. He was so rude. He would probably laugh at her and tell her she sucked. It was nerve-wracking just to think about. Regardless of his personal demeanor, she still admired his talent.

Seth helped Evie clean up after dinner, which greatly surprised her. She and her brother had always had a pretty typical sister/brother relationship. They didn't really have much in common. Seth liked video games and heavy metal music. He was your average rebellious, mouthy, lazy, seventeen-year-old boy. Evie was an artist. She loved anything beautiful. She was fascinated by color and shape. She also loved poetry and theatre. Those things were lost on Seth.

For their entire childhood Seth had always found a way to weasel out of chores and stick Evie with them. The fact that he had helped her clean up instead of rushing back to the game console he had brought along made her wonder if he was feeling alright.

After the kitchen had been picked up, Evie returned to her room, a cold lump of dread quickly forming in her stomach. She took her portfolio, which she had arranged three times, and clutched it in her hands. She squeezed her eyes shut and tried to will her courage to come back. Sure, she was brave beating a gong and demanding money, but showing her life to the Lord of the Dark Tower was a completely different story. She was vulnerable when it came to her work and, whether he was heinous or not, he was still the greatest artist of all time. She knew he could slay her with one unkind word and that thought terrified her.

She took a deep breath and forced herself to start down the hall. She would get nowhere standing in her room. Once she reached his hallway, she stopped, trying to steel herself again. She didn't even know where he was. She hated that she had to go looking for him. It was annoying. If he wanted to see her portfolio, why couldn't he come and find her?

She headed down the hall and stopped at his office again. The door was half open and an amber glow was coming from the room, casting a misshapen shadow on the floor of the hall. She frowned and peered in a little. She blinked in surprise and couldn't help but stare. Traevyn was sitting in a brown leather chair reading a thick book by candle light. His ebony hair fell all around him like a blanket, and the light cast intriguing shadows across his face. It highlighted the dramatic lines and shaded the hollows, making him look even more menacing, and yet, very sensual somehow. He reminded her of a medieval knight sitting in his castle. She swallowed and suddenly found it difficult to breathe. He was magnificent...

She shook her head and forced air into her lungs. What in the heck was she doing? Had she lost it? She raised her hand to the door and knocked lightly.

"Yes?" his erotic voice called.

Evie shivered, then frowned. Good lord, what was wrong with her? She surely hadn't thought his voice was erotic earlier when he had been snarling at her. The man was a nightmare. Why was she marveling at his beauty and shivering at the sound of his voice? She opened the door with caution and stepped in, clinging to her portfolio like a lifeline. "I'm sorry if I'm intruding," she murmured.

He glanced up at her and arched an eyebrow. "A little late for courtesy, don't you think, gong mistress?"

She cracked a smile and thought she might have seen the slightest twinge around his lips as well. "Why are you reading in the dark?" she queried.

"I prefer candle light to electric. Electric is harsh and false. It hurts my eyes at times."

She raised an eyebrow. "Can you go out in daylight? I

mean, you don't, like, turn to dust or anything?"

He heaved a sigh and closed his book, meeting her eyes. "Do you have a purpose in being here, Miss Austin?"

She smiled in amusement. She couldn't help it. She nodded. "You told me to bring you my portfolio."

He nodded. "Let's go into my studio." He stood and started toward her. "Also, you may use the computer in this room for whatever you need." He brushed past her and continued down the hall.

Evie followed. Her hands shook and she hated herself for it. Traevyn led her into the room across the hall. He turned the light on to reveal a room choc full of canvas, paints of all sorts, and any art supply anyone would ever need. It was a disaster, chaotic and disorganized. It made Evie smile. It looked just like her art room.

Traevyn hastily pushed aside the random papers, paints, and charcoal pencils on his desk to clear a spot. He held his hand out to Evie. "Let me see it," he demanded.

She hesitated a moment, then held it out to him gingerly. He took it and opened it, beginning to study the first piece. Evie couldn't watch. She turned and began to look around at the paintings in the room. Many were in various stages of being finished. She marveled over his use of color and how his paintings were so vivid. Even the dark ones seemed to resonate with life, like he had managed to capture his very soul and the canvas was actually living and breathing. She made a slow circle around the room, losing all concept of time. She wished she could just walk into one of his paintings and never come out. Each one looked like a doorway to a fantastic and magical world.

At the far end of the room was the painting that hung in the SOU foyer. She stopped in front of it and sighed. "I love this painting."

She saw him glance over at her out of the corner of her eye. "The chaotic cauldron of my creative drive?" he said, his voice flat.

She wrinkled her nose and frowned. "I never saw that. No matter what my teachers tried to tell me. I mean, art is supposed to be open to interpretation, right? I always saw something different."

"Oh really? And what did you see?"

"I don't know. To me, it always looked like a man

screaming." She shrugged and ignored the fact that he sounded highly skeptical and almost sarcastic.

His head jerked up and he stared at her.

"Everyone's always said it's a reflection of passion, but it never looked like passion to me. Why would you choose such dark shades to portray passion?"

He made a slow turn in his chair and placed his hand over his chest, as if his heart was beating strangely. "What do you think it represents then?" he asked, his voice hushed.

"Torture, torment, the worst kind of pain and sorrow. I mean, the way the black shades swirl together here, they form a distinct shape. I don't understand why no one can see that." She shrugged and looked down, suddenly realizing what she was saying and feeling stupid. He probably thought she sounded like an idiot. Here she was, a junior art student, contradicting what people who were much more proficient than her claimed. She turned back around and was surprised to see him staring at her with an intensity she found more than unnerving. She averted her eyes and stuffed her hands in her pockets, rounding her shoulders in the way a shy little kid on the playground did. "What?"

He dropped his gaze back to her drawing, and clenched and unclenched his fists a couple times. He cleared his throat. "Nothing," he rasped. He shook his head. "There is no denying that you are very skilled. You have a unique style that should make your work stand out. I do notice that you have more pencil sketches than anything else. Why is that?"

She looked away. "Painting intimidates me," she murmured.

"Why? The paintings you have in here are quite good. Who are your influences?"

"You, mainly." She gave a meager smile.

He cast her a brief glance, but said nothing. "We will have to work on this strange fear you have of canvas and paint. Leave this here. As you will be working in here, it would be ridiculous for you to have to keep toting it back and forth." He stood. "I cannot give you a set time as to when we will work. I work when inspiration comes and no sooner. However, when you wish to work, you do not have to ask my permission. Come in here whenever you like, but leave your projects so I can see them in their various stages. I will do the same for you."

She nodded and followed him back out into the hall.

"Goodnight to you," he said.

She turned down the hall, her fingers still toying with her belt loops nervously.

"Miss Austin," he called.

She turned back to look at him.

He hesitated. "You were right."

"About what?"

"My painting." He looked down for a moment before meeting her eyes again. "No one's ever understood it. No one's ever seen it."

"Seen what?" She didn't quite understand what he was talking about.

His pale eyes fixed on hers. "The screaming man. The one in pain. No one's ever seen it until...you. Until tonight."

Her eyes widened. "You mean...?"

"Hundreds of people claiming to be art connoisseurs, art teachers, other artists. None of them saw. You did."

She stared at him in shock and awe. She opened her mouth to speak, but she couldn't. She had been right about that painting? When everyone else much more experienced than her had said something different? She shook her head. "Mr. Whitelaw, I—"

"Goodnight, Miss Austin." He turned and strode up the hall, disappearing into the room at the far end and closing the door. She stood there in stunned silence for a long while before turning mechanically and walking back to her bedroom, trying desperately to process what had just occurred.

# *Chapter Five*

Evie was going to die. She was sure of it. How did people clean houses for a living? She had already been cleaning for seven hours. That was an entire day of work. Her back was screaming at her. Luckily, she only had Traevyn's wing left to do. His office, bedroom, and bathroom. She had been given strict instructions not to touch the studio, which she could understand.

When she'd lived at home, her parents had always been irritated at her cluttered mess of art supplies and had always cleaned and organized it while she was at school. She'd hated it. It would take her a week just to figure out where everything was. For the most part, creative people were organized in a very disorganized way, and she knew that Traevyn probably had a system that she didn't want to mess with.

With a heavy sigh, Evie faced the hallway and lugged her tote of cleaning supplies with her. She was greatly surprised as to how many rooms the house actually had. She had been unaware of the fact that there was an entire basement until that morning. There was a den in it, as well as a wine cellar and another bathroom. The basement was darker than the rest of the house, which was hard for her to believe, and it creeped her out. Though outward appearances suggested it was a room like any other, it really did remind Evie of a dungeon.

The rest of the house had been pretty self explanatory. Kitchen, dining room, living room, three guest bedrooms, two guest bathrooms, and his bedroom and bathroom. She had never seen a bigger house in her entire life.

She pushed open the office door, plunked her tote down,

and set to dusting, taking a moment to study his wide array of books again. She wondered if he'd let her read any of them, or if he would tell her to keep away from his things. Many of them she had read already, but there were many more she would like to.

Her eyes drifted as her hand mechanically dusted things. His Masters in Visual Arts hung framed on the wall, and there was a picture directly under it. It showed a younger Traevyn in cap and gown, apparently at his college graduation. Next to him stood a young boy who looked somewhere around fourteen or fifteen. He had shorter black hair that waved nicely to frame his face, and he had several piercings in both of his ears. On the other side was another young man whose hair looked like liquid gold. It was quite a contrast to Traevyn's dark beauty, but his features resembled Traevyn's greatly. The thing that stood out the most to Evie was the fact that Traevyn was smiling. Grinning, in fact. It looked foreign to her since she had only ever seen his black scowl. His smile was beautiful. It lit up and softened the harsh lines of his face.

Evie let her eyes scan over a picture directly under the one she had been studying. This one was of the same three people, but it was apparently more recent as the young boy was much older and had tattoos running up the length of one of his arms. It appeared as if they were at a party of some kind, but Traevyn didn't seem happy like he did in the graduation picture. He was smiling, but it looked forced and pained, like it had taken all of his effort just to muster it.

She moved on, dusting his desk. There were several pictures turned face down, and curiosity nagged at her. She cast a fleeting glance toward the door to make sure no one was around, then picked up the pictures and started to flip through them. They were all of a staggeringly beautiful blonde woman and an adorable little girl who looked somewhere around five. Her hair was golden and her eyes were light like Traevyn's. She gave a thoughtful frown. This must be Traevyn's daughter and wife. She suddenly felt like she was intruding and carefully placed the pictures back where she had found them.

The book he had been reading the night before was sitting on the brown leather chair, and she glanced at the title. *Les Miserables*. Geez, that was an undertaking. She finished dusting and went to clean the glass on the French doors. After making sure they were streak free, she vacuumed the rugs and swept and mopped the hardwood floors.

The master bathroom and bedroom were her next project. She knocked on the door, just to make sure, then went in. Her eyes nearly bulged out of her head. The bed was a king-sized, four-poster made of dark, molasses-colored wood. The posts stabbed up like carved spires and the bedspread was black with a black brocade pattern on it that shimmered in the right light. The pillows were large and dark blue in color. There was another pair of French doors and dark blue crushed velvet was wrapped around a silver curtain rod and hanging down on either side of the doors. A nightstand sat on either side of the bed draped in black lace, and a beautiful Celtic dragon tapestry hung on one wall. There was an entertainment center, but with no television in it. Instead, a huge vase full of dried roses sat where the TV should be, and more books adorned most of the shelves. The top of the entertainment center was draped in the same crushed velvet as the French doors, and dried rose petals were spread around three large pictures of the little girl she had seen in the office. A sharp pain stabbed at Evie's heart, and she had to look away.

She continued her surveillance of the room, noticing that there were candles everywhere of various shapes and sizes, as well as a large fireplace at the far end of the room. She went into the bathroom and was not greatly surprised to see that everything was black marble. The bathtub was the most enormous thing she had ever seen, and she didn't look forward to cleaning it. With a sigh, she set to cleaning it anyway, and moved on into the bedroom once the bathroom was finished.

When she reached the French doors, she stopped for a moment to peer out at the ocean and fog-encompassed trees. She smiled a little. There was no denying that he had picked a beautiful place to build his home. She looked away for a moment to glance at the clock so she could tell him how many hours she had worked. When she returned to the door, he was standing right in front of her on the other side. She screamed and stumbled backwards, falling directly on her butt.

Traevyn casually stepped into the room, trying not to show his amusement. It bothered him that he even felt amusement, but it was impossible not to be amused at his petite, outspoken apprentice flailing her arms and falling promptly on her backside.

"What is the matter with you?" Evie cried.

He raised an eyebrow. "I didn't do anything. I was merely enjoying the sanctuary of the sea from my terrace. I didn't even know you were in here. It's not like I planned to frighten you." He extended a hand to help her up.

Evie looked surprised at his display of courtesy, but she took his hand and let him pull her into a standing position. "You were out there the whole time?"

He nodded and his lips turned up slightly at the corners as he took in her haggard appearance. She was sweaty, and her brown hair was straying from its ponytail. She reeked of lemon cleaner, and it was apparent that some sort of bleach substance had streaked across her otherwise dark blue t-shirt. Something about it warmed his dead heart in a strange way. He was used to rich, spoiled women. No one he'd ever met would have been willing to get their perfectly manicured hands dirty. It was nice to see a woman not afraid or too proud to work hard. He had come from an average family, a middle-working class family. He and his brothers had all worked very hard to get where they were in life. He admired hard work in all its forms. "How much do I owe you?" he asked.

"Two-hundred dollars," she stated.

He nodded. "Very well. I will give you a check tonight at dinner." He started to leave the room.

"Mr. Whitelaw?" Evie called.

He glanced at her over his shoulder.

She swallowed. "The books in your office...are they off limits, or would you mind horribly if I read one?"

He turned back to face her, intrigued. "My boring classics fascinate you?"

"Oh, yes." She grinned. "I love the classics."

He studied her for a moment. "Do you?"

She nodded. "They are the foundation on which all modern literature was built. A lot of people think they're boring, but I find them very interesting."

He regarded her for a moment longer, then nodded. "You are welcome to read anything on my bookshelf, Miss Austin. Also, as it seems you enjoy the view, you may use the terrace in the office at your leisure. It is a good place to read and draw."

She grinned. "Thank you."

He gave a ceremonial nod and continued out of the room.

Evie gathered her supplies and slipped back out into the hallway. The first place she headed was the shower, which was immediately followed by a trip to her bed, where she slept.

\* \* \*

Seth watched Evie cook with boredom and sighed. "It is really dull around here," he muttered. "There's absolutely nothing to do."

Evie rolled her eyes. "You brought enough video games to entertain a small planet."

He wrinkled his nose. "Yeah, but still." He yawned.

"You could have helped me clean today," she suggested. "That would have been nice."

He shrugged. "You did fine without me."

She scowled and bit her tongue to keep from saying something very rude. Her back hurt so bad she could hardly stand, and her arms felt like noodles from scrubbing. It was all she could do to set the food on the table. She glanced at her watch and groaned aloud when she saw that Traevyn was five minutes late. Great. Now she'd actually have to exert effort to hit the stupid gong.

"This looks good," Seth commented absently as Evie set the food on the table. "I love chicken fried steak."

Evie trudged into the living room and lifted the mallet. She was just getting ready to wallop it when Traevyn came all but running down the stairs. "I'm here!" he shouted. "I'm here, alright?"

Evie smirked and set the mallet down. Traevyn handed her a check and continued into the kitchen. She followed and sat down to eat. She was not all that surprised when Traevyn loaded up his plate and headed out again, leaving Seth and her alone.

It took all her energy to clean up the kitchen. Especially when she had just cleaned it. The thought of doing it twice in one day utterly disgusted her. When she had finally finished, Seth went to his room to watch television and she found herself heading to the office with her sketchpad. She turned the light on and went out onto the terrace, shivering as the foggy ocean air drifted over her. She pulled on a sweater she had brought with her and sat in a chair with a sigh. She couldn't see the ocean because it was dark, and fog covered everything like a surreal blanket, but she could hear it pounding against the cliffs and she could taste the salt in the air.

Evie leaned back in the chair and closed her eyes. She rubbed at a huge knot in one of her shoulders and relaxed to the sound of the waves.

"Peaceful, isn't it?"

She jumped and turned to see Traevyn leaning nonchalantly in the doorway. He was holding a glass of red wine and looked so old world aristocrat to her that she almost smiled. "It is."

He sighed and walked out to the railing. "My house looks spectacular. Thank you."

Evie stared at Traevyn's back. She couldn't help but marvel at how statuesque he was, so tall and proud. "I think I died somewhere around the second guest bathroom," she grumbled. "My spirit cleaned the rest of the house out of sheer pride."

He gave the faintest of chuckles, but kept his back to her. He seemed to lapse into thought and continued to sip his wine in silence.

Evie opened her sketchpad and started to draw him. He made a spectacular sight standing there, his long hair shining down his back, the fog drifting around him. She gave a little sigh. Even though he was rude and surly, his beauty was undeniable. And he was always dressed so elegant. She'd never seen him in jeans or a t-shirt. He was always in slacks and silk button-down shirts that hugged his lean frame. He always looked to Evie like he had stepped directly out of a different time and somehow got stuck in the twenty-first century.

"Do you like wine, Miss Austin?" he asked.

She looked up at him. "I do."

He turned to face her, the movement more like an elegant ripple of his body than a turn. "Red or white?"

"White," she answered. "Red is too dry for me."

His lips quirked. "Then you've never tasted a really good red wine."

She was surprised at his almost playful banter. She was actually wondering why he was even out there talking to her at all. Was he really that pleased with her cleaning abilities? If that was the case then she seriously needed to rethink her career choice. If her skills with a mop and a duster could soften a man like Traevyn Whitelaw even a little, she could make serious bank if she marketed on it.

She set her sketchpad on her lap and folded her arms. "What constitutes a 'really good red wine' then?"

He held up his glass and swirled the contents.

She rolled her eyes. "Oh yes, that tells me volumes."

One corner of his mouth rose in a wry, lopsided smile, and he moved forward, holding the glass out to her. "Try it."

She blinked in bewilderment, but complied. It went down surprisingly smooth without the harsh, bitter bite she was used to.

"Merlot is decent, and I enjoy Cabernet Sauvignon, but my preference is Shiraz," he supplied. "Each vintage is different, of course, but I find it generally enjoyable all the way around."

She handed the glass back to him and nodded. "It's good." She gave a short, nervous laugh and pushed her hair behind her ears in a self-conscious gesture. "I'm used to the five-dollar bottle of White Zinfandel that you get at the convenience store."

He made a face. "That is vile."

She snorted. "Well excuse me for not being a wine connoisseur. You're lucky I drink wine at all. When you went to SOU, were you living it up at the frat parties with your glass of Shiraz?"

A dry chuckle was torn from his lips and he shook his head. "No. My roommate was living it up at the frat parties with his lips suctioned onto the beer tap. I stayed in my dorm and painted..." He slid his gaze over her with a devilish glint in his eyes. "With my glass of Shiraz."

She giggled and fell silent, enjoying the conversation, but not knowing how to prolong it.

"Which is your favorite?" he questioned suddenly.

She frowned. "Huh?"

"Out of all the classics you claim to enjoy. Which do you like the best?"

He wandered closer to her chair, and Evie hastily closed her sketchpad, not wanting him to see that she had been drawing him. She thought for a moment. "*Wuthering Heights*, I think."

He arched an eyebrow. "The tragic romance type, are

you?"

She shrugged. "I don't know. Maybe I just like brooding men." She blushed as she realized what she had just said.

Traevyn's lips turned up at the corners. "Brooding men are dangerous."

She met his eyes and thought that he might be half-teasing, but she couldn't be sure. "What is your favorite?"

"*The Phantom of the Opera*," he replied without hesitation.

She blinked in surprise. "Really?" She had figured he would be more *The Old Man and the Sea*, or *The Grapes of Wrath* type. Something depressing and full of symbolism.

He nodded. "I think everyone can relate to the opera ghost in some fashion. Most of us have felt an outcast at some point in our lives. All of us have suffered the sting of rejection."

Evie nodded, noticing how he stared off into nothingness as he spoke the last part of his statement. "And everyone, regardless of what they may claim, just wants to be loved for who they are."

He met and held her eyes for one long second of silence, then gave a slow nod and took another sip of wine.

She shrugged. "I would have picked the Phantom over Raoul any day."

He frowned. "You would have gone with the broken, disfigured man over the dashing hero?"

"In a second."

He fixed her with a quizzical look. "Why?"

"Well, because," she shot him a glance, "Raoul was just the dashing hero, but the Phantom was beautiful."

Traevyn studied her for a moment. She continued to surprise him. Evie saw things most people would look right over. She was proving to have a depth of soul that was rare. It was like she looked at something and saw straight into the very core of it without even pausing to glance at the surface. His eyes narrowed as he saw her wince and start to rub at a spot in her shoulder. She yawned. He sighed, feeling bad that she had gone grocery shopping early that morning, had promptly come back and cleaned for eight hours, then made a delicious dinner and cleaned up the kitchen alone while her brother had spent the entire day wasting space on his couch with a video game console. She deserved a long soak in a

Jacuzzi. He sighed again and, though it went against his nature, traveled around to the back of her chair and placed one hand over the shoulder she was rubbing.

Evie's eyes flew open and she tensed. Her stomach made an uncomfortable flip as she felt his fingers gently knead at her sore muscle.

"I imagine you have a fondness for Pip in *Great Expectations* as well?" he asked.

She nodded and tried to keep her focus. Her heart beat erratically and she felt stupid for it. "Like I said, I seem to levitate towards the brooding, tormented men. Dangerous or not, they're just more interesting."

He paused for several seconds. "You should soak your sore muscles," he finally suggested. "Otherwise you'll barely be able to move in the morning." He dropped his hand and came around to stand in front of her. "The tub in the guest bathroom is horribly small. My tub has jets in it. Miss Austin, please use my bathroom if you'd like."

She stared up at him, stunned. The fact that he was being nice disturbed her. Maybe it was because he was drinking wine. Hey, she wasn't going to complain, and she definitely wasn't going to turn down a soak in an enormous tub. She stood. "Thank you. I think I will take you up on that offer. By the way, I think it would be safe to call me by my first name. This Miss Austin stuff is killing me."

He nodded. "Very well. I will remain out here or in the office until you are finished. Have a good night, Miss Austin."

Evie put a hand on her hip and sighed. "Didn't we just go over this?"

He gave a small smile. "Forgive me."

She arched an eyebrow. "Come on," she urged, "you can say it. Have a good night..."

"Evie," he answered.

For some stupid reason, she shivered again. Trying to ignore that strange reaction to her name spoken in his deep, velvety voice, she nodded and turned back toward the door. "Goodnight, Mr. Whitelaw."

He watched her go, then sighed and turned back to the sea. He closed his eyes and let the sound of it soothe him, momentarily easing the ache in his soul.

# Chapter Six

The terrace and the office became Evie's favorite spots as the days dragged on. She spent most of her time either drawing on the terrace or attempting to paint in the studio, which never really got that far. She tended to avoid the studio most of the time anyway since Traevyn was in there nine times out of ten, and he made her amazingly uncomfortable. She would go in when she knew he was elsewhere to sneak a peek at his current projects, but she tried to be out of there before he returned. She felt very inadequate next to his artistic genius.

She was pleasantly surprised to find that Traevyn had become much more cordial to her. She couldn't really say why, but she wasn't going to complain. He shared small snippets of conversation with her from time to time, and that was nice. He also joined her often when she was reading in the office. A lot of the time neither one of them said much of anything. They both sat in their respective corners and read until they were tired. At times, Evie would react to something she had read, prompting Traevyn to question her about it. It was during these quiet evenings that she and Traevyn had the most interaction. She came to realize that he loved discussing literature and enjoyed hearing her opinions as well. Some nights, they would share long conversations on a certain character, or something that one of them thought was particularly symbolic. Other nights, Traevyn didn't say much of anything at all, but Evie enjoyed it either way.

She continued to make dinner every night, which Traevyn was always on time for. Most of the time, she didn't mind. There was a side of her that was very domestic. She liked to experiment with new recipes, and it made her feel good to be needed in some small way. Heaven knew Seth would starve if she didn't feed him.

"Crap!" Seth shouted suddenly.

Evie glanced over at him from where she had been trying to read in the living room. He flung his video game controller across the room. She rolled her eyes. "Smart, Seth. Maybe you could aim at one of Traevyn's expensive decorations next time. I'm sure you'd love to work it off."

He huffed. "I've fought that thing six times and I still can't beat it!" he cried in exasperation.

Evie raised her eyebrows. "I'm...sorry?"

"You don't care," he grumbled.

She smirked. "What are you going to do when you beat all the games you brought with you?"

"Die of boredom," he spat. "Seriously, this is like, the worst summer ever."

She sighed. She did feel bad that Seth had to just sit around all day. She could occupy herself with Traevyn's books and her art, but Seth wasn't interested in things like that. "Why don't we go out for dinner tonight?" she suggested. "We haven't had pizza in a week and a half." She flashed him a grin.

Seth looked at her and smirked. "What about Darth Whitelaw?" he mocked. "Won't he cut your pay if you ditch out on his dinner?"

"Screw that. I'll just invite him to go along."

Seth frowned. "I'm sure that'll go over well."

She waved his comment away. "He'll just have to deal one way or another. It's not fair that you can't go out and do anything, and I'm sick of being cooped up in here too." She stood. "I bet the man hasn't had pizza in years. I honestly wonder what he ate before I started cooking for him."

"The salesmen that came to the door," Seth said flatly.

Evie let out a rather loud burst of laughter and shook her head. "You're horrible. I'm going to find him and ask him to go."

"Doesn't that totally defeat the purpose of having fun?"

She scowled. "Seth, come on. Don't be rude. He's not completely awful. Maybe if you spoke to him once in awhile instead of just monopolizing his TV you'd know that."

He rolled his eyes. "Whatever. Just go and ask the guy so

we can leave soon. I'm hungry."

Evie mounted the staircase, smiling to herself as she heard Seth grumble something about needing to get his driver's license. She headed to the office, but Traevyn wasn't there. She checked the studio, but he wasn't there either. That only left his room, since he never ventured down to her end of the house, and she had just been in the living room. Unless he was in the dungeon of the basement, but she doubted that.

She hummed cheerily to herself as she approached his door, but she stopped short just before knocking. Her smile faded when she heard the distinct sound of muffled sobs. Her heart twisted as she put her ear closer to the door and listened while the ever-scowling, ever-poised, dark artist cried as if his heart was breaking. She hesitated a moment, uncertain of how to proceed. She knew she couldn't just walk away and let him cry, but she couldn't let him know she had been listening either. She had a feeling that he wouldn't be very thrilled to be caught in a weakened state.

Evie turned and went back down the hallway. She stopped at the beginning of it, counted to five, and kicked the wall hard enough to make a noise that announced her presence. "Ow!" she exclaimed, making sure she was loud enough to be heard. She counted to five again, then headed back to his room. She took a deep breath and knocked.

"Just a moment," he called from inside, his voice soft but clear.

She chewed on her bottom lip as she waited, still greatly troubled at the thought of him sobbing alone in his bedroom.

Traevyn opened the door looking no worse for the wear. His eyes were red, but his presence was the same. Calm, aloof, icy. He was good at hiding his emotions. "What is it?"

She plastered a grin on her face. "Seth and I were going to go to Monterey and get pizza tonight."

He gave a solemn nod. "Very well. I'll just find something here. Have a good time." He started to turn away.

"Wait!" she cried, taking a step in the room. "We wanted you to come with us."

He stared at her for a moment before his dark brows drew together in an almost confused frown. "Are you out of your mind?"

She arched an eyebrow. "A little. More so since I've been

living here with you."

His features softened and his lips turned up slightly. He sighed. "Thank you for the invitation, but you go and have fun with your brother."

She huffed. "Oh come on!" she exclaimed. "Please? What do you have better to do? Sit in your tower and read?"

He raised his eyebrows. "My tower? Well, yes actually. Perhaps I'll weave some magic while I'm at it," he grumbled.

Evie smiled. It was important to her, now more than ever, to get him to go with them. She would have let it go originally, but not now. She couldn't leave him alone to be at the mercy of his ghosts and demons while she went out and had a good time. It wouldn't be right.

"Why is it so important to you that I go anyway?" he asked in curiosity.

She met his gaze and folded her arms in determination. "Because I have the feeling that you haven't gone out just to have fun in eons."

He averted his gaze. "You're right. I don't have fun when I go out." He shook his head. "Can you honestly picture me sitting in a pizza parlor full of screaming children and loud people? It's completely out of my element."

"Traevyn, sometimes we have to step outside of our element or we forget what life is like."

He stared at her for a long time. He hated when she did that—looked at him or said something that gave him the impression that she saw right through every defense and barrier and could actually gaze upon his inner self whenever she felt like it. It was unnerving and yet, exhilarating somehow. To think that someone could actually see the small remnants of his shattered soul was terrifying, yet it gave him hope. Hope that perhaps one day he could be whole again. A real man and not just a shadow of one.

He opted to change the subject. "Why are you calling me by my first name?" he asked. "I never gave you permission to call me by my first name."

She huffed in obvious frustration. "Like I care!"

He raised his eyebrows. "Aren't I, more or less, your teacher? Do you call all your teachers by their first names?"

She scowled. "Well, I don't see you doing a whole lot of teaching around here. Maybe when you start teaching, I'll start calling you Mr. Whitelaw again, but until then, it's silly for me to live here under such formalities."

"You are very impertinent," he stated.

"And you are a great big pain in my butt! Now that *that's* out of the way, can we move on?"

He gave a small smile in spite of himself.

Evie's exasperation melted into a warm grin. "Come on, Traevyn, just go with us. I promise you won't hate it and, if you do, you'll never have to listen to me again." She studied him for a moment and her gaze turned soft. "I want to see if I can get you to smile. A real smile and not that quirky thing you do with your lips." She pointed to him as he half-smiled. "Yeah, that one!"

He gave a soft chuckle. He didn't understand Evie. It seemed the more he tried to get her to leave him alone, the more she bothered him. His cold demeanor had successfully kept everyone else at bay, but she ignored it. She challenged him in the most unabashed way. It was strange for him to be around someone so open, so fearless.

He looked at her. She stood with her arms folded, waiting. She was so small. She only came up to his chest. A tiny little powder keg. She was not what he had expected the day he'd so rudely accepted her into his home. She had stayed in her room for an entire week. He had barely seen or heard her. Then, when she'd had enough, she'd sought him out with boldness and voiced her opinion of him. She had been continuing to voice that opinion ever since. He was coming to realize that she had many opinions. Their discussions on literature had proven that.

With a sigh, he turned away from her and toward the French doors. He admired Evie for the courageous way she seemed to stride through life, but he couldn't be like her. Not anymore. His time had passed. He glanced back at her over his shoulder and opened his mouth to speak.

"A compromise then," Evie announced, stepping toward him. "We'll get the pizza to go, but we'll eat it down on the beach, away from people. You can read or draw if you want. You don't even have to talk to us. Seth and I can entertain ourselves."

He frowned and turned back to face her. "You want me to go and just sit there like a bump on a log?"

She shrugged. "That's entirely up to you. Do whatever makes you feel comfortable. Just go with us, okay?"

He gazed down into her hazel eyes and had to look away. She had sensed what he was going to say before he'd even voiced it. She had known he would refuse and she sought to change her plans to make *him* comfortable. Why? He was nothing to her, no one. Yet, all she seemed to care about was getting him to have fun, getting him outside of himself, getting him to smile.

Smiling... Just a moment ago he had been sobbing. If only she knew the sorrow he carried within him every day...like an overwhelming weight, like a plague.

He sighed in defeat and nodded slowly. "All right," he murmured.

Evie blinked, as if wondering if she'd heard him right. "All right?" When he nodded again, she grinned and jumped, clapping her hands together. "Woo hoo! All right, come on then. We'll leave soon."

He smiled at her obvious enthusiasm. "Give me just a moment. I wish to take a small canvas and my oil pastels."

"Just meet us downstairs when you're ready." She met his eyes and flashed him a delighted smile before leaving the room.

Traevyn watched her go and sighed. The acute pain he had been feeling moments ago returned. The shadows beckoned him, waited in the darkness to consume any light his soul might hope to steal. He closed his eyes and turned his back on them. Not now. He would not return to them now. They would be waiting for him later like they always were. For now, he would try to pretend. Pretend he was human. Pretend he was whole. He would fail,  but he would try. Evie's kindness deserved at least that much.

# *Chapter Seven*

There was nothing more beautiful than a sunset over the water. Traevyn watched as the sunlight sparkled across the rippling waves and he sighed. It was fog free at the moment, and he relished in the splendor of nature's art. He heard Evie's laughter ring out. It diverted his attention from the sunset to her and Seth. They were down by the shore hitting a volleyball back and forth. The sunlight glinted off of the blonde streaks in her hair and highlighted the brown so it looked bronzed. She screamed as Seth hit the ball too fast at her, and she had to flail her arms erratically to hit it in time. It shot off into the waves as she accidentally punched it at a funny angle.

Seth gave Evie an exasperated look, and she dissolved into giggles. Traevyn looked back down at the drawing he was working on. He continued to add colors and lines, making it come alive, adding dimension.

Evie glanced over at Traevyn as she waited for Seth to retrieve the ball. He was drawing still. It was what he had been doing for the past hour. They had eaten their pizza with she and Seth exchanging most of the conversation. Traevyn had listened quietly, had thrown in a comment now and then. He hadn't been rude or unpleasant, just quiet and reserved. He'd eaten, then started drawing, and that's what he had been doing ever since.

"What are you looking at?" Seth asked, coming up next to Evie as he tried to dust the wet sand off of the volleyball.

"Traevyn," she replied softly. Seth glanced over at him, and Evie sighed. "Right before I went to ask him if he wanted to come eat with us, I heard him in his bedroom sobbing. I

mean really sobbing, Seth. Crying like his heart was shatter-
ing."

"Are you serious?"

She nodded. "It was horrible." She continued to let her
gaze roam over him. He had his knees up, the canvas bal-
anced on them as he drew. He had a slight frown of concen-
tration on his face and his ebony hair spilled all around him,
glistening in the light from the setting sun.

"Why don't you go talk to him?" Seth suggested.

Evie stared at her brother in confusion. Seth was not
known to be all that empathetic.

He shrugged. "Maybe he could use some company."

She chewed on her lip as she glanced back at Traevyn.
"Just put the volleyball back in the trunk when you're done."
She headed up the beach and sat down next to Traevyn.
"What are you working on?"

He gazed at his drawing for a moment, then glanced up
at her. "Tell me what you see."

She studied it. It was a rough sketch of the ocean, the
waves large and chaotic, yet serene somehow. The sky was
gray with fog, and the tendrils of it were reaching out and
curling around the silhouette of a man with long hair.
Through the gray covering was a thin shaft of sunlight,
enough to give the silhouette a shadow. The shadow was a
misshapen heart that was rent in two and looked like it was
bleeding. Evie's heart twisted painfully at the image, but she
tried to keep it professional. She didn't want Traevyn to
know she suspected anything. He didn't know she had heard
him crying. "This person is staring out at the ocean because
it is peaceful to him," she said. "The fog represents darkness
reaching out its fingers to grasp him. The shaft of light shows
that he sees just enough light and beauty in the world to remind him of what hurts him the most, which is symbolized
by the shadow." She looked up at him to see if she had come
anywhere close to the mark.

"Very good," he said, his voice hushed.

Evie pointed to the still blank fourth of the canvas. "It
isn't finished yet."

He gave a thoughtful frown. "You finish it."

She looked up at him in surprise.

"I want to see how you would complete it," he said, setting the canvas aside. "Do it whenever you like and let me

know when you have finished."

She blinked in bewilderment. "A—All right." Her? Finish his own work? How could she even hope to create anything that would complement his extraordinary talent? She was an amateur and he was a master.

He leaned back on his elbows with a sigh; Evie looked away from the drawing and over at him. "Are you happy you came with us? Or are you just humoring me?"

He met her eyes and his lips turned up into a small smile. "I am glad I came. It's very nice out here. Peaceful. The ocean brings such tranquility to me." He turned his gaze back to the setting sun. "Evie, thank you for inviting me...and changing your plans to make me comfortable. It was very thoughtful of you." His dark brows drew together. "May I ask you a question?"

She pulled her knees up to her chest and rested her chin on them. "Go ahead."

"Why do you pursue me the way you do?"

She frowned. "Pursue you?"

He nodded. "I was anything but polite to you on your arrival, and have been nothing short of a complete ogre. Why do you still seek to include me? To talk to me? To give me your kindness?"

"Well, because, Traevyn..." She shrugged helplessly. "I'm living in your home. It's not in my nature to be rude even if it is in yours." She gave him a teasing smile, then sobered and shook her head. "You really are my favorite artist. I've always been drawn to your work. When Professor Roth told me about the opportunity to be your apprentice, I was excited to think I'd finally get to see what the man behind the art was like. I'm coming to realize that you are just as intriguing and complex as your work. So, I guess you could say I'm drawn to you as well."

He sat up and met her gaze again with a kind of befuddled wonder.

Evie blushed and looked down. "Sorry, that kind of sounded like I was hitting on you. I wasn't." She tucked her hair behind her ears in her telltale nervous gesture.

He smiled at her obvious embarrassment. "You're drawn to my work, you say?"

She nodded. "I always have been. The first time I saw your work was when I went to the Museum of Modern Art in

New York. My senior art class went there for this end of the year trip in high school. I saw your painting 'Escape Into Fantasy' and I thought it was the most beautiful thing I had ever seen."

Traevyn swallowed painfully. That painting had been of his wife. Her golden hair had taken up most of the canvas like an aura, and her deep blue eyes had been beckoning, inviting. That seemed like a lifetime ago.

"I bought a bunch of your postcards in the gift shop," Evie continued with a giggle. "After that point, I kept up constantly with your work. I have all of your prints and your art books."

He smiled wryly. "I spawned a fan off of that one painting?"

"Well, not just that one. It was 'Innerworkings of a Creative Soul' that really got me hooked. It was such a contrast to the other painting. A lot of your early work had so much vibrance and color, where the work you've done within the past three years is so much darker. I admire your diversity."

He shrugged and a lump formed in his throat. "It's not talent. I paint what I feel. Simple as that. My life changed, therefore, my work changed."

She seemed to notice the bitterness his voice carried. "Does it really bother you that I try to be your friend? If it does, I'll leave you alone. I just..." She worried her bottom lip with her teeth and shrugged.

He sighed. Sometimes he really wondered what was going on inside the woman's head. He thought of her interpretation of his painting. She was so astute. So astute it was frightening. He didn't exactly know how to handle her unique ability. It made him uncomfortable and piqued his curiosity all at the same time.

"No, Evie, it doesn't bother me," he murmured. "Do not take my cold demeanor as annoyance. When you first came here, I resented it because I feared change in a life I was very used to, but I am not irritated by your presence any longer. You are very intelligent and very kind. I do enjoy your company." Against his better judgment, he had to admit it was true. He had grown to look forward to their discussions. Evie was in a class all of her own. She was not one of the mindless, witless masses. She walked her own path, spoke her mind, and did so with abandon.

Evie looked at him and smiled. She jumped as the volleyball suddenly made contact with the side of her head, sending her glasses flying. Seth's laughter quickly followed. "Thanks a lot, Seth," she grumbled.

Traevyn picked up her glasses with an amused smirk and handed them to Evie, who had just hurled the ball as hard as she could, sending Seth running after it. "You have to love him. He's your brother," he stated.

She snorted. "Doesn't mean I have to like him." She shoved the glasses back on her face in annoyance.

"I have two younger brothers. They used to drive me crazy."

Evie briefly thought of the pictures she had seen in his office. She wondered if the two men in the photos were his brothers. They had all resembled one another. "What are they like?" she questioned.

He gave a whimsical smile. "Julian works at an animal clinic. He's an assistant until he finishes school to become a veterinarian. He has a very gentle soul. Talis is a tattoo artist, and he travels with renaissance faires pretending to be a knight and playing guitar for the belly dancers."

Evie raised her eyebrows. "That's an interesting profession."

He chuckled. "Talis is the sort of person who wants to sample as much life as he can. He's very much a free spirit."

"Are you close to your brothers?"

"Yes. They are the two stabilizing rocks in my life. They are the support beams on which I stand. They are all I have and everything to me."

Evie thought of the deBoer family. With the exception of Barrett, that was how they viewed one another. She envied that.

She watched as Seth started to walk back up to where they were sitting. She wondered if she would ever be able to view him as a stabilizing rock and support beam. Maybe when he wasn't seventeen. "My family's not really close," she said. "My parents have jobs that keep them away a lot of the time. My friend Meg has this family and circle of friends I've always been horribly jealous of. They're all so close. That's something I've always wanted to have one day." She stared out at the ocean wistfully and sighed as the last remnants of the sun dipped beneath the horizon line.

"The stars will be out soon," Traevyn remarked. "If you ever get a clear night, there is nothing more magnificent than the night sky away from city lights."

"I know. It's breathtaking."

"At times, I paint on my terrace. Usually when the moon is full. It gives everything a different perspective." He glanced at her. "Perhaps at the next full moon you could join me. See what inspiration the nocturnal world has to offer you."

She grinned. "I'd like that."

"When we return, I think we should get you started on painting. You need to get over your fear of it."

Evie looked away. She studied the patterns in the sand. "All right," she said, her voice sounding meek and tiny. The truth was, she was horrified to paint in front of him. Painting on her own in her apartment where no one could laugh at her was one thing. Even painting for class was safe, but to paint in front of the greatest artist in the world? What if he thought she was no good? Traevyn was anything but tactful. He would call her a talentless amateur right to her face. She didn't think she'd be able to handle that.

Seth sat down next to her and put the volleyball next to him. "I dare you to jump in the ocean," he said.

She rolled her eyes. "Yeah, right. It's freezing."

"Wuss," he taunted.

"You go jump in it if you're so tough."

"I would."

She met his eyes in challenge. "Do it then."

He shrugged. "I don't feel like it."

She shook her head. "Whatever. You're the real wuss."

Traevyn smirked. "You know, it's not very manly to go against your word. You'll never be able to woo a girl if you claim false things or make empty promises just to make yourself look better."

Seth stared at him and snorted. "Are these words of experience? I don't see the chicks lined up outside your door."

"Seth!" Evie scolded. Her face burned with embarrassment over what Seth had said. She had finally gotten Traevyn to associate with them on some sort of amicable level and now he was being completely out of line.

Traevyn gave an enigmatic smile. "I am not actively pursuing a lady, but even though I'm not, I still do not claim false things."

Seth frowned and folded his arms. "Let's see you jump in the ocean, tough guy."

Evie sighed and rolled her eyes heavenward. "Seth, I think you're missing the point."

Traevyn stood without a word and calmly began to unbutton his shirt.

Evie's eyes widened. "Don't listen to him!" she cried. "He's a bratty teenage boy!" He looked down at her, and she thought she might have detected the faintest glimmer of mirth in his light eyes.

"A real man also never backs down from a challenge." He removed his shirt and handed it to Evie. "Hold this for me, if you would."

She stared up at his now shirtless body and her mouth went dry. His shoulders were broad and his waist and hips were narrow. His arms were well-defined and muscles rippled across his back as he moved. Every line of his body seemed etched in elegance. He was just as beautiful as one of his paintings.

Seth frowned and stood as well. Evie tore her gaze from Traevyn and looked over at her brother. "What are you doing?"

"Like I'm gonna let him make me look like a pansy," he grumbled. He threw his shirt down at her.

"You are both out of your minds!" Evie cried. She watched as Traevyn started to make his way down to the shore. "You're going to ruin your pants!" she exclaimed. "At least take your pants off!" The minute the words left her mouth, she felt her face flush with color. She shook her head and mentally kicked herself. Had she always been such an idiot? Traevyn stopped and turned to look at her over his shoulder. She waved her hand. "Can you just forget I said that?"

He stared at her for a moment as she continued to squirm with embarrassment. The corners of his mouth quirked and, then, it was like a flower blossoming before her eyes. A slow smile spread across his lips and split into a grin. He chuckled.

Evie watched him in awestruck silence, unable to believe what she was seeing. His entire face lit up with his smile; the brooding lines softened. Her heart melted at the sight of it. If her constant idiocy had caused that smile, it had all been worth it. She grinned warmly back at him.

Traevyn turned back to the ocean and waded out into it.

When it was deep enough, he merely dove forward, directly into an oncoming wave. He didn't hesitate, didn't act like he was reluctant to get wet and cold. He just launched himself with grace right into the water and began to swim.

"Hey! Wait for me!" Seth shouted. He tramped through the waves after him, splashing water every which way, and sort of belly flopped into the water. He jumped out almost immediately, screaming. "That is friggin' cold!"

Evie laughed as Seth stumbled out, trying to escape the freezing water as soon as possible. He had a strand of seaweed tangled around his leg, and he tried to kick it off. He only succeeded in tripping himself, and he collapsed right into the sand. Evie fell backwards, laughing hysterically. She looked up just in time to see Seth fling the seaweed as far as he could and curse.

Traevyn had stopped swimming and was treading water, watching the scene unfold. Seth turned to him and gave a dramatic salute. "You're a better man than me!" He ran back up to where Evie sat, shivering. "Gimme my shirt!" he demanded.

Evie handed him his shirt, still laughing until her stomach hurt. He was only in his boxer shorts, and the backs of his legs and butt were completely covered in sand. She glanced over at Traevyn, who was making his way out of the water, shaking droplets from his long hair. He walked leisurely back up to where Seth and Evie were, a small smile still playing about his lips. Evie held his shirt out to him, and he took it with a nod.

Seth still shivered and he looked at Traevyn, who was buttoning his shirt back up with calm, sure fingers. "You're not even cold?" he cried. "Man, I don't think you're human."

"I swim in the ocean sometimes," Traevyn stated. "The cold is invigorating. It wakes your body up. It makes you feel, reminds you that you are alive."

He said the words softly, and it made Evie look up at him. It was so different from the bite that his voice usually had to it. He gave her a gentle smile and offered his hand to help her up. She took it, and marveled over how the iciness surrounding him seemed to have melted slightly.

"I don't feel invigorated," Seth grumbled. "All I feel is sand up my butt crack."

Traevyn gave a soft laugh. He patted Seth on the back as

they headed to the car. "It was a very valiant attempt."

Seth glanced up at Traevyn and shook his head. "I think the real lesson you were trying to teach me is not to be such a macho big mouth."

Laughter flew out of Traevyn's mouth and it startled both Seth and Evie. Evie wanted to cry at hearing his laughter. It was beautiful. Deep and resonant, like music. All the shadows of pain and sorrow on his face seemed to vanish and, for a brief moment, he resembled that picture in his office. Hearing his laughter was so much better than hearing him sob. She wished she could keep him laughing forever.

She unlocked the car and opened the trunk so they could load their stuff in it. Seth got in the back seat and, as she went to close the trunk again, Traevyn came to stand beside her. "Evie," he murmured. She looked up at him, and he lifted her chin with his forefinger. He bent to press a light kiss to her cheek.

Evie froze and her heart made a dull thud in her chest. As he pulled away, she gazed up into his light green eyes in confusion.

"There was a time when I most certainly thought I would never laugh again," he said. "Truly, I had forgotten what laughter felt like. Thank you for reminding me again... Even if it is just for a moment."

She stared up at him, finding it difficult to breathe all of a sudden. Who said stuff like that? And who said it like they were from a different century? She wondered if Traevyn really had time traveled at some point. She couldn't think of anything to say in response so she just gave a lame nod.

He smiled. "We shall paint when we get home, all right?"

She nodded again. There went that formal, medieval speech again. She didn't know why, but she found it terribly sexy. He brushed past her and went to get in the car. She headed to the driver's seat, wondering why her hands were shaking so much and why her heart felt like it was going to explode at any given moment. She touched her cheek absently, thinking it was a little bit strange that she could still feel the soft impression of his lips there.

# Chapter Eight

Evie hated that she was a nervous wreck while waiting for Traevyn in his studio. She twisted her fingers, then adjusted the canvas on her easel again just to try and give herself something to do. The door opened and she jumped as he strode in with clean, dry clothes on and his hair pulled back in a damp ponytail. He looked at her and smiled.

"Are you ready to get started?" he asked.

She heaved a sigh. "I guess so."

"You guess so? You are an artist, correct? Do you plan to make your living off of sketches alone? I somehow doubt that you would be Professor Roth's chosen one if you did." He pulled a fresh canvas out and set it on his own easel. "Why does painting intimidate you when drawing does not?"

She shrugged. "It's more permanent. If I mess up, I can't erase it. Not everything's in black and white. Color is important. I'm always afraid I won't be able to convey what I'm trying to."

He shook his head. "Don't worry about trying to convey anything. Art shouldn't be about thinking. Art is self expression. Colors represent feeling. Close your eyes and think about how you feel, then choose a color to represent your emotion. It doesn't matter what color it is. Some people may choose blue or gray to represent melancholy, but there is no set standard for what you have to choose. That's the beauty of art. To you, maybe chartreuse is a depressing color. No one has the right to tell you otherwise. It's your self expression."

She felt color creep into her cheeks for no reason at all. Even though her experience with Traevyn had been anything but what she had expected, the fact that she was still learning from the greatest artist of their day floored her. Sometimes, she couldn't believe she was actually there.

"There are no limits in art," Traevyn continued. "This"—he held up a paintbrush—"is just an expression of this." He placed his hand over her heart. "You paint what's inside here and nothing else. Let this guide you and you will never make a mistake. The trouble is you have to free yourself. Remove all of your own limitations and criticism. Just let what's inside of you come out."

She nodded, looking at him with rapt attention. Her heart beat out an erratic pattern beneath his palm and she hoped he didn't notice. She realized that one long strand of his hair was free of the ponytail and hanging loosely in his face. She stared at it and had the insane urge to reach out and tuck it back. His jaw was defined and his chin had a small cleft in it; for some reason, she found that very attractive.

"Evie?"

She snapped out of her wandering thoughts and met his eyes. "I'm sorry. What did you say?"

His lips came together in a thin line of disapproval. "I can see my words make a real impression on you."

She blushed. "No, I'm sorry. I was just—" She shook her head. "Please go on. What you have to say is very important. I'm just...tired, I guess."

"Well, choose the kind of paint you want to use and we'll get started." He turned away and began to gather his supplies.

Evie looked around and decided on acrylics. She didn't think she could manage oil with her suddenly trembling hands. She selected her brushes and put a small amount of several colors on a pallet. She dipped her brush in red and poised her brush over the canvas, but couldn't seem to hold it steady enough to draw a straight line, or anything else for that matter. Her hand shook like she was having a seizure. She frowned, put the brush in her mouth, and rubbed her hands together. This was stupid. So she was working with her idol. No big deal. He said himself there were no limits in art. He technically couldn't laugh at her for her own "self expression" unless he wanted to be labeled a hypocrite.

Evie saw Traevyn glance at her out of the corner of her eye after she had prepared her materials. She knew she looked ridiculous. She pointed her brush at the canvas like she was trying to cast a spell on it and her hand trembled badly. She made a frustrated growl and tried to shake her hands, only to assume the same position with the same result.

Traevyn smirked, set his tube of paint down, closed it, then went over to her. "Evie," he said softly. She jumped and whirled to look at him. He gave her an amused expression and placed his hands on her shoulders to steady her. "For goodness sake, take a deep breath."

She closed her eyes and forced air into her lungs, letting it out in a powerful rush.

He took the paintbrush from her fingers and set it aside, then took her hands in his and rubbed them lightly. "Why are you trembling so much?"

She looked down, a little more than humiliated at having him notice, and a little more than flustered at having him touch her. "I—I—It's just..."

"You don't have to prove anything to me, Evie. This is not a job interview and I am not appraising you for your worth. Just paint. I would never criticize, never condemn. Here, turn around." He turned her toward the canvas and went to stand behind her. He picked up the paintbrush and put it back in her fingers, keeping his hand over hers. "Just let it flow through you," he instructed. "The vision, the emotions, the inspiration. Let it come from within you. You are just the vessel the image is using to tell its story. Listen to it; let it guide you."

Evie closed her eyes as she listened to his deep voice. It was like black seduction, and he was standing so close to her. She felt the heat of his body, and her fingers tingled from the touch of his hand on hers. She opened her eyes, swallowed hard, and applied the brush to the canvas, drawing out a sleek line of red.

Traevyn smiled. "Good," he murmured, keeping his hand in place over hers. "Just feel it, Evie."

Her heart refused to beat in a normal way, and she kept getting flashes of Traevyn at the beach shirtless and wet, laughing, grinning, kissing her cheek...of his voice, and the feel of his touch, and that stupid strand of hair in his face... Before she knew it, she was painting almost wildly, her hand moving on its own.

Traevyn stepped back, watching her. After a moment, he returned to his own canvas and began to work.

An hour went by before Evie stopped. When she had exhausted her inspiration, she stepped back and looked at her work with a frown. It was the image of a heart being consumed in flames, but it was camouflaged in a background of blazing red and orange. She scratched her head. She knew it wasn't finished, but she couldn't think of anything else to do.

"That's very good, Evie," Traevyn remarked as he glanced over from his own project. "What is it?"

"I—I don't know." She gave him a nervous glance. There was a strong possibility that it might be lust, but she was not going to tell him that. "I don't know how to finish it. I don't feel it anymore." Maybe if he came and stood close to her like he had done before... And speak to her in those sensual tones...

"That happens," he said. "Just leave it be. Finish it when it comes back to you."

She silently hoped it never did. Lusting after Traevyn Whitelaw was not something on her to-do list. It troubled her that she had felt it so strongly in the first place. The man was thirty years old, and she was pretty sure that lusting after the person who was technically your teacher was ethically wrong somehow...even if he was amazingly good-looking.

She glanced over at his painting and raised an eyebrow in surprise. She wasn't sure what it was going to be yet, but the colors were bright and vivid, something she had not seen in his work in quite some time. She smiled.

The phone rang and he stepped away from his painting with a frown. Setting his brush down, he went to answer it. Evie studied his work while he was gone, then looked at hers some more. She smiled as she thought of how he had instructed her with such patience. She felt bad that she had thought he would be harsh and critical. The past several hours had shown her a side of Traevyn that she was eager to learn more about.

The door opened and he came back in. Evie turned toward him with a smile. "Anyone import—" Her smiled faded and morphed into a look of concern. He was horribly pale, and no trace of the momentary happiness he had been experiencing remained. He looked drawn, fatigued,  and so sad. "Are you all right?" she whispered.

He said nothing. He walked slowly to the painting he had been working on and stared at it for a long moment. Then, without warning, he grabbed a pocket knife that he used to sharpen his charcoal and drove it into the canvas.

Evie let out a shriek and jumped backward in horror.

Traevyn's hand was shaking as he released the knife. He stared at the marred painting, breathing heavily. "I call this one *Death of Passion*. What do you think?" He fixed her with a sinister look.

Evie let out a slow breath. "I think I need to go change my pants," she grumbled. "Because I'm pretty sure I just crapped 'em."

He kept his eyes on her for a breath or two, then lowered his gaze and gave a weak, sad smile. He sat down in his chair and rested his head in his hand wearily.

Evie watched him, unsure of what to do. It was only after a moment that she realized he had tears running lonely trails down his cheeks. She stood frozen, immobile. What was she supposed to do? Traevyn was such a loner. She was still, more or less, a stranger. She had no idea how to offer comfort to someone who could be so cold and distant. She didn't know how he would react to her attempt at comfort. Would he be offended? Feel intruded upon?

"Do you know what today is, Evie?" he murmured.

She said nothing.

"Three years ago today, my daughter was killed."

Her eyes widened and she brought her hand to her mouth.

"I usually spend this day either drinking myself into oblivion, or contemplating suicide. Today is the first day since it happened that I've laughed, which is what my daughter was all about. Laughter." His smile was small and pained. "She loved to laugh. She loved the beach. She loved to play. When you invited me to go with you and Seth tonight, my immediate reaction was that it would be disrespectful to attempt to have any semblance of a good time on such an awful day, but the more I thought about it, I realized that Leanna would have chosen laughter and light over dark sadness any day. I went with you because it was something she would have loved, and because I couldn't say no to your kindness, Evie. I just couldn't." He met her eyes. "Once I was there, with you and Seth, watching the two of you interact, I was reminded of what it felt like to have a family. And it hurt. But, strangely, it also felt nice. It felt nice to not be so isolated with my sorrow. It's not that I forgot the acute pain in my heart at her absence, for that will be with me forever, but it was just..." He sighed as he searched for the words.

"Nice to not have to be so alone," she murmured. His eyes held so much pain when he looked at her. Pain and sorrow, and an enormous amount of guilt. He gave a slow nod, then put his face in his hands.

"It didn't feel wrong at the time," he whispered. "To laugh... I'm so sorry."

Evie didn't think he was apologizing to her. He was apologizing to his daughter, for daring to laugh, to try and move forward. She took a tentative step toward him, her heart breaking as she watched him cry softly. Who had he spoken with? Who had made him feel like he should punish himself for celebrating his daughter's love for life? She reached out slowly and placed her hand on his shoulder. When he didn't pull away, she extended it across his back so her arm was around him.

"Traevyn," she breathed, "there is nothing wrong in what you did. There is nothing wrong with laughing, especially when it's what your daughter would have loved. Whoever made you feel like it was wrong is stupid." She felt so at a loss. She knew there were no real words of comfort she could offer. Not for a situation like this. She sighed and rested her forehead against his shoulder. "I'm so sorry, Traevyn," she whispered. "You know I didn't know."

He shook his head. "Evie, you saved me from horrible pain this evening. You and your brother made me remember the beauty of my daughter's life and not just the tragedy of her death. I will never forget that."

She closed her eyes, swearing she could feel his pain in her own heart. She hesitated only a moment before she wrapped her other arm around him and held him in an awkward embrace.

Traevyn closed his eyes as Evie's warmth surrounded him. Warmth. It was so foreign. He was so used to cold solitude. Evie. He didn't even know why he had just told her all he had. He didn't know why he had decided to come back into the room after he'd hung up the phone. Any other time he would have just taken his leave, would have isolated himself to cry alone, would never have involved her—a near stranger—in his sorrow. He didn't know why he had returned, why he felt comforted by her. It was strange, so out of character...

He sat up and wiped his eyes. "Forgive me." He stood abruptly and knocked her off of him. "My problems are not your problems. I shouldn't have involved you." He turned and headed toward the door.

Evie could hardly comprehend what was going on. One minute she was holding him, and the next she was stumbling backwards trying not to fall on her butt. "Traevyn!" she cried. She lunged forward without thinking and grabbed his hand. "You can't just walk away! I can't let you go and suffer alone." He was always alone. No one should have to be so isolated.

"I am used to being alone," he almost snarled.

Her grip on his hand tightened as he tried to move away from her. "You shouldn't have to be. Traevyn, it's okay to talk to me. I would never criticize or condemn you either. You do a good enough job of doing that to yourself. Please, I know you're stubborn and prideful, but don't shut me out just because talking to someone instead of brooding alone is foreign to you. It might do you some good to have some company." She couldn't stand the thought of him going in his room and sobbing again. It hurt her heart.

He heaved a sigh and turned to face her. His icy demeanor softened somewhat, and he took her hand between both of his. "Evie, I mean no offense," he said, his voice soft. "I understand your point, I do, but I can't talk about it. It amazes me that I was able to say as much as I did. When I speak of what happened three years ago, it's like someone is taking a razorblade and dissecting my heart. It hurts too badly. You must understand."

She gave a slow nod and gazed up into his eyes. It made a dull ache settle into her heart to look at the hurt in their amazing depths.

He shook his head and gently touched her cheek with his fingertips. "You are a good person. I know you're concerned, but I need to handle this on my own. It's what I'm used to."

She nodded again because she didn't know what else to do. "Whatever you need, Traevyn," she murmured.

His lips upturned in a pained smile. "Thank you." He turned away from her and walked slowly out of the room. Away from warmth. Away from light. Back to the shadows. Back to his familiar darkness. Back to hell.

# Chapter Nine

There was a winding trail through the eucalyptus trees that led to a small plateau overlooking the ocean. Evie had discovered it that morning by accident. She hadn't been able to sleep very well after what had happened with Traevyn. She'd dozed mostly, and at five o'clock she'd realized, as she stared wide-eyed up at the ceiling, that there was no hope of her getting back to sleep anytime soon. So she had taken a walk, deciding to explore the surroundings a bit.

It was evening now and she stood on the same plateau. She hadn't seen Traevyn all day, but she hadn't gone looking for him either. She didn't want to bother him, even though everything within her was screaming to find him and see if he was all right. She didn't want to pry. He had insisted on his solitude, and she'd told him she would respect that. She just couldn't shake the image of him slumped wearily in that chair, crying and hurt. It haunted her.

Curiosity nagged at her. Who had been on the phone, and why had they called? What had they said to hurt Traevyn so badly? She sighed and folded her arms as tendrils of fog curled around her, misting her face. The waves lapped their rhythm up onto the shore below and crashed against the cliffs. Everything else, aside from the pounding sea, was quiet and serene. She couldn't decide if the thundering waves and the cries from the gulls wheeling above in the sky were tranquil or mournful. She imagined it must be either very therapeutic, or very dangerous to be all alone with only your thoughts.

Feeling like someone was watching her, Evie turned to look up toward the house. She spotted Traevyn standing on his terrace like a lonely sentinel. His long, flowing hair blew gently in the breeze. A shiver went through her. He always stood so tall and proud, even though his shoulders carried such a heavy burden. She raised her hand in a tentative greeting, wondering if he could see her. Slowly, he raised his hand in return and she shivered again.

What was it about him? What made her react that way to him? She turned back to the scenery and frowned. There was something about him she found so...unnerving? Fascinating? Alluring? Unimaginably sexy? She shook her head. What was the matter with her? He was almost ten years older than her. And he was issue-ridden. She snorted and turned to head back. She had serious problems.

Evie started dinner as soon as she returned to the house. She was running a little short on food so she cooked steaks for Seth and Traevyn and used what was left of some chicken for her meal. As she was setting the table, Seth came wandering in and plopped into a chair with a yawn. "What's for dinner?" he asked.

"Steak and baked potato for you and Traevyn. Fried chicken for me."

He frowned. "Why are you eating something different?"

"Just wanted to use it before it went bad."

Traevyn came in suddenly and made his way toward the table. He was silent, as usual. Evie sat down and dished up her food, trying not to pay too much attention to him. She blinked in surprise when he sat down across from her. She and Seth exchanged a confused look before she glanced up at Traevyn.

"May I join you two at the table tonight?" he asked, his voice quiet.

"O—Of course," Evie stammered. She met his eyes and flashed him a warm smile.

"Good to have you, dude," Seth put in.

Evie glanced at Seth and felt warmth well up inside of her at his sudden kindess for their host.

Traevyn looked down and gave them his trademark half-smile.

Dinner was quiet. There was no way around that, but it made Evie feel good to know he was there. He had never eaten with them before. It was customary for him to just heap his plate and leave. It made her happy to think that maybe he was beginning to enjoy their company. Maybe she

had actually managed to say something right the night before. That would be a first.

She was cleaning up when Traevyn came up behind her
and placed his hand gently on the small of her back. "I've
never told you how good of a cook you are," he said. "Your
food is fabulous. I always look forward to dinner."

Evie turned and looked up at him with a grin. "Thanks,
Traevyn."

"I'll clean up," he offered. "You are not my servant."

She frowned. "It's all right. You pay me—"

"I pay you to clean once a week and cook one meal a day.
I do not pay you to wait on me like a common slave while I sit
on my throne. Not to mention the support you gave me yes-
terday was going above and beyond the call of duty."

She blushed and looked down, surprised he had brought
it up. "Oh, I—"

"Evie, go work on your drawings or something. Please,
just let me clean up. All right?"

She gazed up into his eyes and nodded.

He flashed a gentle smile and finished clearing the table
for her. It really was the least he could do after losing it the
night before. He expelled a deep sigh as he recalled the way
she had listened to him, how she had been so compassionate
and concerned.

Evie radiated a warm light that he was unfamiliar with, an
aura of gentleness surrounded by fiery passion and spunk.
She was bold and dynamic, yet could soothe his wounded soul
with little effort. It stunned him, and he even found it a bit
frightening. No one had been able to reach him since Leanna
had died and Amy had left him. No one but his brothers. He
let no one close enough to try. Evie seemed to see right past
his barriers and, somehow, she just knew. Knew how to touch
him, knew how to make him feel, even for one small second,
that his heart was beating again. He didn't understand it, and
he didn't know what to do with it. It terrified him. *She* terrified
him, yet she intrigued him. It was a paradox he couldn't get
away from.

Once he had finished in the kitchen, he went to his studio
to paint for awhile. He saw the painting he had mutilated the
night before, pocket knife still sticking out of it. He sighed
and removed the knife, setting it back on his desk where it
belonged. He winced as he remembered the words spoken to

him. His heart ached at the absence of his daughter. Persistent, ever-present. There was never any relief from it. It was his curse.

He removed the marred canvas and pulled out a new one. He painted. For four straight hours, he painted. His release. His passion. His emotions flowing onto the canvas. When he had finished, he stretched, studied what he had done for a moment, and headed out. It was eleven-thirty. Another day he had survived. He went downstairs to get a glass of wine when he heard what sounded like someone throwing up in the bathroom. He frowned and turned down the hallway just as Evie stumbled out of the bathroom looking pale and weary.

"Evie? Are you all right?"

She slumped against the wall and put her hand over her stomach. "I think the chicken I ate may have already been bad," she grumbled. "I need to lie down."

"Would you like me to get you anything?"

She shook her head, then seemed to turn a shade of green and ran back toward the bathroom. Traevyn followed after her without even thinking about it, and he knelt down next to her. He pulled her hair back out of the way while she threw up and ran his hand gently across her back. When it subsided, she slumped down onto the floor and groaned.

"I just love praying to the porcelain god," she moaned.

He smiled a bit and stood to wet a washcloth. He applied it to her forehead, smoothing her hair back.

"This is humiliating," she muttered.

"Nothing to be embarrassed about," he assured her. "If my stomach was turning inside out, I would want someone to help me."

"Somehow, I can't see you ever wanting anyone's help in anything."

He met her eyes briefly. "Everyone needs help sometimes. There are just some circumstances that are more difficult than others. Do you think you can stand?"

She gave a weary nod and let him help her up. Her stomach must have roiled in protest because she groaned.

"Let's get you upstairs," he suggested.

She shook her head. "No. I don't want to have to run all the way to the end of the hall every five minutes. Just get me to the couch. I'll watch television and try to distract myself."

He put one arm loosely around her shoulders and guided her to the living room. "Here, sit down." She obeyed, and he grabbed a blanket from a nearby chair. It was fleece, and he thought it might be comfortable to her. He knelt and pulled off her shoes, then swung her legs up so she was lying down. He placed the blanket around her and offered a small smile. "Are you comfortable?"

She looked up at him, obviously amazed at his considera-tion. "You must have been a very good dad," she murmured.

He averted his gaze, but the smallest of smiles touched his lips. "Thank you," he whispered.

She started to nod when her stomach somersaulted. She flung the blanket off and bolted back down to the bathroom. Traevyn didn't follow, but when she managed to pull herself together and shuffle back out into the living room, he was waiting on the couch with a brush in his hand.

"Come here, Evie," he invited. "Let me help you with your hair."

She eased herself onto the couch and turned her back to give him access. "You can braid hair?"

"Have you seen the length of mine lately?"

She smiled weakly. His gentle hands gathered her thick mass of hair and he began to brush it. She closed her eyes, enjoying the feeling. "You don't have to do this," she mur-mured.

He sighed. "Evie, I am not going to leave you to be mis-erable. What you did for me last night..." He let the sentence hang, apparently unable to find words. "Just let me help you, all right?"

She nodded and loved how his fingers moved through her hair. He was so careful and gentle, not tugging or pulling. Any knots were untangled with care and smoothed.

"You have lovely hair, Evie."

She smiled. "Thank you. So do you. If I could get my hair to look half as good as yours, I would be one happy girl. I know many women who would be jealous of your hair. How do you get it so perfect? It doesn't look like you have any split ends at all."

He gave a soft chuckle as he began to braid. "I don't re-ally do anything to it aside from the usual. My father is Cher-okee. I suppose it might have something to do with that."

So he *was* Native American. That explained his dramatic facial features, as well as his last name. "Is that why your hair is so long? Does it have something to do with your heritage?"

He finished her braid and tied the end. "No, I just look funny with short hair. It's been long since I was sixteen. My brother Julian has long hair also. Goes better with the Whitelaw features."

She turned to face him and gave him a meager smile. She leaned back against the couch cushions and groaned as her stomach protested the movement. "So, your brothers share your Indian features?" she asked, trying to distract herself from the bile rising in her throat.

"My brother Talis has the dark hair. Julian has the features, but he took after my mother as far as his coloring. He is very blond."

So those were his two brothers in the pictures in his office. She would have to remember to take a better look when she cleaned next. She grasped for the remote and pulled the blanket up over her legs. Traevyn's house got cold at night with the ocean and the fog.

"Let me get you a glass of water," he offered.

She groaned and shook her head.

"You need to stay hydrated, Evie. Besides, throwing up water is better than throwing up nothing."

She remained silent. He had a point. Nothing in the world was worse than dry heaves. As he went into the kitchen, she started to turn on the TV, but quickly realized that the worst was not over and booked it back to the bathroom.

She heard a light knock on the bathroom door after several seconds, and she eased herself onto the floor, leaning against the wall. "Come in," she croaked. She knew she had to be ghastly pale, and she was exhausted.

Traevyn gave her a tender look as he entered, wet the washcloth he had been using before, and knelt in front of her, applying it to her face again.

Evie watched him with curiosity. At times, he seemed so rough and cold. After shutting her out the night before, she had expected him to go back to being aloof and icy toward her. She had not expected him to treat her the way a long time friend would. Not even Seth would have stayed in the bathroom with her while she threw up. He might have been helpful in other ways, but he would have lost it too if he'd actually been in the same room as her digestive pyrotechnics. "Traevyn," she croaked.

He met her gaze.

"Thank you." She said it seriously. She hated to be alone when she was sick. She always had. It was the worst feeling in the world. The fact that he was taking care of her meant more to her than she could express at the moment.

Traevyn gave her a gentle smile and set the washcloth on the sink. "Come on," he urged, holding his hand out to her. "Let's get you back to the couch where you can rest."

Evie put her hand in his and let him help her up, but she slumped against him without meaning to. She was so tired. She felt like she had turned inside out. His arm came to wrap around her shoulders, and he guided her back into the living room. He placed the blanket over her once more, then stood back. "Did you want to watch television?"

"I guess," she grumbled.

He handed her the remote, but remained. He was uncertain of how to proceed. He felt awkward and stupid. He knew he should leave her in peace and return to his room, but she looked so small and frail lying on the couch all alone. It dawned on him that he didn't like seeing dynamic Evie small and frail. She had shown him nothing but kindness, despite his abhorrent behavior. He couldn't bring himself to leave her all alone. He sighed. "May I keep you company?"

She glanced up at him. "If you don't mind having a vomit faucet as a companion."

He smirked and sat on the end of the couch. Without even really thinking, he took one of her feet and began to gently rub it.

Evie frowned. "What in the world are you doing?"

She sounded more perplexed than anything. She probably thought he was trying to give her a heart attack on top of her food poisoning. He wouldn't be surprised if she suspected that he really just wanted to kill her so he'd be rid of her once and for all. Massaging someone's feet was somewhat intimate, and it definitely wasn't a practice he made a habit of doing. He actually felt slightly embarrassed, but he tried to hide it. He was acting on pure instinct and trying not to think too much about it. Thinking just made him analyze, which made everything seem more complicated than it needed to be.

"Do you know reflexology?" he asked.

"I know of it."

"Every part of the body is supposed to be represented by different parts of the foot," he replied.

"You know where my stomach is?"

He shrugged one shoulder. "Well no, but I figured if I tackled the whole thing I'd hit it sooner or later."

She studied his face while he wasn't looking at her. She knew it was stupid, but it took her breath away every time she looked at him. No man on earth should be so divinely beautiful.

"Evie," he said suddenly, his voice serious. "I'm sorry about just leaving you the way I did last night. I feel rude for it, but I was having a difficult time—"

"Traevyn," she interrupted, "you absolutely do not have to explain yourself to me. I understand. Besides, you've never had a problem being rude before. Don't start caring now." He met her eyes and she gave him a teasing smile.

He smiled and looked away. "So tell me a little about yourself, Miss Austin," he said. "You are a junior in college, correct?"

She nodded. "One more year to go and I'll be unleashed on the world. Frightening, isn't it?"

"Do you plan on staying in Oregon?"

"I don't know. I've lived there my whole life. It would be nice to get away. I'd love to travel, see the world."

"Traveling is a love of mine as well. I get so much inspiration from beautiful places. Where would you most like to go?"

"Italy," she replied without hesitation. "I want to drink wine, eat pasta, and paint everything."

He chuckled. "By 'drink wine,' I hope you are not referring to five dollar bottles of White Zinfandel."

She raised an eyebrow. "I think I might manage to branch out a little."

He grinned with ease. "And do you have a young man to have a romantic adventure with while you are there?"

She giggled. "No, unfortunately."

He frowned. "No one? You have no one you are interested in?"

"No one I can have is more like it. My best friend Meg's brother has been the object of my affection for years. Maxim deBoer..." She shook her head and sighed. "He's married. It sucks."

He gave another soft chuckle and began to rub her other foot. "And why is this Maxim deBoer so special?"

"He's intelligent, first of all," she said. "Very literate. He's a novelist. And he's quiet and gentle. He isn't loud and obnoxious and flirty. He's just...Maxim. He just always seemed so beautiful to me, so genuine and real." She shrugged. "I don't know. It's stupid."

"No, it isn't," he countered. "Our world is full of fake, shallow people. Depth and uniqueness are refreshing. That's how you are. Genuine and real. No pretenses. I admire that."

She met his eyes and grinned. "Thank you." For some reason, his words made her feel warm all over.

"How are you feeling?" he asked.

"A little better. Just exhausted." She eased herself up into a sitting position and reached for her water glass. She forced down a few swallows, then turned on the TV. "What do you want to watch?" She flipped blindly through the channels until she recognized a movie she loved. "Oh!" she exclaimed. "*V for Vendetta*!"

Traevyn smiled and sat back. "You like political movies about revolution?"

"I love this movie," she commented. "Besides, Natalie Portman's character is named Evey. I mean, come on."

He chuckled. "We'll watch this then."

She scooted closer and offered some of the blanket to him. He accepted and they watched a little of the movie before Evie's eyes started to feel heavy. Hardly realizing it, she leaned her head on Traevyn's shoulder.

He glanced down at her and put his arm around her. "Put your feet up. Lie down," he said gently. "I don't mind."

She obeyed and rested her head on his lap. She knew she should feel awkward, but she didn't. For some reason, when she was with him, it just felt right to her somehow. Natural and easy. Even when he was being sullen and brooding. Even when he was barely speaking. She closed her eyes as she felt his fingers begin to caress her hair. She was starting to realize that she felt the most comfortable with him when he was being warm and gentle. It was rare and fleeting, but she liked it very much.

* * *

Traevyn knew that Evie had fallen asleep, but he remained there for awhile. He watched the movie, but didn't really pay attention to it. His mind was spinning with the realization that he enjoyed having her close to him, touching him, trusting him. It was troubling.

How? How could she affect him the way she did? He had made himself a recluse, a loner, a cold, dead man. He had done it to protect himself, to keep the pain away. How was it that she made him feel warmth and tenderness without doing anything at all? When had she gone from being an annoyance to being dear? How was it that, when she was around, he felt like he could breathe again instead of feeling like he was suffocating? Maybe because she saw him. Maybe because she saw his art. Maybe because she cared. Or, maybe it was like he had said. She was genuine and real. Whatever it was, it was beautiful.

He slowly eased Evie off of him and turned the TV off. He gathered her in his arms and carried her up the stairs and down her hallway. Seth apparently heard him coming because he opened his door, rubbing the sleep from his eyes. "Evie, where—" Traevyn shushed him softly and he blinked up at him. "Is she okay?"

He nodded. "She has food poisoning. She's resting now," he whispered.

Seth frowned. "You should have woken me up. Evie doesn't like to be by herself when she's sick."

"It's all right. I took care of it. Go back to sleep, Seth."

He nodded. "All right. Hey, thanks, man."

Traevyn gave him a small smile and nodded. He continued into Evie's room and set her down on the bed. He pulled the covers over her before standing back. He reached down, removed her glasses, folded them, and set them on the nightstand. He took a quick glance at her room and smiled at all the papers and books she had strewn everywhere. Several of them were his. His own art book sat on the dresser, and he ran his fingers over it on his way out. With a sigh, he closed the door and headed back down to his bedroom. He still felt empty inside, but he also felt slightly more human than before.

# *Chapter Ten*

Traevyn was in the kitchen when Seth trudged in still half asleep and wearing only boxer shorts. He sat down at the table and yawned.

"Morning, dude," Seth muttered.

Traevyn smiled. "Good morning." He turned back to smearing jelly onto a piece of toast.

"What are you doing?"

"Making Evie breakfast," he replied.

Seth frowned. "You sure she's gonna want to eat after barfing her guts out all night?"

"It's just toast. And the ginger ale will settle her stomach."

Seth nodded, then smiled mischievously. "What did you make me?"

Traevyn turned his gaze to the teen and raised an eyebrow. He glanced around the kitchen for a moment, then grabbed a banana and threw it to him. "Bon apatite."

Seth stared at the banana. "Gee, thanks," he grumbled.

Traevyn smirked and carried the plate and glass out of the kitchen and up the stairs. He knocked softly on Evie's door, figuring that if Seth was awake, she should be awake also.

"Go bother someone else!" came a shout from within.

Traevyn raised his eyebrows, then knocked again.

Evie let out an annoyed snarl. "Why are you knocking, you idiot? What's the matter with you?"

He chuckled softly and opened the door just enough to stick his head in. "I beg your pardon, madam. I will leave you in peace shortly."

Her eyes widened. "Traevyn!" she cried. "I'm sorry! I thought you were Seth!"

He opened the door wider and stepped in. "Good to know. I brought you some breakfast."

Evie put her hand over her stomach and made a face. She set aside the drawing she had been working on, turning it face down so Traevyn couldn't see it, and she smoothed her hair self-consciously. It was still bound in the braid he had put it in the night before.

"How are you feeling this morning?"

"Like I did about a million crunches."

He smiled. "I brought you toast and some ginger ale. The ginger ale should help settle your stomach."

She looked up at him and he met her gaze. She smiled, tenderness radiating from her eyes. Traevyn's heart did something funny at the way she looked at him. Something it was not accustomed to doing. It seemed to stutter like a car engine trying to turn over. It took his breath away and he averted his eyes. He cleared his throat uncomfortably. "Think you can eat?"

She nodded and reached for the plate. "Thank you. And thank you for being so thoughtful last night. Having you keep me company made me feel better."

His lips quirked and he glanced at her sketch pad. "What are you working on?" he asked, reaching for it.

"Nothing!" she all but shouted, slamming her hand down on top of it.

He raised an eyebrow and smiled devilishly. "Well, now I have to take a look."

"No you don't. Leave it alone."

"I'm supposed to be the master, aren't I? And you my lowly apprentice. Let me see it." He reached for it again.

"Traevyn, come on." She tried to push his hand away. "I'm just messing around. They're just stupid sketches. They aren't even a big deal."

He flashed a smile that he knew reflected the mischief he felt. "Then you won't mind me taking a look." He grasped the corner of the sketchpad and started to pull it toward him when a pillow met the side of his head. He shook his head, grinned, and yanked the sketchpad to him. He dodged Evie's next swing and stood quickly, sauntering over to the dresser. He leaned nonchalantly against it and gave her a pointed looked. "Eat your breakfast," he commanded.

Evie stared at him in dismay. She averted her gaze to her lap and started playing with her fingers.

Traevyn smirked at her, then opened up the sketchpad and flipped through it absently. There were sketches of various people he didn't recognize and several of Seth. There was one of his house, which was quite good, and several of the view from the terrace. He turned a page and saw one of himself. He blinked in surprise.

He was on the terrace with his back turned. It must have been that first night he and Evie had actually shared a conversation. He turned the page and there were more of him. Different angle sketches of his face. When had she done these? Had she silently been watching him from the shadows? He turned the page to see the one she had been working on when he'd come in. It was a larger sketch of him smiling. He peered closer at it. The detail was incredible. It was like looking in a mirror. Although, he was not accustomed to seeing himself smile.

He glanced up at Evie and smirked at her obvious discomfort. She was doing everything in her power to avoid looking at him. She was actually pretending to be very interested in her toast. He closed the sketchpad and went to set it back down beside her.

"I have been...uh...trying to work on faces. That's why there are some of Seth in there. There's a lot of you because you're features are so...um, dramatic." She stole a glance up at him.

He sat back down on the foot of her bed and smiled. "They are excellent. When did you start the latest one?"

"This morning," she murmured.

"What were you drawing off of?" he asked in amazement. "I'm pretty sure I don't have any pictures lying around with me smiling like that."

She wanted to invert. "My...memory," she all but whispered. She loved to remember his beautiful smile. It was something she liked to revisit and, while he did seem to be smiling more now than before, she had yet to see another grin like the one she had seen on the beach. She wanted to capture the image while she still had the details in her mind.

He arched an eyebrow. "Your memory? That's incredible, Evie."

She felt her cheeks turn hot. Because she couldn't think of anything else to do, she flung her pillow at him again. It hit him in the face, then fell in his lap. He blinked and Evie giggled.

"You're awfully ornery for being so sick last night," he commented.

She shrugged and took another bite of her toast. She couldn't believe that Traevyn had actually hand-delivered her breakfast. She remembered how kind and attentive he had been to her the night before. She remembered falling asleep on his lap while he stroked her hair, feeling like it was the most natural thing in the world for her to be there. She also knew that he must have carried her to bed because she did not recall getting there herself.

He cracked a small smile. "Maybe I could sketch you sometime."

The bite that Evie had been swallowing lodged in her throat. She looked up at him. Okay, she didn't know what was wrong with her, but the way he had said that... Soft, gentle, his voice sounding almost like a lover's caress. It was wrong. How could someone say something so simple and have it come out so sexy? She forced a smile and swallowed her toast with a gulp. "Why in the world would you want to do that?"

An enigmatic, almost teasing smile flashed across his face. "I want to study your dramatic features." He stood, anticipating that the pillow he must have sensed was heading his direction again. He chuckled. "No, really. Let me sketch you sometime. All right?"

She gave a bashful smile. "If you really want to."

"It would be good for me to practice faces as well. I haven't worked on them for some time." Evie nodded and he sighed. "In a few days I have to go to San Luis Obispo. Some of my work is in a gallery there, and I need to deliver some new paintings. I'd like you to come with me." She looked up at him with a quizzical expression that made him smile. "It would be good for you to know the ropes of the business end of being an artist as well as the artistic end of it. It's roughly a three and a half hour drive. We should be there and back in a day."

She smiled at the thought that he actually wanted to take her along on something that he was used to doing alone. The knowledge that he had even thought of her made her feel like he actually considered her worthy of being his apprentice. "When are we going?" she asked.

He smiled. "Wednesday. Three days from now."

"All right, it's a date!"

His smile faded and he paled considerably.

Her cheeks burned. "Well, not a date like a date, obviously." She swallowed and looked down. "I just meant..." She shook her head. "Yes, Wednesday sounds good." She plastered a smile on her lips.

His smile seemed slightly pained, but he nodded. "All right. I will leave you in peace. Take it easy today. Rest."

She nodded. "Thanks again for breakfast." He gave a little bow, which made her giggle. Then, he turned and left.

Evie spent the rest of the day lounging, watching television, and taking it easy, just like Traevyn had said. She figured she had earned it. She didn't make dinner either, much to Seth's dismay. In an attempt to be nice, he had made pancakes, but they had come out burnt on the outside and goopy in the middle. Traevyn actually managed to down two of them, which made Evie think he was either really hungry or a lot nicer than she gave him credit for.

The next two days went by fairly normal, and Tuesday night found Evie and Seth in the living room as they watched a terrible martial arts movie. Seth burst out laughing at a cheesy part and Evie grinned. She knew she should go to bed. She and Traevyn had to get up early to leave the next morning, but she wasn't tired. Besides, she could always sleep in the car.

"Oh my gosh!" Seth cried. "Did you see the way that guy just punched? That looked so gay!"

Evie smirked. "Like you could do better," she teased.

Seth frowned, then delivered a mean punch right into her shoulder. Her eyes bulged and she grasped at her now dead arm. "Oh my gosh!" she cried. "That hurt *so bad*!" She turned to her brother to retaliate, but he was quickly retreating. "Come back here!" she shouted, jumping up after him.

Seth laughed as he continued to evade her, but he wasn't fast enough and Evie shoved him. He stumbled backwards into a bookcase that was against one of the walls. It sent a vase wobbling on top and two large photo albums tumbled to the floor. One of them landed open. The other one had a wedding picture of Traevyn and his wife on the front. Evie blinked in surprise and stared down at the picture. He looked so happy, blissful even. She knelt down and picked the album up, running her fingers across the front. "Traevyn's wedding album," she murmured.

Without even thinking, she opened it up and began to look through it. There were so many pictures of him laughing, pictures with his brothers and his friends. His wife was beautiful with alabaster skin and golden hair. What a stunning couple they had made. In all of the pictures, he was staring at her with such adoration. It was plain to see how much he had loved her.

"Look, Evie," Seth said. He handed her the other album.

She glanced at the front. It was a baby book. "Leanna Alison Whitelaw," she read softly. She opened it and stopped when she saw a black and white photo taken of Traevyn holding his baby girl. He was asleep and she was sleeping on his chest. She reached out to touch it. It was the most beautiful thing she had ever seen.

"What are you doing?" Traevyn's voice came.

Evie jumped and snapped the book shut. "Oh." She stood and put the albums back in the shelf. "Seth and I were messing around and he accidentally knocked them down." She frowned as she realized that Seth seemed to have taken a convenient leave of absence.

Traevyn's scowl was fierce. "So you decided to take a guided tour?" His voice was a snarling hiss.

She shook her head. "Oh no! I was just curious—"

"I did not give you permission to look at those!"

Evie was taken aback. She knew she shouldn't have been snooping, but he really didn't have to yell at her like that. "I—I'm sorry...I just—"

"Keep out of my things!" he exclaimed. "You take enough liberties as it is!"

She stopped for minute, and her apology died on her lips. She felt anger well up inside of her. Liberties? What the crap? "Excuse me?" she cried. "I take enough liberties as it is? There is not one thing I've done in this house that I haven't cleared with you first, and I didn't know that trying to be friends with you was taking a liberty!"

He met her gaze, his eyes cold and flat. "I never asked you to befriend me, Evie."

She stared at him, unable to believe what he had just said. Hurt washed over her. She had been so certain that they'd been growing closer, building a relationship that went beyond the student/teacher role. Had he just been tolerating her all this time, pretending to care when he really didn't? "Oh, okay," she said, her voice full of bitterness. "I guess that's why, when I asked you if it bothered you that I was trying to be friends with you, you said no. You said you enjoyed my company." She folded her arms and looked away. Had that all just been a bunch of bull? Had his compassion the night she'd been sick just been a temporary lapse of sanity on his part?

He sighed. "Evie, those pictures..." He indicated the albums she had replaced. "Those memories... They are from another lifetime. They are the memories of a man I don't even know anymore. I don't want to remember them."

Evie watched as he drew in a shuddering breath and hung his head. She felt her heart soften. "Traevyn," she said quietly as she approached him. "You can't deny your own memories. Embrace them, learn from them, grow..." She placed a hand gently on his arm. "Become whole again."

He whirled, anger and pain burning in his eyes. "I will never be whole again!" he cried. "What could I possibly have to learn from those memories that I haven't already learned? I learned that love is pain! It is a razor sharp blade! A scorching, burning dagger that stabs and stabs again! And the wound never stops bleeding!" Tears brimmed in his eyes and he shook with the violent torrent of his emotions. In the brief second before Evie had closed the book, he had seen. He had seen the picture of him holding his daughter, and below it, he had seen a picture of the three of them in a park together. Amy, Leanna, and him. His family. The one he no longer had.

He looked down, feeling lost and hopeless. He wanted to leave, to lock himself in his room and not emerge until he got a grip on himself. But Evie...she was staring at him with such compassion and concern. A very small remnant of his shattered heart wanted to reach out to her, to cry within her embrace. He didn't know why, but her arms seemed the only place that was safe at the moment. That horrified him more than anything. That he would even have that desire meant trust. Trust meant friendship. Friendship of any sort meant love. Love meant pain.

"Traevyn," Evie murmured, stepping forward. "Tell me what happened. Help me understand. If I understand, I can help you." She laid her hand on his arm again, a gesture of comfort.

Everything inside of him tensed at her touch. Too close. She was too close. She was asking him to trust her, confide in her. He couldn't. He wouldn't. He pulled away from her touch and met her eyes. "Stay away from me." His voice was much more sinister than he had ever heard it sound.

She couldn't mask the hurt in her eyes. "I only want to help you."

"I'm broken!" he shouted. "Something inside of me died! I can't fix it! You *definitely* can't fix it! Who are you anyway? Nobody. Just a college student I'm supposed to train for the summer. I'll never see you again. You know those memories you told me to learn from? You know what they taught me? Let no one close enough to hurt you! No one! And that's what I have done. No one but my brothers can get close to me. Certainly not you. You are no one to me. Just my apprentice. Not my psychiatrist, and definitely not my friend."

Evie folded her arms as he turned and started to walk away. Hurt from his words was replaced quickly with her flaming temper. She snorted in disgust. "I guess that's why you went to the beach with Seth and me and laughed and played. I guess that's why you took care of my while I was sick. Or, here's one in case you forgot, I guess that's why you poured your heart out to me on the anniversary of your daughter's death! You did all of those things because I am nothing to you, right?"

He met her eyes with a dark glower. He said nothing, but he had no problem dismissing her as he turned his back to her again.

Evie reached down and pulled her shoe off. It was just a flimsy, black flip-flop. She hated the image of his retreating form, of him walking away from her. She wasn't finished yet! He was going to listen to what she had to say whether he wanted to or not. Stubborn, prideful, ridiculous man.

She flung her shoe at him and it hit him between the shoulder blades. He whirled, looking half perplexed and half infuriated.

"I am so stupid!" she bellowed. "I am a stupid, stupid

woman to think you could be anything other than the insensitive jerk you were when I met you! You know what, Traevyn? You can tell yourself whatever you need to make you feel better, but the real reason you won't revisit your memories or let me in has nothing to do with me. You just take it out on me because I'm a good scapegoat and me being here to lash out at prevents you from having to face the culprit in the mirror. The real reason is because you're a coward."

He strode back to her, his green eyes smoldering with anger. "I am no coward."

"You are a coward! It's easier for you to lock out the world and miss out on everything beautiful in life than it is to just take a chance and risk getting hurt again." She shook her head. "You're pathetic." The words flew out of her mouth before she could stop them, heated words of anger that she never would have said otherwise. She saw hurt flash across Traevyn's features, but she didn't show weakness. After all, he had said hurtful things and not cared.

They stared at one another for an agonizing moment, then Traevyn stood to his full height and fixed her with an icy scowl. "Go to bed. We're leaving early in the morning."

"Oh, you're still taking me?" she said with sarcasm.

He started out of the room and up the staircase. "Not out of desire, out of obligation."

"Oh! Well I'll be sure not to sit too close to you in the car!" He said nothing and she watched him disappear up the stairs. She sat down on the couch, still fuming. After a moment, her anger abated and she sighed. Instant regret over what she had said set in and she pondered whether or not she should apologize. She decided against it. After all, she had only been trying to be supportive! He was the one that had gone off like a loose cannon! If anything, he owed *her* an apology!

She grumbled to herself and made her way up to her room. Seth better not even think of showing his face to her. The little turncoat. If he'd stayed, Traevyn might not have lashed out at her like he had. It had been just as much his fault as it was hers anyway. He'd been the one trying to kung-fu her on the couch.

She thought seriously about apologizing several more times before she went to sleep, but she told herself she was too pissed to give him that much. In her heart, she knew the real reason why she wouldn't do it. Other than her own stubborn pride, he had hurt her. She'd thought she was at least a friend to him, and he, more or less, said she meant nothing. That stung, stung more than it should have, but she tried to ignore it and pawn it off as anger. It was an easy emotion to hide behind.

# Chapter Eleven

The ride to San Luis Obispo was a silent one. Neither of them spoke a word the entire drive down and, when they got there, all Evie got to do was stand around while Traevyn talked to the art dealer for upwards of two hours. When she decided she couldn't take it anymore, she just left. She walked out of the gallery and wandered the streets until she found a coffee shop that caught her interest. San Luis Obispo reminded her of a coastal Ashland so she felt very at home. She went inside and lodged herself into a corner where she just drew. It was the only thing that would make her feel better.

\* \* \*

Traevyn's first reaction when he realized that Evie was missing was great irritation, but as the hours went by and he still couldn't find her, his irritation grew to concern. A cold lump of guilt sat in the bottom of his stomach as he searched. He had driven her away. He couldn't find her because she didn't want to be found. He wouldn't either if someone had spoken to him the way he'd spoken to her the night before. He hated how cruel he had been to her, and had thought seriously about apologizing, but she had hurt him too and didn't seem to show great remorse for it.

Besides, she had pelted him with her shoe.

Still, he couldn't help but feel like her hurtful words were more of a retaliation than an assault. He'd absolutely lost it when he'd seen that picture. It had caused such inner turmoil that all he'd wanted to do was shut it out and run. Evie's presence made it impossible to do that. So, because she wouldn't let him run, he'd attacked her. It was his defense. It was what he was used to...and it made him feel terrible.

After nearly two hours of searching, Traevyn went into a coffee shop that was almost invisible it was so small. He scanned the premises and spotted Evie in a corner with her sketchpad. He suddenly felt like he could breathe easier. He strode to her out of elation, but halfway there remembered he was angry at her and scowled. "What do you think you are doing?" he spat.

She looked up at him and gave him an icy glare. "Drinking an iced mocha. What does it look like?"

"I have been looking for you for two hours!"

"And I had to listen to you BS with that art guy for two hours! We're even now!" She looked back down at her sketchpad.

"You could have at least told me where you were going. Something could have happened to you." *I'm lecturing her. Why? She isn't a child. She is a grown woman. I'm not her keeper.* A tiny voice in his head told him to stop being ridiculous. He'd been worried. That was all there was to it.

She turned her eyes up to him in a lazy movement. "What do you care? I mean nothing to you, remember?"

He sighed in exasperation. He really couldn't argue with his own words hurled back at him. "Do you want anything to eat?" For some dumb reason, that was all he could think of to say.

"I already ate. Thanks." Her words were laced with venom. "But by all means, go find yourself something."

"Will you be here when I get back?"

She rolled her eyes. "As your lordship commands," she mocked.

He let out another sigh and started to walk away.

"Jerk," she muttered.

Traevyn gave her a frigid glower over his shoulder, but she just gave him a giant fake smile and fluttered her eyelashes at him. He let out a growling sound and went on his way.

* * *

They left San Luis Obispo around seven in the same state

of silence as when they'd arrived. The fog was rolling in, thick and unrelenting. By the time they were about an hour away from Traevyn's home, it was completely dark save the soup they were driving through, and Evie was a nervous wreck. She couldn't see more than a foot in front of the car and had no idea how Traevyn was managing to navigate. After several minutes of her almost chewing her lip off out of sheer terror, Traevyn pulled the car to the side of the road and shut off the engine.

"What are you doing?" Evie asked.

"I don't really want to die tonight. I can't see anything. We'll have to wait here until the fog lifts."

"Great," she muttered. She was happy they weren't continuing their suicide mission through the fog, but was not thrilled that she was stuck with him for who knew how long.

"If you hadn't disappeared, we could have left when I wanted to and avoided this," Traevyn grumbled.

"Oh cram it," she shot back.

He sighed and stared out the window at the all-encompassing fog. For some reason, his mind returned to the night he had told Evie about Leanna. He remembered how she had held him, offered him comfort, a soft place to fall. He had felt such warmth from her that night. And that had been after she had lured him out with her and Seth, after they had made him laugh. It had felt so good to laugh.

She had told him she would never criticize or condemn him, that she would give him space if that's what he needed. Evie never pried. She had only ever been understanding...

She had never done anything to deserve the words he had shouted at her the night before.

Returning to the past was not something Traevyn liked doing. In fact, he avoided it at all costs, but he couldn't run from it forever. He actually couldn't run from it at all. Try as he might, his ghosts always caught up with him. Evie didn't deserve his venom. She had done nothing to him. She was not the enemy. He shouldn't take his anger at his wife and his anger at life in general out on the one person who had offered him genuine, unadulterated friendship.

He closed his eyes and let out a heavy sigh. "My wife was one of those women men would have done anything to be with," he began softly. "One of those blonde goddesses straight from Mt. Olympus."

Evie frowned and looked over at him in bewilderment.

Traevyn didn't look at her. He couldn't. Keeping his eyes away from hers was the only way he was going to make it through this. "When she showed an interest in me, the stoic artist, I was dumbfounded. She was spectacular, so elegant and sophisticated. The day she became my wife was the day I felt like my life had started. The day she left me...time stopped.

"Four years into our marriage she began to act strange. Distant and cold. I tried everything in my power to make her happy, but nothing seemed to work. We were living in San Diego then. One day I came home and found her with another man...in my bed. Actually, it wasn't just any man. It was my best friend. Someone I had trusted and relied on since high school. Naturally, I was pretty upset. Amy and I started fighting. She told me she didn't love me anymore, that she hadn't for the past year. She said she wanted a divorce." He winced as her stinging words reverberated through his memory. "She told me she had been seeing Robert for the whole last year of our marriage." He shook his head. "For one whole year she lied to me. While I was lying beside her at night, whispering my undying words of devotion, she was sleeping with my best friend.

"She told me that she couldn't be with someone who put his family second to his career." He looked at Evie then, out of necessity, as if to convince her. "I *never* put my family second, Evie. Never. I would have done anything for that woman. If she'd told me that in order to keep her, I had to stop painting, I would have laid down my brush and become a... I don't know, a janitor, or an accountant. Anything! Nothing was more important to me than that woman and that little girl." He whispered the last part as raw emotion gripped him and his eyes filled with familiar tears.

Evie nodded, indicating that she believed him.

"As we were fighting," he choked, "Amy took Leanna and started to leave with her. She told me that she was going to live with Robert and get full custody of Leanna, that I would never see her again. Leanna didn't know what was happening. She was only four years old." A tear streaked down his cheek and he closed his eyes, his chest feeling tight. "Amy took her out of the house and across the street to Robert's car. Leanna was upset; she didn't know why her mother was making her leave..." He drew in a shaky breath. "Leanna was...Daddy's girl, you see..." He shook his head as waves and waves of agonizing grief washed over him. "She was crying for me, reaching out for me. I was still on the other side of the street, waiting until it was clear to cross. Amy set Leanna down to open the car door and she bolted...straight across the street without looking... Straight to me..."

Evie stared at Traevyn in horror, obviously figuring out and dreading the next part of the story.

"Straight into the path of a diesel pickup truck... It snapped her spine and killed her instantly."

A tear rolled down Evie's cheek, and she put her hand over her mouth.

Traevyn fought to maintain his composure, but he was crying freely now. He was just trying not to go hysterical. "After the funeral, I begged Amy to come back to me. I humiliated myself in front of her. I didn't want to lose her too. I loved her so much... She looked me right in the eye with no emotion except malice and said in the coldest voice I have ever heard, 'You deserve to be alone. It's because of you Leanna is dead. I hope you die miserable and alone.' I didn't hear from her after that except on the anniversary of Leanna's death when she called to remind me it was my fault. She called me both years. This year, too, the night we were painting. I wouldn't have picked up the phone, but I wasn't paying attention. I didn't look at the number." He let out a muffled sob and his heart twisted in agony as he remembered Amy's cold, heartless tone and vicious words. He shook his head. "Why would someone say that, Evie? How could someone be so cruel? It wasn't my fault... It was just an accident..." He repeated it over and over like a mantra, trying to convince himself, trying to believe.

Evie moved to Traevyn and caressed her hand across his shoulders. "No, it wasn't your fault. It was just a terrible, tragic accident. Traevyn, I'm so sorry." She understood now why he didn't want to let anyone close. He had lost the three people he loved most all in the same day.

"So I moved here to Big Sur," he said. "Built my house and my barrier, shut out the world in an attempt to shut out pain, but it always finds me. It lives in me." He drew in another shuddering breath and hung his head in exhaustion. "And that's my story."

Evie's heart bled for him, it wept. "I'm so sorry," she whispered. It was all she could say and it sounded so inadequate.

Traevyn turned to her suddenly, meeting her eyes with force. "I'm so sorry about what I said to you last night," he blurted. "I didn't mean it. I was angry. I was terrified."

She touched his cheek and shook her head. "Traevyn, it's okay."

"No, it's not okay. I was horrid. You were right. I am a coward."

She continued to caress his face in an effort to get him to stop. She couldn't stand to see him groveling. "No, you're not."

"Yes, I am," he insisted. "I *am* a coward and I *am* pathetic."

"Traevyn, no. Shhh."

"It's just that—"

She acted without thinking. All she knew was that she couldn't listen to one more word out of his mouth. She couldn't take his unbearable sorrow for one more second. She lunged forward and planted her lips boldly to his.

Traevyn froze and his eyes drifted closed as the warmth of her lips touched his. It seemed to make some sort of difference, like her touch stayed with him even after she pulled away. It stopped his tirade and seemed to bring him back to the present.

Realization at her own actions slammed Evie. "Oh!" she cried in horror. She sat back and put her hands over her mouth. "I'm so sorry!"

He opened his eyes and let his breath out in a slow sigh. "It's all right," he whispered.

"No it's not! I'm humiliated!"

He gave a small smile. "Don't be humiliated."

"I am!" she cried. "I *am* humiliated! I took advantage of you in a weakened state! I should be shot!" He closed his eyes and laughed softly, as if he was unable to contain it. She stared at him, stunned. "Have you lost it completely?"

He took her face in his hands and stared into her eyes. "Evie." His voice was a sinful whisper. "You are so beautiful."

She blinked. "Wh—What?" she squeaked. Beautiful? That was not something she was used to hearing.

"You're killing me," he breathed. "Killing me slowly with

your gentleness. How is it that you are always bringing me laughter and light?" He shook his head. "What I just told you no one else knows aside from my parents and my brothers."

"And why did you tell me?"

"Because you *are* my friend," he said. "And you do mean something to me even though I tried to tell myself otherwise. For some reason, you can see straight through me, and I don't like it. It terrifies me, but it's true all the same."

She sighed. "It doesn't hurt to confide in someone. We all need someone. No one should have to be so alone."

He stared into her eyes for a long moment, then gave her a soft smile. There was something in his eyes... When she had first seen him, she'd noticed the sorrow and loneliness reflected in them, but now, it looked as if some small part of him felt relief, at peace.

He leaned back against the seat. "The fog isn't letting up."

Evie looked out at the milky whiteness. "No, it isn't."

"There are some blankets in the back seat," he said. "I use them sometimes to sit on when I go down to the beach to draw. Let's just stay here until morning when we can see again."

She nodded and grabbed the blankets from the back. She handed one to Traevyn and spread the other one across herself. She reclined her seat and stared up at the roof for a long time, re-hashing all of what Traevyn had just told her. She looked out the window and sighed. Everything was so silent. It felt like she was floating in a cloud, surreal and eerie. She glanced at Traevyn, who was also reclined and staring out the driver's side window. Her heart ached in her chest as she thought of the horrible pain he had endured. His left arm was draped across his stomach, and she turned on her side, reaching her right hand over to touch his fingers lightly.

He turned his head and looked down at her. She blushed, but didn't pull away. After a moment, he raised his fingers to hers, brushing across them with a soft caress. He pressed his palm to hers and grinned when his hand dwarfed her small one and his long fingers stuck up about an inch more than hers. Evie smiled as well.

He slowly curled his fingers to twine with hers and closed his eyes as if he was savoring something. "Thank you, Evie," he whispered.

"For what?"

"For listening. For being here. For being you."

She gave him a small smile. "I'll always be here, Traevyn. That's what friends do." She frowned. "And...I'm sorry about the kiss."

He grinned. "That's all right. I needed it. I couldn't seem to shut myself up."

She smiled wider and her heart jumped when he let go of her hand and reached up to caress her cheek.

"Goodnight, Evie."

"Goodnight, Traevyn." He reached for her hand again and she scooted as close to him as she could get without being on the arm rest and the stick shift. She lay there for a long while, just enjoying the feel of his hand on hers. She frowned. Something had changed in her, something she couldn't quite place, but she knew after this night, she would never be able to feel the same way toward Traevyn again. She closed her eyes and let sleep overtake her, her last conscious thought being that his presence there beside her felt so right it was unnerving.

# Chapter Twelve

It was the soft rays of sunlight breaking through the fog that first woke Traevyn. His fingers were still clasped with Evie's, and she was proportioned so that the upper part of her body was lying across the armrest while her head was resting against his shoulder. He smiled, wondering how she had managed to situate herself that way. He studied her face for a moment, then slowly pulled his hand away from hers and tried to push her gently back into her seat. She turned and curled herself toward the window almost instantly.

He pushed his seat up and winced at the stiffness in his neck and the pain in his back. Not to mention his legs felt completely numb. He glanced out the window at the fog, which was just as thick, but slightly less menacing now that it was daylight. He smiled and pulled the blanket off of his lap. He wrapped it around Evie, whose breath was coming out in white puffs. He opened the car door and was blasted by icy dampness. He got out quickly and shut the door so cold air wouldn't flood the car.

Once outside, he took a deep breath and smiled. He relished the cold fog. He stepped out into the white mist and let it swallow him.

* * *

Evie awoke disoriented and aware of a great pain in her lower back. Her eyes fluttered open and it took her a minute to remember where she was. Then, everything came flooding back to her like a tidal wave. She immediately looked over for Traevyn, but he was gone. She frowned and glanced at her watch as she rubbed the remaining sleep from her eyes. Six A.M. Where in the heck could he be at six A.M. trapped in a fog bank? She pushed her seat up and opened the door, but almost screamed aloud as the icy morning air attacked her. She grasped one of the blankets and wrapped it around her like an Indian.

"Traevyn?" she called as she stepped out of the car. The fog rolled by, touching her skin and lips with the salty spray of the ocean. She walked around the car. "Traevyn?" she called again. Tentatively, she ran across the road to the other side. "Traevyn, where are you?" She took a few steps forward, then decided she was too cold and turned to head back. She blinked as she realized that the fog had swallowed the car. She spun in alarm, but everything looked the same. "Traevyn!" she shouted. She let out a deep sigh as no reply came. "Great," she muttered.

Suddenly, her eyes caught something moving up ahead of her, parting the mist and emerging like he was stepping through time. Tall and elegant with his spectacular mane of raven black hair falling around his shoulders and down past his waist, the ocean air tugging on it ever so gently. Evie couldn't breathe. The breath she would have taken caught in her throat and all she could do was stare.

He strode up to her, a small smile on his provocative and arousing mouth. The breath that she was trying so desperately to take turned into a soft gasp as he towered over her.

"Evie, what are you doing out here?" he asked.

She didn't speak. She just stared up at him, into his alluring green eyes.

He frowned. "Are you all right? Evie?"

She gave herself a mental shake, and her heart remembered it was supposed to be beating. She snapped back to the present. "Uh... Y—yes, I'm fine." She averted her eyes, trying to keep from blushing.

"What are you doing out here?" he repeated.

"What are *you* doing out here?" she asked.

"Walking."

She frowned. "Walking where? To the nearest 7-11? How can you even see?"

He smiled. "I don't need to see." He closed his eyes. "I just feel where I am going."

She arched an eyebrow. "Just when I thought you

couldn't get any weirder..."

He reached for her hand. "Come with me. I want to show you something."

She let him guide her through the fog, wondering if he'd completely lost his mind. In a few short minutes, he stopped and Evie looked up, keeping her blanket clutched tight around her with her free hand. Her eyes widened. They were on top of a high cliff. She could see the ocean below, spraying water up into the air as the waves pounded against the cliff base. The slowly abating fog shrouded everything, making it all seem like she had stepped into a dream.

"This is my world," Traevyn said. "This is what inspires me." He closed his eyes as he listened to the sound of the powerful waves. "It's music."

Evie glanced up at him and smiled at the blissful look on his face. She looked down at their entwined fingers and she tightened her grip just slightly, studying how his fingers felt. She had never held hands with a man before. Seth didn't count. He was her brother. And he definitely wasn't a man. Besides, even Seth didn't hold her hand unless they were at a funeral, or one of them was really scared.

"This is me, Evie," Traevyn continued. "My heart is that ocean, my passion like those crashing waves. Intense, dangerous, forever flowing. My mind fills with so many images when I'm staring out at the violent beauty of the sea. I want to paint everything." He sighed and looked down at her. She gave him a gentle smile and his eyes, usually so distant and sad, filled with a tender warmth. "What inspires you, Evie?"

At that precise moment, her stomach made a very audible growling sound. "Breakfast," she joked.

He arched an eyebrow. "Breakfast?" He chuckled and looked back out at the sea.

She studied his profile. *He* inspired her. He was a living work of art. There was so much to see when she looked at Traevyn. Such depth, such wicked, dark beauty. "You," she whispered. He looked down at her with a curious frown, and she felt her face turn hot. Had she just said that out loud? Fantastic. She tried to lighten the moment by laughing, but the sound was nervous and awkward. "But mostly, breakfast."

He gave her a half-smile and turned to face her. "I shared with you the darkest shadows of my soul last night," he said, his eyes gazing intently into hers. "You have a part of me now."

Evie again seemed to decide that staring was the best course of action. How did stuff like that just roll off of his tongue? She let out a slow breath and shook her head. "Oh geez," she muttered.

"What's wrong?"

She took a deep breath and met his eyes. "All my life I've loved Gothic novels. The dark classics like *Wuthering Heights*, *Rebecca*, *Jane Eyre*. I always loved the dark, brooding characters because they had so much substance. They were intriguing, and possessed a depth that people like my brother, for instance, lack." She let her eyes travel over his gorgeous face one more. "Traevyn, you leave them all behind." At his thoughtful frown, she went on. "Your soul is deeper than that ocean." She pointed out toward the sea. "I imagine it would take someone a lifetime to find the bottom."

He gazed down at her, obviously touched by her words. "No one's ever tried," he said.

"Someone should," she murmured. "I imagine the journey would be unforgettably beautiful."

For several heartbeats, all they did was stare at one another. The fog floated listlessly by, and everything was complete silence save the thunderous crashing of the waves below them. Then, Traevyn took Evie's hand in his own and brought it to his lips. He pressed a slow kiss to her knuckles and curled her fingers around his own, holding their interlocking hands over his heart.

Evie's heartbeat was sluggish and she felt lightheaded. She was also really embarrassed. Why couldn't she just keep her mouth shut? She was always spewing ridiculous words out of her mouth. Words that she would much rather keep to herself. Did she possess no self-control at all?

"Come on," Traevyn said, putting his arm around her shoulders. "Let's go get some breakfast. Should we get something for your brother also?"

She sighed. "I guess. Hopefully he hasn't burnt your house down."

He smiled and guided them back to the car. The fog had lifted enough so they could see, and he warmed the engine up while she flung the blankets in the back seat. Doing this caused the end of one blanket to hit her in the face, and managed to send her glasses flying to the floor under Traevyn's seat. She reached for them on instinct, as did he, and they smacked their heads together. "Ow!" Evie cried, rubbing her forehead. He winced and rubbed at his as well. "Here, I'll get them," she volunteered. She leaned forward to reach for them, but it was difficult with Traevyn's long legs in the way. She felt around under the seat until she realized that she was practically lying on Traevyn's lap with the side of her face pressed up against a rather private area. Her face flushed horribly and she sat up. "Maybe... uh...you should get them." She cleared her throat.

He glanced at her slyly and smirked. "Oh by all means, don't let me rush you."

She was positive that she turned more shades of red than a crayon box had in it. She put her hands over her face.

Traevyn chuckled and retrieved her glasses. "Here."

She grabbed them and shoved them on, not able to look at him out of sheer humiliation.

He cast her a sidelong glance and smiled. "You should wear red more often, Evie," he teased. "It suits you."

She heaved an exasperated sigh. "I'm always wearing red around you, Traevyn," she grumbled.

He grinned and pulled onto the road.

* * *

Evie had decided that she wanted to make breakfast rather than just raid a McDonald's, so she and Traevyn hit a grocery store. When they arrived back at the house, they were laughing about something, and Evie was taken aback as her brother flew down the staircase and stopped to stand in front of them. He looked more annoyed than she had seen him look since their mother had first informed him that he would have to spend the summer with Evie.

"Where were you guys?" he cried.

Evie blinked in surprise. "We got caught in some bad fog and had to pull over and wait it out for the night," she explained.

"And you didn't have the decency to at least call me?" he shouted. "I thought you were dead somewhere!"

Evie raised her eyebrows. She couldn't pretend that she wasn't completely caught off guard by Seth's concern. She'd imagined he would have slept through everything and barely even noticed that they were late.

"What's this for?" He held up his cell phone. "Come on, Evie! You say I'm irresponsible? At least I would have called you! You might have thought of that too considering you're like thirty and used to be a father!" He stabbed an accusing finger at Traevyn.

Traevyn adopted the same surprised expression as Evie.

Seth snorted and threw his cell phone down onto the couch. "You know, whatever." He strode out of the room and back up the stairs.

Evie blinked in bewilderment and looked up at Traevyn. "Geez, I didn't even think he cared."

He smiled. "He is your brother. You've been stuck together for the past month. He probably feels closer to you now than he ever has."

"Well I'd better start cooking. Apology food should do the job."

"I'll help you," he volunteered.

She cast him a suspicious look as they made their way into the kitchen. "Do you cook better than Seth?"

He made a face. "I could be blindfolded and drunk and I'd still cook better than Seth."

She giggled.

* * *

Evie knocked softly on Seth's door.

"Dude, go away!" he shouted. "I am so friggin' pissed at you right now!"

"Seth," she called. "Come on, open the door."

He huffed. "It's unlocked. I can't keep you out, but I don't have to sit here and listen to your lame excuses either."

She rolled her eyes and opened the door. "Seth," she called in an enticing tone, "I made you breakfast."

"Woo friggin' hoo," he grumbled, changing the television station.

"Oh come on, I made you apology pancakes."

"I made pancakes a couple nights ago," he stated.

She wrinkled her nose. "Yeah, but they were awful."

He gave a mighty sigh and fixed her with a scowl. "I did

it to help you out at the time, but I'll be sure never to do that again." He angrily stabbed at the channel button on the remote again.

Evie sat down on the bed. "Come on, Seth. I said I was sorry. What more do you want?"

He flicked off the TV and sat up with a frustrated noise. "Evie, listen," he said, looking like he was trying to figure out exactly what it was he wanted to say. "You and I have never really been all that close. We have nothing in common and, since you're four years older than me, that kind of killed us ever running in the same circles. I've never understood you and I did not want to come on this trip with you, but I did, and here I am." He huffed again. "For one whole week we were stuck here in this dungeon with no one but each other. Even after you started making nice with Traevyn, I still only had you. After you went away to college, I felt like I didn't know you anymore because you were never around, just like Mom and Dad were never around, and I hated you for it. At least when you were living at home, you were there. I may not have understood you, but I had you." He shook his head, as if trying to centralize all his thoughts into one main point. "What I'm trying to say is that being stuck here with you has forced me to get to know you again and, for the first time in my life, I feel like you're actually my friend instead of just my sister."

Evie stared at him, dumbstruck.

"You know when I knocked Traevyn's picture albums down—"

"And you conveniently disappeared?" she interjected. "Yes."

"Well, I heard him yelling at you. I heard him talk about how broken he was because of losing his family. When you didn't call me last night and I thought something could have happened to you, all I could think of were his words." He looked up at her. "Evie, you're my only sister. You told Traevyn that no one should have to be alone. If something happened to you, that's what I would be." He looked down for a second, then snorted and waved it away. "Aw, never mind."

She smiled. "No, Seth, listen to me." She put her hand on his arm. "I'm sorry I didn't call. Traevyn was having this soul outpouring, and I didn't think. I was selfish. I'm sorry. I won't do it again...okay?"

He glanced up at her, stared at her in sour silence for several moments, then huffed. "Whatever, dude. Just don't do it again. I'm giving you a warning."

She arched an eyebrow and raised two fingers to her forehead in mock salute. "Aye, aye, Captain!"

He pursed his lips and hunched his shoulders, continuing to look disgruntled, but she could have sworn it was somewhat forced. She grinned. "And I love you too." She grasped him around the neck and noogied him.

"Ugh! Get off!" he shouted, shoving at her.

She giggled and sat back. She couldn't deny that Seth's words surprised her. She had never thought she actually meant anything to him at all.

"So did you guys do the wild monkey dance?" he asked.

She frowned. "Huh?"

"You and Traevyn. You were stuck together all night. You had to have done *something*. Did you at least make out?"

Evie felt her face flame, and she grabbed Seth's pillow, bludgeoning him with it.

He laughed and jumped off the bed, bolting out the door. She followed.

* * *

Traevyn was eating at the table when Seth tore in, laughing. Evie followed, crashing after him. She chased him around the table, then back out again. Traevyn blinked, then chuckled as he heard Seth laugh then make an *ooof* sound, which was promptly followed by, "Dang, Evie! You just took out my kidney!"

As much as he had come to relish his solitude, he thought that it was nice to have life back in his home.

# Chapter Thirteen

Life went on rather uneventful for the next week or so. It was now late June and Evie had been in Traevyn's home for a little over a month. Since the night they had spent stranded on the side of the road, Evie and Traevyn had been more friendly. Traevyn ate dinner with her and Seth every night and joined them sometimes in watching TV or a movie afterward. Many nights he and Evie still sat and read, or painted.

Traevyn remembered the day after the night they had spent in the car. After Evie and Seth had finished wrestling in the living room, she had disappeared into the art studio for most of the day. Traevyn had left her alone with her creativity, knowing that sometimes the best work was done in solitude.

When he had gone into the studio later that evening, he'd almost stopped breathing. There, sitting on his easel, was the oil pastel he had been working on at the beach. Only she had finished it. The once blank fourth of the canvas now had the silhouette of a woman mirroring that of the solitary man. Her shadow was stretching out in a contrasting angle, but that wasn't the point. The point was that her shadow was shaped like two hands reaching out to hold the broken heart that his shadow portrayed.

He'd stared at it for what seemed like an eternity, filled with such emotion over her astute symbolism and her selflessness. He could say with all honesty that he had never met a person as kind as Evie. Her compassion was enough to cradle the world.

He hadn't said anything to her about the painting because he couldn't find the proper words. He knew that probably unsettled her, made her wonder if he liked it at all, but a simple thank you just seemed too bland. He wanted to do something for her in return, something to show her he cared, that he could give back kindness instead of just taking it from her. He just hadn't figured out how yet.

It was now a rather boring Thursday, and Traevyn sat in the living room reading while Seth played an acoustic guitar and Evie cleaned. She was finishing up his wing of the house and he wanted to stay out of her way. She looked mean with that duster and mop, and he didn't want her yelling at him if he accidentally walked across her wet floor or something.

He glanced up at Seth and smiled. "How long have you been playing?" he asked.

Seth looked up at him. "A little over two years. I still kinda suck."

Traevyn shook his head. "You sound fine to me, but then again, I know nothing about music. I remember when my brother Talis was learning to play, I thought the scales sounded good."

Seth smiled. "Your brother plays guitar?"

He nodded.

"Acoustic or electric?"

"Acoustic mostly. He plays for the belly dancers at renaissance fairs."

Seth raised an eyebrow. "Hey, that's a sweet way to make a living. I have my acoustic with me because Evie didn't think it would be good to bring my amp and electric, but I prefer electric. I would love to be in a band."

Traevyn smiled. "You look like a rocker."

Seth grinned. "I love Bleeding Passion. Do you know who they are?"

Traevyn chuckled and shook his head. "Sorry."

"Well, they're my favorite band. They rock the universe. Van Marshall is the front man and an awesome guitar player. I've seen them in concert three times. He's a genius."

Evie came down the stairs out of breath and frazzled-looking. "Done," she stated. "By the way, I'll be gone tomorrow."

Seth frowned. "Where are you going?"

"I'm going to Cambria for the day. I was looking at it on the Internet, and I'm going to go have a nice day to myself."

"And you're not taking me with you?" Seth cried.

She frowned. "Since when do you like antique shops and art galleries?"

He snorted. "Hello! Van Marshall lives there!"

"Who's Van Marshall?"

"The front man for Bleeding Passion," Traevyn supplied.

Evie looked at him in bewildered surprise, but shook her head and turned her attention back to Seth. "I am not stalking rock stars, Seth. Tomorrow is *my* day." With that, she went into the kitchen.

Traevyn frowned. "What was that all about?"

Seth rolled his eyes. "Oh, tomorrow marks the sixth year anniversary of when Evie did her first real painting. She celebrates it by herself every year for who knows why. To celebrate the birth of her creativity, or something like that."

Traevyn pondered that for a moment and closed the book he was reading. "She celebrates it every year alone?"

Seth looked up at him and shrugged. "Yeah. No one else understands it."

Traevyn smiled. "I do."

"Yeah, well, you're just as much of a nut job as she is."

"Seth, since you're stuck with me tomorrow, do you think I could enlist your help?"

Seth gave Traevyn a suspicious look. "With what?"

"I want to surprise Evie with something. I want to celebrate with her."

Seth blinked as if Traevyn's words had surprised him. "Really?"

He nodded.

Seth shrugged. "All right. That'd be cool. She deserves a nice surprise. She's always doing things for everyone else."

"Precisely."

Evie walked back into the room, carrying a bottle of water. She glanced at the two men and frowned. "What are you two doing out here anyway?"

"Male bonding," Seth replied.

She raised her eyebrows. "That horrifies me."

Seth grinned and Traevyn chuckled. "Evie, do you think you could be home by six tomorrow?" Traevyn asked. "I'd like to work on something with you."

She shrugged. "Yeah, sure."

"Good."

She continued on her way up the stairs, and Seth and

Traevyn exchanged a conspiratorial smile

\* \* \*

By six o'clock, Evie was tired, but pleasantly so. She had spent the entire day strolling leisurely through the small town of Cambria shopping, drawing, and relaxing.

Every year she stopped to reflect on the day she had first started considering herself an artist. She thought of how far she had come, what she had accomplished, and what her goals for the future were. It was *her* day. Her one day to stop worrying about everything and everyone and just focus on her and her own creativity.

She sighed as she walked up to Traevyn's door, wondering how he had fared with Seth all day. She was just reaching for the knob when the door swung open, and Traevyn stood before her in a black suit with a loose black necktie. He looked stunning. Stunning in a way that made her make sure her mouth was closed for fear she might drool all over herself. "Geez," she breathed. "Where are *you* going?"

He smiled devilishly and offered her his arm. "Come with me."

She frowned, but obeyed and allowed him to lead her inside. She let out a little shout of surprise. Most of the furniture had been cleared out of the living room, and the dining room table had been brought in and set in the center of the room. The lights were dim and there was a candle in an amber holder on the table, which was set for two. A white tablecloth covered the top, and wine glasses were turned upside down next to cloth napkins held together with elegant napkin rings. The dark, medieval tapestries were gone from the walls, and several Mediterranean paintings hung in their place. Italian music played softly in the background.

"What's this?" Evie murmured.

"Italy," Traevyn replied, "or the next best thing." He guided her over to the table and pulled a chair out for her. "I figured that, until I have the time to show you the real thing, this will have to do." He pushed the chair in as she sat, and he leaned over her. "Happy anniversary, Evie," he whispered in her ear.

She shivered at the feeling of his warm breath against her skin, and stared at him in wonderment. "How did you know about that?"

He grinned and sat down across the table from her. "Seth told me."

Her eyebrows shot up. "I didn't even know *he* knew about that." She looked around again, dumbstruck. No one had ever given her such a thoughtful surprise. "This is incredible. Where's all the furniture?"

"In the kitchen and dining room. It's not like I don't have enough room."

"I feel so underdressed." She glanced down at her teal, hippie-style skirt and black tank top. She'd dressed for a casual day in an artsy, coastal town. She had even used a matching teal scarf as a headband. Sure, she imagined she looked okay, cute even, but Traevyn was dressed so upscale. She definitely didn't want to feel "cute" in the midst of all the splendor he had created.

Traevyn's gaze traveled over her and he smiled. "You look perfect, Evie."

She met his eyes, then looked down shyly. "Why did you do this?"

"An artist should always celebrate the birth of their creativity."

She turned her eyes back up to him and grinned.

Just then, Seth walked in from the kitchen wearing a white dress shirt, black slacks, and a black bow tie with a white apron around his waist. His usually spiked blond hair was slicked back and he had a bottle of white wine nestled in the crook of his elbow like he was carrying a child. In the crook of his other elbow, he held a bottle of red. "Good evening," he greeted.

Evie took once glance at him and burst out laughing. She covered her mouth and dissolved into giggles.

Seth kept a straight face. "Could I interest you in a glass of wine? We have our finest—" he looked down at the bottle of white "—Pe-nut griggio."

Evie had to bite down on her lip to keep from guffawing.

Seth looked at the bottle of red. "Or we have..." He glanced at the label and let out a little huff. "Shy—razz."

Traevyn winced. "Give the lady a glass of white and me a glass of red, please," he instructed.

Seth filled both Evie's and Traevyn's glasses—almost to the top. It was the largest glass of wine Evie had ever seen in her life. "I will be back shortly to take your order," he said suavely before sauntering back into the kitchen.

Evie glanced at Traevyn, who watched her with a smile on his lips. "That is fantastic," she said. "How did you get him to do that?"

"His idea," he replied.

She just stared at him. "Are you serious?"

He nodded and his lips turned up in a wry smile. "Guess I should have told him how to pronounce wine titles before I gave him the job." He lifted his glass of red and peered at it, then raised an eyebrow. "And maybe told him we didn't want to get drunk until *after* dinner."

She laughed. "Yeah, I've got to say, I've never heard of Peanut Griggio before." She lifted her glass of white and took a sip. "But at least they arent' stingy with the portions here."

Traevyn chuckled.

Evie shook her head. Despite his lack of finesse, her brother was really surprising her lately. She looked up as he came back into the room with a basket of bread and a dish of olive oil.

"Olive oil with garlic and rosemary," he announced.

Evie grinned so wide that she thought her face might split in half.

"All right, may I take your orders, please? We have some excellent choices for you this evening. We have chicken marsala, chicken marsala, or may I suggest my favorite, the chicken marsala?"

Evie had to fight not to laugh in a very undignified manner. She resorted to a giggle instead. "Hmmm," she teased. "I think I'll take the chicken marsala."

"Excellent choice. And for you, sir?"

Traevyn was grinning more than Evie had ever seen as he nodded at Seth and replied that he wanted the same.

Seth nodded. "I'll bring that out shortly."

Traevyn glanced over at Evie as Seth disappeared again. "I think he's enjoying this."

"It's scaring me a little. Please tell me he didn't do the cooking."

He made a face. "Lord, no. I wasn't looking to kill you tonight."

She giggled and met his eyes across the table. She sobered and shook her head slowly. "This is very overwhelming."

"Enjoy it, Evie. Seth told me you celebrated this every year alone because no one else understood. I understand. I wanted to celebrate with you."

She averted her eyes, fighting sudden tears. No one had ever validated her passion except for the deBoers, and even then, they only supported her and believed in her as fellow creative people. Traevyn truly understood her.

He stood as a slow Italian melody started to play, and he offered her his hand. "Would you care to dance?"

Her breath hitched at the seductive note his voice carried. She knew he hadn't done it on purpose. His voice resonated sensuality all on its own, but that almost made her reaction to it even more powerful. She braved a look up at him and her mouth went dry. He was so amazingly elegant, even more so than usual. Traevyn Whitelaw was the most beautiful man she had ever seen.

She reached out slowly and placed her small hand in his, remembering the warmth of it from the night in the car. He smiled and led her out to an empty space on the floor, pulling her into his arms so that Evie had to close her eyes and remember how to breathe. She had tried to forget almost everything about the night they had been stranded. How she had kissed him on instinct; how having him sleep so close to her felt so right; how his touch made her heart beat in strange and erratic patterns. She had tried to write off all those things as being caught up in such an emotional moment, but they came flooding back to her at the warm contact of his body against hers.

"I wanted to thank you for the painting," Traevyn murmured.

She frowned in question.

"The one of mine that you finished."

"Oh..." She looked away, her face flaming. She had done that on impulse and had almost immediately thought it had been too bold. He had never said anything to her about it, which had been more than okay with her, but she had wondered what he had thought. She shook her head. "It was just—" She made a face. "It was nothing really."

He stopped dancing and lifted her chin so he could look into her eyes. "Nothing?" He shook his head. "Evie, it was everything."

She stared up at him and her eyes scanned his gorgeous face. They came to rest on his perfect lips, and she realized that she wanted to kiss him very badly. That alarmed her. It was easy to deny feelings in normal, day-to-day life, but in a setting like this... When had she come to care for him so much? The realization that her affection for him was much deeper than she thought swamped her and she had to look away. What was the matter with her? Was she out of her mind? Like Traevyn Whitelaw would actually go for someone like her. His ex-wife had been a goddess. He had said so himself. Elegant and sophisticated. She was anything but elegant and sophisticated. She was loud and opinionated and definitely not goddess-like. Plus, he was almost ten years older than her. He probably thought of her as a child. Was she completely stupid?

"Evie?"

She looked up at Traevyn, who was frowning in concern.

"Evie, you're trembling." He ran both of his hands lightly across her shoulders and down her arms.

Oh, right, like *that* was going to make things better. "I—uh—" she stammered. "I just..."

"Dinner is served," Seth announced, returning to the room.

Evie breathed a sigh of relief and all but bolted back to her seat. Being in close proximity to Traevyn was dangerous. It was better if she just sat down. Seth set the plates in front of them and Evie managed to give Traevyn a small smile. He gave her a warm look that made her heart somersault, and she turned her attention to her food.

"You made this?" she asked as she took a bite.

He nodded. "I hope it's not too awful."

"No, it's delicious!" Her eyes narrowed. "You can cook like this, and yet, I've been making all your meals?"

He grinned. "I never said I couldn't cook. I just don't like to."

She rolled her eyes, and he chuckled. They lapsed into pleasant conversation as they ate, and Evie was certain she had never seen Traevyn smile and laugh so much. It warmed her heart. What progress he had made in such a short amount of time. Perhaps he had just needed someone to actually care, and take the time to listen.

Dessert was raspberry crème brulee, which Evie loved,

and when everything was finished, she was stuffed and content. "That was fabulous, Traevyn," she said with a stretch. "Thank you."

He smiled and dipped his head in a nod. "Would you care to keep me company up in my bedroom?"

Her eyes bulged and the air slammed out of her lungs as she stared at him.

Traevyn closed his eyes and cleared his throat. "Forgive me, that came out..." —he frowned— "slightly different than I expected. What I meant was, I have a fireplace in my bedroom, and it's cold tonight. You and I spend many evenings reading together. Would you like to join me in my room instead of the office?"

She gave him a curious frown, wondering why he sought to prolong the evening.

His smile was almost bashful. "I find myself reluctant to part with you," he admitted, his voice so quiet he almost couldn't hear his own words. How could he tell her that, when he was with her, the pain that plagued his heart seemed lessened? And the shadows receded?

Evie grinned as a soft blush touched her cheeks. "I would love to. We can bring the wine." She giggled as she grabbed the bottle of red that Seth had left on the table.

He chuckled and stood. "Just give me a moment. I have to tip the waiter." He gave her a playful wink, delighting in how she laughed.

Traevyn entered the kitchen where Seth was lying on the couch, drinking wine directly out of the bottle. He frowned. "Decided to help yourself, did you? To my finest bottle of Peanut Griggio?"

Seth glanced up at him lazily. "Hey, I dressed up in this ridiculous outfit and served you all night. Plus, I made an idiot out of myself because reading those wine labels was like reading Greek. I think I at least deserve to drink your booze."

"You're only seventeen," he reminded him.

Seth raised an amused eyebrow. "You gonna call the cops?"

Traevyn sighed. "Don't be ridiculous. Just don't drink too much. If you throw up anywhere other than the toilet, I'll make you clean it."

Seth chuckled.

"Tonight went well," Traevyn said with a pleased smile.

Seth grinned. "Yeah... You know, you're pretty cool, dude."

Traevyn raised an eyebrow. "Well, thanks... Look, I'll give you fifty dollars if you clean everything up."

Seth groaned. "I take it back."

Traevyn chuckled.

Seth sat up with a sigh. "Look, I'll clean up, but I am not moving the furniture by myself. I'm strong, but I'm not friggin' Hercules."

"Agreed. Thanks for your help, Seth."

"You gonna make a move on her?"

"Pardon?"

"On Evie. You invite her to your *bedroom* with the *fireplace* and you don't plan to make a move?"

He blinked in bewilderment. "It's not like that at all. Evie and I share stimulating conversation."

Seth raised an eyebrow. "Is that what you call it? Stimulating conversation? I'm sure you find lots of things stimulating, especially given the size of my sister's gazangas." He made a mountainous gesture with his hands.

Traevyn opened his mouth to speak, but resulted in a short sigh. "Seth, that is a very disrespectful thing to say."

"Oh, like you haven't noticed."

"That's not the point." Of course he had noticed Evie's...assets. It was impossible to miss them... He shook his head and let out a frustrated growl. "Why were you listening to our conversation in the first place?"

Seth snorted. "Like there's anything else to do back here."

Traevyn folded his arms. "I respect your sister very much and have nothing but honorable intentions. Besides, I highly doubt that Evie thinks of me as anything other than a mentor and friend so 'making a move,' as you say, would be greatly overstepping boundaries."

Seth snorted again and rolled into a standing position. "Traevyn, you're cool," he said, coming to stand in front of him, "but don't be an idiot."

Traevyn frowned.

Seth held his hand out. "Gimme my fifty."

Traevyn pulled a bill out of his wallet and handed it to him, then turned and went back into the living room, perplexed and slightly flustered. Don't be an idiot. What did he mean by that?

"What's Seth doing back there?" Evie asked with a grin.

"Getting plastered," Traevyn muttered.

She raised her eyebrows in alarm.

He chuckled. "He's fine. Don't worry about it. Shall we?"

She nodded. "Just let me go get my book from my room, and I want to change my clothes."

"Come in whenever you're ready." He made his way to his bedroom, removed his tie and jacket, and un-tucked his shirt. He started a fire, then sat back against the headboard, kicked off his shoes, and pulled his sketchpad up onto his lap. He sighed and mulled over Seth's words. *Don't be an idiot.* Was he trying to tell him that Evie did feel something other than friendship for him? He frowned, not entirely sure how he felt about that possibility. The realization that he was unsure was very unsettling to him. Any other time, with any other woman, he would have put a screeching halt to anything that might have the slightest chance of developing into something, but with Evie... Everything was different with Evie.

A soft knock on the door brought him out of his thoughts and he smiled. "Come in."

Evie entered with a smile and she held the bottle of wine up enticingly.

He chuckled and motioned her inside.

She crawled up onto the foot of the bed and set the wine on the nightstand. She set her book down, then poured them both a glass.

"What are you reading now?" he queried as he took the glass from her.

"*Pride and Prejudice,*" she answered.

"Good choice."

She sighed and took a sip of wine. "Traevyn." She looked up at him. "Thank you for tonight. Every year I celebrate the day I painted my first real painting. You know, one that wasn't done with finger paints or those horrible goopy things you use in grade school."

He smiled.

"It was an oil painting on canvas. I was fifteen." She smiled at the memory. "I celebrate it because, in a sense, it's like celebrating the day I became who I am. Everything I dream of and stand for started that day." She sighed. "It was very nice to celebrate it with you."

He raised his eyebrows. "Don't forget, a great deal of credit goes to your misfit brother. He was my partner in crime all day."

She shook her head in disbelief. "Seth continues to surprise me." She set her wine glass down and opened her book, lying diagonally across the bottom of the bed on her side. Sitting next to Traevyn on his own bed just seemed too intimate to her at the moment. It was something married couples did. She briefly wondered if Traevyn's wife had ever sat up and read next to him while he drew. She sighed and lost herself in her book.

She read for awhile and Traevyn sketched away. After a bit, she glanced up at him in curiosity, unable to fake disinterest any longer. "What are you drawing?" she asked.

"You," he replied with a smile.

She blinked in surprise.

He met her eyes. "I'd like to paint your portrait, but I need something to go off of. I can't just paint from memory like you can."

She gave him a weak smile. "Why do you want to paint me?" she queried with a puzzled frown.

He looked up at her again. "Because," he said enigmatically.

The firelight reflected for a moment in his eyes, and it made Evie draw in a soft breath. She looked down and swallowed hard as her heart skipped a beat.

"In about two weeks time I have to go to Sedona, Arizona," he stated, changing the subject. "I am opening a gallery there."

Her eyes widened. "That's wonderful!"

He smiled. "I'll be there for a few days. My brother Talis lives there and I would like to visit with him while I'm in town."

She nodded.

"I would, of course, like you to join me. Seth can come too."

"Really?"

"You are my apprentice. It would be stupid to leave you here during such a big event."

She grinned. She'd never been to Arizona before. She'd

never been to a gallery opening either. It all seemed very exciting.

"It's going to be a very formal affair," he continued. "With mostly other artists and rich people who can afford to buy our art."

She giggled. "I'll find something to wear between now and then."

"Excellent. Now be quiet and read so I can keep sketching."

She grinned and went back to her book, turning on her stomach so she could bend her knees and swing her legs in jubilation.

Traevyn looked at her and smiled. Seth's words continued to echo in his mind, but he pushed them away. After all, the boy was only seventeen. What did he know?

# Chapter Fourteen

A week and a half later found Evie sitting down by the beach in Monterey. She had gone shopping with Seth to see if she could find anything for the gallery opening. So far, it wasn't looking very good. She leaned back against the rock she was sitting in front of and smiled as she watched Seth chase around some children who had been playing down by the shore. Two of them had been throwing a Frisbee while Seth and Evie ate lunch. It had veered off course and nearly scalped Seth. He threw it back, but the kids must have liked something about him because they kept throwing it at him.

After about three times, he'd gone down to play with them and had been at it ever since.

Evie sighed and looked down at her bag. She reached into it, pulled out a brown leather journal, and ran her fingers over the front before she opened it and glanced across Traevyn's elegant cursive. Over the past week and a half, he had continued to open up to her, sharing small bits and pieces of his past. He was still reluctant to discuss the events surrounding his divorce and his daughter's death, but he did relate stories of his daughter once in awhile. He would tell Evie of silly things she had done, or things she had liked. Evie hated the sadness that washed over his features whenever he spoke of Leanna, but she was glad he trusted her enough to tell her such things.

She remembered so well the night Traevyn had entrusted the leather journal to her. They had been in the office, reading their favorite poems to one another and discussing what they thought they meant. He had read a lot out of the Shakespeare's Sonnets book that she had first discovered in his office.

"It's funny," he said after studying the well-worn front of the book. "I used to read to Amy out of this. I couldn't even look at it for the longest time." He shook his head as if slightly puzzled. "It's strange, but since I've been talking to you, I've come to realize that I shouldn't shut myself off from good literature just because of the painful memories I associate with it... The same could be said for anything, I guess."

To think that she had made some sort of small difference in Traevyn's life.

After reading many more of their favorites, he read her a poem out of the brown leather journal. When Evie asked who it was by, he informed her that it was one of his own. Later, when she had been heading to bed, he'd stopped her at the door and slipped the book to her.

"I want you to take this," he said. "Read it if you want to. Anything you might want to know about me is in there." At the questioning look in her eyes, he had merely shrugged. "You already own part of my soul, Evie. You may as well know what it is you have."

She had been beyond stunned. Poetry was a very private thing, and the fact that he would entrust his own work to her spoke volumes.

"What is that?" Seth asked suddenly.

Evie jumped, startled by his unexpected presence. "Oh," she said, closing the journal on instinct. "It's Traevyn's poetry book."

He frowned and sat down next to her. "He writes poetry?"

She nodded and opened up to a poem that was her favorite. She had already read through the entire book, but she kept coming back to this particular piece. "Look...

"*Beauty is an open canvas that spreads across my mind, causing shattered glass to pierce my broken side.*

*We all paint upon the canvas with colors of our desire, perfecting the picture until we are able to see music, feel love, hear kindness.*

*My canvas is blank as I look in the mirror, attempting to portray who I am in poetic beauty. The paper is too small and simple to hold such a complexity.*

*And so I paint, making the best of the situation. Waves upon waves of color, a little of everything here, a portion of something there, all ending up in nothing.*

*And as I look upon myself in the mirror, I still cannot see the beauty others have placed upon me. It has been lost for so long. Yet I try and draw it to the best of my knowledge and ability.*

*The reflection changes constantly as I paint, yet I try and stop the change from changing, trying to remain myself. Then I realize, change is what started it all...*

*Change brought upon love at one time in my life. So I add the sweet, sadistic color of love, and I find myself lost inside the screaming agony of the color that is held within the painting.*

*And as the mirror shatters across time and space, unable to hold the complexity of me, I finish the painting and find myself saddened.*

*Upon the canvas is an empty face because I know not who I am. Love and change caused me to lose myself at some point in time and so in my painting I depict that.*

*Others may see differently, but that is because I paint them a different picture. One with a face and a smile. One without a past. One with a marvelous future.*

*The truth is, I am nothing, I am nowhere. I am lost within myself. The painting falls to the floor and I collapse in sorrow at what I've become.*

*I know not who I am, or what I shall ever be, and I am frightened..."'*

She finished with a sigh and turned to look at Seth. "What do you think of that?"

Seth shook his head. "That's pretty heavy... Is that whole book full of his poetry?"

She nodded. "He told me I could read it. Can you believe that?"

Seth glanced up at her. "I believe it."

Evie frowned, wondering how he could be so nonchalant about it. "I just think it's an awfully big deal." She closed the book and ran her hand across the cover. "These are all his deepest thoughts and feelings. He entrusted them to me."

Seth smirked. "You like him."

She met his eyes. "Of course I like him. He's my mentor and my friend."

He rolled his eyes and groaned dramatically, flopping down onto his back. "No, I mean you *like* him. Don't even try to deny it, Evie. Contrary to popular belief, I'm not stupid."

She turned to give him a pointed look. "Seth, you don't know what you're talking about."

"No, *you* don't know what you're talking about!" he exclaimed. "Geez, is this what I have to look forward to? I grow out of my teenage years and automatically become ridiculous? You people are killing me!"

She frowned. "You people? Who else is pissing you off?"

He snorted and sat back up. "Look, from where I sit, it seems pretty simple. You like him. He likes you. You make him not evil and heinous, and he actually gets you. Why don't you just hook up already and give my gag reflexes a rest?"

She looked out at the rolling waves. "Life isn't that simple, Seth."

"So you do like him?"

She rolled her eyes. "Okay, yeah, but that's not really the point." She shook her head. "Someone like Traevyn would never go for me."

"Why?"

She huffed. "Okay, well, first of all, I think that Traevyn Whitelaw is about the last person on the planet who is looking for a relationship at the moment. He had his heart ripped out and stomped on."

"That happened three years ago."

She met his eyes again. "Does it seem like he's coped well to you?" She shrugged. "Besides, even if he was looking for someone, I doubt he'd look my direction."

Seth appeared to contemplate strangling Evie for a minute, but decided against it. "Why wouldn't he? Evie, gimme a break. You guys love the same things, you laugh together, he opened up to you when he's been living like Quasimodo in the bell tower for the past three years. You spend hours every night in his *bedroom* by the *fireplace* reading classics and drawing! Come on! Do you not see the signals?"

She shook her head vehemently. "It's not like that. I think Traevyn would have opened up to anyone who just cared a little. He doesn't like me that way. He couldn't. I'm totally not his type. You've seen pictures of his wife. She was beautiful and elegant. I'm neither. I would look frumpy and ridiculous in Traevyn's world."

Seth frowned. "Evie, don't be stupid. Who gives a crap if his wife was beautiful and elegant? She was a sleazy ho who turned him into a complete loner. I mean, come on, the girl had no shape. She was like an anorexic stick. You, on the other hand..." He made the shape of an hourglass with his hands. "Va va voom."

She smacked him in the arm.

He laughed. "Seriously, Evie. Don't get all down on yourself. He opened up to you for a reason. He turned his living room into Italy and celebrated your crazy anniversary with you for a reason. He let you read this"—he pointed to the journal—"for a reason. Don't ignore all of that."

Evie chewed on her bottom lip as Seth's words rolled around in her head. Could he be right? Could Traevyn really feel anything for her besides friendship? She thought of how badly she had wanted to kiss him that night they had danced and how many times she had wanted to kiss him since then. She thought of his laugh and how she would do anything, give anything, if she could make him laugh every day for the rest of his life. She thought of the many innocent touches they seemed to share. How he would stand behind her to watch her paint and rub her back just before he walked away. How she liked to rest her head on his shoulder if they happened to be watching a movie or something on television. How sometimes he would absently play with her hair if she was near him while they were reading together. Sometimes he would even just touch her arm briefly when he would walk past her in the kitchen. Could those be signals? Small signs that maybe he could care for her?

She shook her head and let out an aggravated growl. "Seth, you're insane," she stated. "This is just my lot in life. I always fall for guys I can't have."

Seth frowned again. "What's stopping you from having Traevyn? He's not seeing anyone... Unless you want to count me since I'm the only other person he's ever in contact with."

"Well, I could never compete with you," she teased.

He puffed his chest out. "I am a sexy stud in a waiter's uniform." He sniffed.

She laughed.

"I'll make a deal with you," he said. "I bet that Traevyn will make a move on you by the time we come back from Sedona. If he doesn't, I won't play anymore video games for the rest of the summer."

She raised her eyebrows. "You are going to be one bored guy."

"I really doubt it, but I guess I'll have to be proven right for you to believe me."

"Whatever." She glanced at her watch and sighed. "We'd better keep shopping because I've got to find something. At this rate, I'll be going to the gallery opening naked." She stood and brushed the sand off her pants.

"That would definitely ensure Traevyn making a move," Seth remarked.

Evie giggled, and they headed back up toward town.

* * *

The bedroom was on the top of Evie's list of places to mope as she entered the house exhausted and empty-handed. She heaved a sigh and headed into the kitchen to try and figure out what she was going to make for dinner. She took a step back in surprise when she entered and saw Traevyn standing over the stove, stirring something.

He glanced over at her and smiled. "Welcome home."

She fought a shiver at those words. "What are you up to?" she asked, pushing her feelings aside.

"Making dinner," he replied.

He smiled at her. A soft, gentle, affectionate smile that tugged at her heart. An entire scene snuck up and played through her mind like an excerpt from a movie. One of her coming home to this exact situation, only it really was her home, and when Traevyn smiled, he bent to press a soft kiss to her lips. He would whisper how much he had missed her and nuzzle her neck, then pull her into his arms...

She sighed. Great. Now the romantic fantasies were starting. If she had to count how many times she'd had imaginary romantic interludes with Maxim deBoer over the years...

Evie forced herself back to the present. "So, why are you making dinner?"

"You were shopping all day. I thought I'd be nice and let you rest. Why don't you go up to your room and relax? I'll come get you when it's ready."

"What is it?" she asked, peering into the pot.

He glanced down at what he was stirring. "Well, this is

mac and cheese."

She raised an eyebrow. "Gourmet."

He gave her a playful scowl. "It's just a side dish."

She giggled. "All right, I'll go upstairs and wait till it's ready." She shot him a warning look. "And don't use the gong to call me to the table."

He chuckled.

She wandered her way up the staircase and into her bedroom. She swung the door open and started as her eyes fell on the closet door. She stared in bewildered wonder at it. A gown was hanging there. A shining gown of shimmering turquoise. The sleeves weren't really sleeves, but sheer strips of material that tied at the elbow, then flowed freely. She walked over to it slowly and touched one of the gossamer sleeves. Tiny, sparkling rhinestones spilled down the skirt, and all she could do was gape at it. It was the most beautiful garment she had ever seen. Elegant, but romantic and medieval, like a drawing out of a fairty tale.

"Do you like it?"

She spun to see Traevyn standing in the doorway. She pointed to the gown. "You got me this?" she squeaked.

He looked down in a shy gesture. "Seth told me you weren't having any luck in Monterey so... I thought I'd look."

She frowned. "Seth?"

He nodded. "I called earlier today from the grocery store to find out what we needed."

She tried to ignore the fact that he had just said *what we needed* like they were a family. "And you called Seth?"

"Well, I called your cell phone, but Seth answered. He said you were trying on gowns and having no luck. There's a small formalwear store I know of so I thought I'd take a look." He shrugged. "If you don't like it, I can return it."

"Oh no!" she exclaimed, catching the faint glimmer of disappointment in his eyes. "No, Traevyn, I love it. It's gorgeous. How did you know I love this color?"

"You wear turquoise often. And you use shades of blue and green a lot in your paintings."

She stared at him in awe. "You pay that much attention to me?"

He averted his eyes to the floor and shrugged. The gesture was completely self-conscious, and awkward, very non-Traevyn.

Evie blushed and looked away in much the same fashion that Traevyn just had. "Thank you," she murmured. "It's perfect."

He gave her a soft smile and glanced up at her. "I hope it fits all right. Seth told me your size, but you can never be sure."

She frowned, looking even more perplexed than before. "Seth knows my size?" She shook her head. "I'm beginning to realize that he pays more attention than I thought too."

Traevyn grinned.

"Well, I'll pay you back for the dress," she stated.

He frowned and waved away the suggestion.

"Come on, it's your own money anyway."

"No, it's a gift. Please, Evie, just take it."

She met his eyes and chewed on her bottom lip. "Thank you, Traevyn. You have impeccable taste."

He smiled and gave a slight shrug. "This dress told me to buy it. It just looked like you...like something you would wear."

Evie approached him tentatively and laughed in apprehension. "Well, thank you so much." She held her arms out to indicate an embrace. He moved forward and caught her up in his arms, holding her closer than she had expected. He bent his head to rest his cheek against the top of her head and, with great care, ran one hand down the length of her hair.

Evie had only intended it to be a thank you hug, but as his arms wrapped securely around her, she melted against him without even thinking. She had wanted her entire life to be enfolded in the embrace of a beautiful man and, in her opinion, there was no man more beautiful than Traevyn. She sighed and tried to memorize the way he felt. He smelled like paint, like the passion that made him who he was. It was intoxicating.

She started to tremble against her will and wished she could just stay in his arms forever. She'd always been such a hopeless romantic, and she'd only ever been looked upon as a "great friend." She hated it. She hated the fact that this would probably be the only time she could be close to Traevyn like this. She hated that she was ninety percent sure that Seth was wrong when she wanted him so badly to be right. But what could possibly make this situation different than all the others? Traevyn was so out of her league. She was just fooling herself to even think she was more than a passing thought to him.

"Evie?" Traevyn pulled away gently and looked down at her in concern. "You're shaking again. What's wrong?"

She felt the horrible, betraying sting of tears and shook her head, trying to fight them off as long as possible. "Nothing, I just..." She wanted to die as one tear succeeded in trailing down her cheek.

His eyes widened. "Evie..." he murmured. "Why are you crying?" He reached up and, with tremendous tenderness, caressed her tear away.

Of course, this only made her want to cry more. She forced a smile. "Oh, I think I'm just tired, or...hormonal, or something." She gave a little laugh.

He smiled and framed her face with his hands. "Are you sure?" He tucked back a strand of her hair. "Want me to get you some chocolate?"

She forced a laugh. She couldn't take it anymore. He really needed to leave before she lost it. She nodded emphatically. "I'm fine... Shouldn't you go check dinner?"

"Oh!" he exclaimed. "Fantastic. It's probably on fire. I'll come back when it's done."

She waved away the suggestion for fear he'd come in when she was blubbering. "I'll just come down in a minute."

He nodded and left the room.

Evie waited until she knew he was down the staircase and then plopped onto her bed. She cried. She felt like an idiot, but she didn't care. "Seth!" she shouted. She must have sounded very demanding because he rushed into the room within seconds.

"What is it?" he asked, looking worried.

She stabbed an accusing finger at him. "I hate you," she declared.

He raised an eyebrow. "Why?"

"Because you messed me up, that's why! Look, Traevyn bought me a dress! Then I said thank you and he hugged me and I freaked out because of you! I was fine before you insisted that he liked me, and now I'm all screwed up because this is going to be just like every other guy I've ever liked and I'm going to end up really, really hurt!" Tears ran tracks down her cheeks, but she didn't bother to wipe them. She was entitled to a moment of girlish weakness once in awhile.

Seth stared at her, then sat down next to her. "Evie, you didn't exactly make a whole lot of sense there. Did he say something to you?"

She shook her head and sniffed. "No, but there is no way on this planet that *that* man would go for me. He's so talent- ed and high class. I'm just 'fun' and 'nice.' I've always been 'fun' and 'nice.' Evan Woods started it in the fourth grade and it was followed up by every guy I was ever interested in from that moment on. Lee Harris, Jeremy Frost, Steve Jackson, Robert Warner. 'Oh, you're a great pal, Evie. I just don't think of you that way.' 'You're a great friend, Evie.' 'I'm sor- ry, but you're like a sister to me.'" She let out a frustrated growl. "I am sick of being a great friend and a sister! I want to be a goddess from Mt. Olympus!" She dissolved into soft sobs, feeling humiliated, upset, and in dire need of some- thing chocolate, even though she had denied Traevyn's offer to get her some.

Seth stared in bewildered silence for a moment, then sighed. "Evie," he started, "you *are* a great friend and, well, you *are* my sister, so this whole conversation is kind of awk- ward for me, but that's not really the point." He sighed again and shook his head. "Evie, you are a goddess from Mt. Olym- pus and any man who doesn't see that is not worth having."

She looked up at him in surprise. Seth was not, by nature, a sensitive person. He was, more or less, a typical guy. The fact that he had just said, not only the nicest thing he'd ever said to her, but the nicest thing she'd ever heard in her life, floored her. She gave him a wobbly smile. "Thanks, Seth."

He grinned and winked at her.

She sighed and rested her head on his shoulder. "You know, you're not such a bad brother."

He chuckled.

# Chapter Fifteen

Evie still clung to Traevyn's hand as they waited in the airport for Seth to get out of the bathroom. She'd been holding onto him like a lost little girl ever since they'd boarded the plane. She hated flying. She hated it with a passion. She had only ever flown once, but it terrified her. It didn't matter that the flight from San Luis Obispo to Phoenix was relatively short. Flying was still flying. She hated the take off the most. When the engines revved up and the plane started to climb, she swore it always sounded like it was going to explode.

Traevyn glanced down at her. She knew she still must look scared to death even though they had been on firm ground for ten minutes. He smiled a bit and lifted her hand. He gently pried her fingers away and took her hand between both of his, rubbing it. "Evie, we're on land now," he reminded her. "You're alive."

"I hate flying," she stated.

"Yes, you've made that very clear, but you're on ground now. You're all right."

She glanced up at him dismally.

He smiled and brought her hand up to kiss her fingertips.

Evie's stomach lurched, and she looked away. Why did he have to do that? It only made her have more unrealistic fantasies that, in turn, made her very sad.

Seth emerged from the bathroom and they all headed off toward the baggage claim.

"How far is Sedona from Phoenix?" Seth asked.

"About two hours," Traevyn replied. "We could have flown into Sedona, but this was less of a hassle. Talis is picking us up and driving us the rest of the way."

"Bummer, I would have liked to check out Phoenix," Seth said. "They have a great metal scene."

Evie nudged Seth with her elbow. "Hey, do I look okay?" she whispered.

He glanced at her. "You look fine. What, did you decide to go for the other brother now?"

She rolled her eyes. "Gimme a break. I don't want to look all frazzled and awful."

Traevyn started to go ahead of them and Evie glanced after him. He was heading toward a shorter man with black hair and two full sleeves of tattoos. She smiled. The man from the picture. Traevyn's brother. One of the only people who knew him completely. The two men embraced, and she stood back, watching.

"Hey, Traevyn," Talis greeted with a wide grin.

Traevyn smiled. "Hello, little brother."

Talis pulled back with an almost puzzled expression. "You look different." He frowned as if trying to figure out the change. "You're...smiling. Like a real smile. Not one of those forced polite ones you usually give me."

He looked down and gave a bashful shrug.

Talis raised an eyebrow. "Okay, now *that* is a gesture I haven't seen in decades. You're freaking me out."

Traevyn gave his brother a playful scowl and turned. He held his arm out to indicate Evie and Seth. "This is my apprentice, Evie Austin. She's been staying with me for the summer."

Evie stepped forward to shake Talis's hand, noticing that he had several more ear piercings than he'd had in his picture, and Celtic rings of all patterns adorned most of his fingers.

"I'm Talis," he greeted with a warm smile.

She smiled in return. "It's good to meet you. This is my brother, Seth."

Talis reached out to shake Seth's hand.

"Dude," Seth breathed in wonderment. "Check out all your ink! Where did you get all of that done?"

"I did some of it myself," he explained. "My friend did the rest."

"You're a tattoo artist?" Seth sounded awestruck.

He nodded.

"Can you give me one?"

"Seth!" Evie reprimanded. "I'm sure that would just make

Mom and Dad's day. You coming home with a tattoo. They'd never trust me with you again."

Talis chuckled. "All right, let's get your luggage and get out of here. I don't want to hit rush hour. Evie, after you." He motioned for her to go first with a graceful sweep of his arm.

Evie raised her eyebrows in surprise. "I take it you're the courteous Whitelaw brother."

"Don't let him fool you," Traevyn remarked, shoving his brother out of the way in a playful gesture. "He spends all his time jousting and sword fighting. He gets paid to be chivalrous."

Evie giggled and glanced at Talis again, interested in his occupation, but too self-conscious at the moment to voice her curiosity.

They retrieved their luggage and loaded it into Talis's car without many delays. In no time, they were driving through the huge city of Phoenix, Arizona. Evie had never seen a city so stretched out over such a vast area. When they had been flying in and she had gathered the courage to take a quick peek, she had been overwhelmed by the sheer enormity of the city. The landscape also amazed her. As a native of Oregon, she had never seen the desert. Now, huge saguaro cactus loomed on barren hills dotted with brush and other mean-looking cactus with thousands of sharp, long spines that grew low to the ground. It all seemed very foreign to her.

"Ever been to Arizona before, Evie?" Talis called from the front seat, as if reading her thoughts.

She glanced toward him. "No, this is a first for me."

"Well, Sedona is the prettiest place in the entire state, in my opinion."

Evie smiled and continued to watch the strange scenery whiz by.

"There are over fifty art galleries in Sedona alone," Traevyn supplied.

That got Evie's attention and she raised her eyebrows in surprise. "Are you serious?"

Talis nodded his agreement. "It's a very arts oriented community. That's why I love it there."

"So, what do you have planned for us while we're here?" Traveyn drawled, leaning his head against his hand and glancing toward his brother.

Talis grinned. "Well, I have this crazy friend who lives in

Flagstaff. He wanted to go pine needle boarding in the mountains tomorrow."

Traevyn frowned. "Pine needle boarding?"

"Hey, I've heard of that!" Seth exclaimed. "It's like snow-
boarding only on pine needles instead. You take the wheels
and trucks off of a skateboard and use the deck, right?"

Talis nodded, meeting Seth's eyes in the rearview mirror.

"That is the most absurd thing I have ever heard,"
Traveyn muttered. "Can you honestly see me doing something so ridiculous?"

Talis shrugged. "You don't have to do it if you don't want
to, but go anyway. My friends want to meet you."

Traevyn snorted his disapproval.

Evie giggled and reached around to the front seat. She
squeezed Traevyn's shoulders. "What's wrong?" she teased.
"Don't tell me you don't like sports. And you seem so typical
male."

Talis and Seth both laughed.

"No one in my family likes sports." Traevyn said, giving
Talis a pointed look.

Talis shrugged. "I like everything."

Traevyn sighed. "I'll probably end up breaking my neck
just from watching."

The thought of tall, elegant Traevyn anywhere near a
skateboard did seem rather...contrasting, to say the least, but
Evie was glad Talis had planned things for them to do. Sure,
she was there for the gallery opening, but she had never been
to Arizona before and she wanted to have some fun.

The drive to Sedona was mostly boring. The cactus was
cool when she'd first seen it, but one could only stare at cactus for so long before it became very dull.

Around ten minutes before they reached the city, Evie
noticed the soil turn from a pale brown to a rich, red color.
When they reached Sedona, Evie stared in awe as monolith-
ic, jagged red rocks jutted out of the earth and towered
around the small city like guardians. It was breathtaking, and
she instantly wanted to rummage through her things and
find her sketchpad, but all of her stuff was in the trunk. She
imagined it would be hard to sketch while in a moving car
anyway. She made a mental note that, sometime during the
trip, she would need to find a good spot to draw.

Talis's home was small but nice, with a porch in the front

and a pool and hot tub in the back yard. The interior reminded Evie of a lair. Swords and medieval weaponry adorned one entire wall, and a mannequin with full armor sat displayed in a corner. There was a gigantic black beanbag chair sitting off to one side, as well as a black leather chair next to the beige sectional, which was the only light thing in the entire house. There were video games strewn everywhere in front of the TV, as well as three different video game consoles. Seth immediately started to drool.

The walls that weren't covered in weapons were full of Traevyn's art and pictures of dragons, fairies, and other mythical creatures. A large orange, yellow, and black Celtic wall hanging was tacked to the ceiling, and the enormous yellow sun in the middle of it seemed to glow down on them.

What surprised Evie the most was that, even though it was cluttered, it was clean. No wrappers or empty containers on the floor. No weird, foreign things breeding on the carpet. That and the fact that there were no role-playing game books anywhere were the only things that saved it from looking like geek-haven.

She could smell incense burning from somewhere and she smiled. Talis's house reminded her of some of the hippie, new age stores in Ashland, and she loved it. She decided right then that she adored the Whitelaw brothers, even Julian, even though she hadn't met him yet. She had no doubt he would be just as awesome in some other way.

Talis scowled as he entered and accidentally kicked a CD that was lying in his path. It skidded across the floor and hit the leg of the couch. "Ash!" he shouted. "Dude! I told you to bloody clean up the place!" He started to grumble incoherently as he shut the door and set down Evie's bags, which he had been carrying.

"Sorry!" someone shouted from one of the bedrooms.

Talis rolled his eyes. "Well, what the crap are you doing? Get out here and meet my brother, you jerk!"

Evie giggled.

"Sorry," Talis said to them. "He was supposed to pick up a little."

Traevyn shrugged with a smirk. "Talis, your place has always looked like this. No need to start apologizing now. Just be sure you put all the weapons away this time." He gave Evie a pointed look. "Last time I was here, I sat on an arrow...point up. That is not something I want to repeat."

She laughed and glanced over to the hallway as a blond man came bounding out. His ankle apparently caught on something because he tripped and came stumbling into the living room. He cast a perplexed glance at whatever the culprit had been, then looked up at everyone and smiled.

"Traevyn, it's a pleasure to finally meet you," he greeted. "I'm Ashton, Talis's roommate."

Traevyn smiled and shook his hand. "Good to meet you, Ashton. This is my apprentice, Evie, and her brother, Seth."

Ashton met Evie's eyes and his grin widened. "It is definitely a pleasure to meet you."

Evie felt her cheeks grow warm. He was very attractive. Sun-bleached blond hair that fell somewhat shaggy around his face and ears and a build that suggested he worked out regularly. His eyes were a warm blue-gray, and his smile lit up his handsome face. A small, silver hoop looped around his left earlobe, and she could see the markings of a tattoo around his right bicep. She briefly wondered what it was and if Talis had done it.

"Uh, we don't have a guest room," Talis said. "Just throw your luggage into a corner. I guess..." He scratched his head. "I guess you'll all have to sleep on the hide-a-bed in the sectional. Unless someone wants to sleep on the recliner or the floor."

After some arguing and a game of rock, paper, scissors between Seth and Evie, it was decided that Seth and Traevyn would share the hide-a-bed and Evie would sleep on the regular couch part of the sectional since she was the only one short enough to fit.

Evie had been hoping that Seth would take pity on her and let her sleep next to Traevyn, but his selfishness apparently won out over his out of character niceness.

Since they had arrived in Sedona rather late in the day, the first thing they did was find a place to eat dinner. They all decided on a Mexican restaurant that had a man playing people's requests on a guitar and interacting with the audience. The atmosphere was pleasant, and all of them had the opportunity to relax after their travels.

"So, you're Traevyn's apprentice?" Ashton asked Evie as Seth studied all of Talis's arm tattoos in mesmerized silence.

Evie nodded. "For the summer. My art history professor

chose me for the program."

"What school do you go to?"

"SOU in Ashland, Oregon." She met his eyes and gave him a little smile.

"SOU is my alma mater as well," Traevyn interjected. "Evie's professor was mine years ago, and I agreed to take on an apprentice as a favor to him."

"How do you like living with my brother so far?" Talis grumbled with a knowing smile.

"He's actually been very hospitable."

Traevyn chuckled. "Yes, after you ripped me another one about my abhorrent behavior, I decided it would be in my best interests to be more agreeable."

Evie met his eyes and she gave a shy smile, feeling her cheeks turn pink. "So, what do you do, Ashton?"

"Please, call me Ash. Everyone else does." He grinned. "I'm a waiter during the renaissance faire off season, but when the faires start up again, I'm off with Tal."

"What do you do at them?"

"I joust," he replied.

Talis rolled his eyes. "You joust. Sounds like you're baking a cake." He met Evie's eyes. "Ash is the best jouster I have ever seen. He's won more contests than I could even count."

Ash chuckled and waved it away. "Evie, would you like a drink? I was going to get something for myself. Want anything?"

She gave him a broad grin. "Yes, thank you. A strawberry margarita, please." She had been eyeballing the drink menu earlier and was more than happy to take Ash up on his offer.

He winked at her and headed to the bar.

Traevyn watched Ash walk away with a disgruntled expression before he gave a slight huff and turned his attention back to his brother. "Talis, when are you planning on dragging us up to Flagstaff for this ridiculous sport tomorrow?"

Talis shrugged. "I was thinking maybe around noon or so."

"Can we leave earlier and go to the Grand Canyon? I'd like to show Evie."

"Sure. Everyone should see it at least once."

She grinned and held Traevyn's gaze for a moment before Ash returned with her drink. "Thank you," she said with a bright smile.

Ash flashed her his beautiful grin.

Evie bobbed her head in time to the song that was currently being played, even though she had no clue what it was. "I wish they'd play 'Stairway to Heaven,'" she said to no one in particular. "That's my favorite."

Seth frowned. "You like Led Zeppelin?"

"What's wrong with Led Zeppelin?" she asked.

He shrugged. "Well nothing, but it doesn't really go with your mood music and your Lenny Kravitz."

Talis chuckled and Traevyn smiled.

Evie scowled at her brother. "Whatever."

Suddenly, Ash, who Evie hadn't even seen leave the table, sat back down, and the musician said, "This song is for the pretty girl in the pink shirt."

Evie looked down at her shirt, then blinked in bewilderment as "Stairway to Heaven" started to weave its way through the restaurant. She looked over at Ash, who winked at her again.

Seth glanced from Ash to Evie and frowned. Then he looked at Traevyn, who suddenly seemed to be rather interested in the napkin on the table.

The rest of dinner went by pleasantly, and afterward, everyone headed back to Talis's house to unwind. It was decided that everyone would go to sleep early since the Grand Canyon was two hours away from Sedona and no one wanted to be rushed the next morning.

Evie thought that Traevyn had been rather quiet since dinner, but she didn't say anything about it. Traevyn was, after all, known to lapse into brooding silence every once in awhile.

After Talis and Ash turned in for the night, Traevyn pulled out the hide-a-bed where Seth fell asleep almost instantly and started to snore. Traevyn and Evie exchanged a glance and laughed softly.

"We have all these crazy pictures of him when he was little," Evie said. "He can fall asleep anywhere in seconds. It's always amazed me." She spread a blanket across the couch and tried to figure out where to put her pillow. Either way, one end of her body was going to be really close to Traevyn's face since her part of the sectional was attached to the hide-a-bed. "Do you want the feet or the head?" she asked.

He arched an eyebrow. "Well, I think the head would be

the best choice."

She giggled and set her pillow down. She went to brush her teeth and wash her face in the bathroom while Traevyn changed, and she took her time getting into her pajamas and going about her nightly routine.

When she was finished, she opened up the door to see Ash standing on the other side in only a pair of blue plaid pajama pants. "Oh!" she exclaimed. "I'm sorry! I didn't know you were waiting." She tried to keep from gaping at his perfect upper body. Good lord, he was buff. Six-pack and everything. She could see his arm band tattoo now. It was some Celtic pattern, and he had a double bladed battle axe tattooed right in the middle of his chest. It was insanely sexy.

Ash smiled. "No, it's okay. I wasn't waiting long." He pointed to her pajamas, which were pink and had karate chopping monkeys on the pants. The equally pink shirt had Girls Kick Butt written across it. "Cute PJs," he commented.

A faint blush touched her cheeks as she looked down at them. She realized she wasn't wearing a bra either, which made her blush worse. She wasn't worried about Traevyn. She had been living with him for two months now, and she was usually in her PJ's when they spent their evenings together. She was comfortable with him seeing her, but Ash was a complete stranger. A hot stranger who had been flirting with her all night.

"Hey, the air conditioner panel is in the kitchen," he stated. "I know you guys live by the ocean so it's probably a heck of a lot cooler there at night. It gets pretty sweltering here, so if you need to turn it up, go ahead."

"Thanks."

He grinned and maneuvered past her into the bathroom. "See you tomorrow. If you need anything, just ask."

She smiled and nodded. He shut the door and she turned to go back into the living room. Traevyn sat on the edge of the bed, brushing out his shining hair. She grinned and went to him. "Can I?" she questioned, holding her hand out.

He looked up at her and smiled. He handed her the brush and turned his back to her. "Braid it, if you would," he said. "I don't need it strangling you and Seth in your sleep."

She giggled and gathered his thick mane in her hands. She sighed as she began to brush it. "I love your hair, Traevyn," she commented. "It's so beautiful."

Her words sent warmth into his heart. "Thank you."

"It was what first caught my attention when I saw you," she continued. "I'd never seen a man with such long hair. It was a surprise. That and the fact that you were towering over me in such a menacing fashion."

He chuckled. "I hated you that day, hated you intruding on my solitude." He shook his head. That seemed like forever ago. He couldn't fathom ever hating Evie now. She was the only beautiful thing in his world. "Evie," he said softly, "I can never repay you for what you've done for me."

"Like what? Clean your enormous house and cook you dinner?"

He smiled. "No... Since day one, you have seen me, seen through every barrier, every harsh word or action. Your friendship...it means so much to me."

"I don't know what I did, really," she murmured.

He turned to look at her just as she finished braiding his hair. "You made me open up," he said. "You forced me to face what I was hiding from. You have shown me warmth and compassion and understanding when I offered you nothing but cold resentment. Evie." He took her hands in his. "You did nothing more than be yourself, which ended up being the best gift I could ever receive." He shook his head. "You and Seth...you are both so special to me." For some reason, his heart felt heavy in his chest, and his chest felt constricted and pained. It was as if his heart was trying to tell him something, but he was unsure of the message. It had been bothering him all night. Since dinner actually. For some reason he couldn't quite place his finger on, all he wanted to do was have Evie as close to him as possible. It was strange and out of character, and Seth's blasted words kept ringing over and over again in his mind.

Evie averted her gaze and smiled, but it looked forced. "You are very special to me too, Traevyn," she murmured. "A very special friend."

Her voice caught on the word *friend*, but he didn't ask her about it. He smiled and pressed a gentle kiss to her cheek.

Evie's eyes fluttered closed and, without thinking, she leaned in and wrapped her arms around his neck.

Traevyn's eyes widened, but he pulled her into his arms and held her. Warmth filled him, that delicious warmth that he cherished. The warmth that always chased the shadows from his heart. He breathed in the smell of her, a feminine, clean smell that attacked his senses in a dramatic, yet subtle way. He pulled away and gazed down into her hazel eyes with a sigh. He had his palm against the side of her face, rubbing his thumb across the soft satin of her skin. He let his eyes roam over her before they fell on her lips, supple, full and soft-looking. He could barely remember what they had felt like when she'd kissed him in the car. It had been so fleeting. He imagined they were perfect. Perfect and warm and gentle, just like everything else about Evie... Well, except maybe her fiery temper.

Traevyn realized with some confusion just exactly what he was thinking, and he dropped his hand. He cleared his throat. "Get some sleep, Evie," he whispered.

She nodded and pulled away, but seemed reluctant to do so. "I'll see you in the morning." She lay down and pulled the cover over her.

Traevyn turned out the light and climbed under the covers, all too aware of Evie's head lying perpendicular and very close to his. The smell of her hair attacked him once again, and he closed his eyes. He clenched his jaw as feelings he had thought dead to him came flooding back in a torrent. Desire... It had been so long since he had desired anyone, but the feeling was unmistakable. Where had it come from? Why so suddenly? Had it been lurking close to the surface for some time just waiting to pounce? Something inside him already knew the answer was yes.

He turned on his side, trying to get away from her alluring fragrance, but was met by Seth who was on his side facing Traevyn. His mouth gaped open and he was snoring like a troll or some other hideous beast. He quickly turned back over onto his back and let out a frustrated sigh. He was trapped. His body felt painfully tight and he closed his eyes, trying to relax. It didn't work. He glanced up at Evie again. She was facing the couch so she didn't see him. He slowly reached his fingers out to capture a strand of her soft hair. He rubbed it between his fingers, feeling the texture, then brought it to his lips. He frowned, feeling foolish, and covered his face with his hands.

He needed to go to sleep. Maybe he would be able to think clearer in the morning.

# Chapter Sixteen

The first thing Traevyn was aware of as he awoke was that things were not where they should be. He felt a strange pressure across his throat, and a body was against his back. His eyes fluttered open and he frowned, trying to blink away the sleep and focus. Dark hair obscured his vision. Dark, perfumed hair that had taunted him all night. He brushed it back and realized that Evie was lying on her stomach with one arm flung across his neck. He smiled and lifted her arm, gently setting it aside. Next, he investigated the pressure against his back and almost laughed aloud as he realized that Seth was curled up against him with his arm wrapped around his waist. He deftly moved away from Seth and slipped out of bed, chuckling softly under his breath.

He stretched and made his way into the kitchen where Talis was already dressed and making a cup of coffee.

"Good morning, darling," Talis teased with a smile.

Traevyn yawned. "Why didn't you wake me up sooner?" he asked, leaning against the kitchen counter.

"You just looked so comfortable spooning with Seth."

Traevyn shook his head. "He would never believe us if we told him."

"I should have snapped a picture." Talis chuckled as he leaned against the counter next to Traevyn. "So, what changed?" he queried.

Traevyn frowned. "What do you mean?"

"You're different. You smile, you laugh. There's light in your eyes for the first time since Leanna died and Amy left. What happened?"

Traevyn looked down and sighed. "Evie happened."

Talis gave him a questioning look and took a sip of his coffee.

"Talis, no one has ever seen me like she has. I tried to push her as far away from me as possible and she just saw right through it. She saw through everything right into the core of me. She is the most understanding, loving person I have ever known."

"You seem very close," he observed with a smile.

"She's a good person with such a big heart. I think Evie would befriend the entire world."

Talis slid his gaze over to Traveyn, obviously realizing he had avoided the statement. He smirked. "You know, Traevyn, I'm very proud of the strides you have made. You let someone close to you, a stranger. That's very commendable. Especially when Julian and I thought you would never glance at someone other than your family ever again."

Traevyn smiled at his brother's words.

"Just don't be afraid to open up fully."

He frowned in confusion. "I don't follow."

Talis turned to face him. "You have had to endure more in your lifetime than anyone should have to. Amy was your first love. She hurt you in unspeakable ways."

Traevyn swallowed and looked away as familiar pain washed over him.

"Being hesitant is understandable," Talis continued. "But you're a different person with Evie around. It's a noticeable change. You can't tell me you don't feel it."

"Of course I do," Traevyn almost snapped. Not out of anger, but out of frustration at not being able to decipher anything he was feeling lately. He sighed. "Evie is a ray of light, bringing warmth and hope to all around her. She is young and vibrant and—"

"You're an old, jaded man?" Talis grinned. "Traevyn, come on. Don't be an idiot." He patted him on the shoulder and headed back down the hallway toward his bedroom.

Traevyn frowned. There were those words again. *Don't be an idiot.* Seth. Talis. He felt like everyone on the planet knew something he didn't. He let out an irritated sound and headed toward his suitcase. After finding something to wear, he went to take a long shower. Afterwards, he went to wake Evie, who was still sleeping soundly.

He knelt in front of her and watched her for a second, a

small smile touching his lips. She looked so angelic and peaceful. He reached out to brush a strand of hair out of her face. "Evie," he murmured. "Evie, wake up."

Her brows drew together in a disapproving frown, and she tried to turn away from the sound of his voice and go back to sleep.

He smiled and ran his hand along her shoulder. "Evie," he persisted.

"Dude, that won't work," Seth yawned suddenly. He sat up and motioned Traevyn out of the way. He grabbed a pillow. "Evie!" he shouted. "Rise and shine!" He flung the pillow down onto her head with a dull, thwacking sound.

Traevyn winced.

Evie sat bolt upright, her hair disheveled and falling in her face. She blinked rapidly, then scowled with ferocity. She picked up her pillow and hurled it back at her brother before turning her fiery glare to Traevyn.

He held his hands up. "Innocent," he stated.

She grumbled something under her breath and shuffled into the bathroom. Seth looked at Traevyn and gave a triumphant grin. Traevyn chuckled.

* * *

Seth winced as he pulled a pine needle out of his butt. Then he rubbed at his elbow. "That really kinda hurt," he muttered.

Evie laughed. "That's what you get for not letting Draco teach you. You wiped out because of your own arrogance."

Seth scowled and stood up, retrieving his board from where it had skidded into a bush.

They had headed up to the Grand Canyon that morning, which Evie had found absolutely breathtaking. Traevyn had walked the trail with her while Seth and Ash had taunted a squirrel with potato chips and Talis had gone to the lookout area by the gift shop.

Evie was dizzy standing on the edge, staring down into the chasm that seemed never ending. She almost felt as if she was staring straight into the middle of the earth. Traevyn had taken her hand protectively, like it was instinctual, and she had welcomed his touch, as well as his care.

"You really need to see it at sunrise," he had said. "The

colors are so beautiful. We'll come back sometime, just the two of us."

Evie didn't know if he actually realized what he'd said, but she wasn't going to ask him about it. She just liked the invitation.

After they had spent sufficient time marveling at one of the Seven Wonders of the World, they had all headed back to Flagstaff where they'd met up with Talis's friends, Draco and Leila. Apparently, they both traveled the renaissance faires with Talis and Ash. Draco was a leatherworker and a musician. He was tattooed, pierced, and gothic, which made Seth like him almost instantaneously. Leila was a dance instructor who did belly dancing at the faires. She was petite, blonde, and easy-going.

Evie learned a lot about renaissance faires while they drove up to the mountains, and she found the entire lifestyle fascinating. All summer they got to travel like modern day gypsies. It seemed very exciting and free to her.

Once in the mountains, Draco had given them a brief demonstration of how pine needle boarding was done. He made it look so easy that Seth had just plowed ahead and ended up on his back before he knew it, sliding down the mountain.

Traevyn adamantly refused to get anywhere near one of the wheel-less skateboards, and he stood casually by, content to watch everyone else make idiots out of themselves.

"Are you going to try, Evie?" Ash asked her with a wide grin.

She giggled. "I'm not sure yet. I'm going to have to have Draco give me a lesson."

He smiled. "I can teach you. I've done this with Draco loads of times. Here, come stand on this and try to get your balance."

Traevyn watched as Ash grasped Evie's hand to keep her upright while she got a feel for the board. He said something that made her laugh, and Traevyn frowned. He folded his arms and started to walk through the trees, down the slope, and away from the group. He sighed when he came to a stop a good distance away. He leaned against a tree and looked back up at everyone. Talis and Leila were talking while Draco tried to show Seth how to properly operate the board. Evie was starting to head her way down slowly, listening carefully to Ash's instructions and giggling the entire time. As she gained more confidence, she picked up speed.

"Great job, Evie!" Ash called. "You're a natural at this!"

Evie grinned and came to a stop close to where Traevyn was standing. She threw her arms up in the air. "Woo hoo!" she shouted. She laughed. "I'm gonna go again!"

Traevyn watched her run back up to Ash, who gave her a high-five. He sighed again and turned his back on the scene, wondering why seeing her laughing and playing with another man made his heart twinge. He rubbed at his temples, feeling so confused. It was like his heart was trying to tell his mind something that his mind was trying very hard to deny.

"Woo hoo! Go, Evie!" Ash's voice shouted, followed by Seth and Talis's laughter.

"Watch out, Traevyn!" Evie called down to him. "I'm gonna getcha!"

Traevyn turned lazily at the sound of Evie's voice, a small smirk on his lips. She maneuvered the board with finesse down the slope, picking up speed. She grinned, then suddenly lunged forward as the edge of her board hit a protruding rock and came to a complete stop. Her eyes widened as she was propelled through the air.

Traevyn really didn't have time to react. All he saw was her body catch air as she hurtled toward him. He held his arms out to catch her just as she plowed into him, knocking them both to the ground. Traevyn landed hard on his back, holding Evie on top of him. He grunted as pain worked through his body. He blinked a few times as the dust they had kicked up settled and the pain reduced in intensity. He looked at Evie. "Are you all right?" he croaked.

She raised her head and winced. "Yeah," she muttered. "You broke my fall."

"I think I broke my back," he groaned.

Evie smiled and tried to get up, her chest no doubt hurting from where the wind had been knocked from her on impact. She put her hand on the ground beside Traevyn's head to stabilize herself as she tried to stand, but the pine needles caused her to slip and she landed on him again, this time pressed intimately close with her face mere inches from his.

Traevyn sucked his breath in at the sudden contact, and he looked up into Evie's eyes. She stared down at him, bewildered. Her eyes...they were so beautiful. So full of life and love, so soft and compassionate. He reached for the hand that had caused her to slip and he slowly pulled it up over his head, stretching her out and pressing her body even closer to his. He relished the feeling. He had felt nothing for so long. Nothing but ice. She was all fire. She melted him and set him ablaze.

Evie's heart threatened to explode right there. She couldn't tear her gaze from Traevyn's. He was looking at her with such intensity. She couldn't have pulled away if she tried. She drew in a shaky breath as she felt him let go of her hand and run his fingers in a painfully slow course down her arm and her side. Her skin burned where he touched her, and her always active mind filled with about a hundred wanton images she did not need at that particular moment. His hand came to rest on her hip and a small smirk touched his lips before he squeezed her side.

Evie let out a yell, which only encouraged him. He squeezed again, tickling her until she was screaming. He flipped over with a playful snarl, rolling her beneath him. He buried his face in her neck and tickled her there with his nose as he continued to squeeze her sides. She squealed with laughter, writhing beneath him. He grinned and continued his assault, playfully nipping at her neck. This made Evie gasp and stop laughing. Traevyn suddenly went very still, as if overcome by her, by being near her, by the moment in itself. He closed his eyes and gave in. He lowered his lips to her neck, kissing and nuzzling it gently.

Evie's eyes rolled back into her head and she seriously thought she might die. She felt him run his tongue up her neck and nibble on her earlobe, and she made a small, incoherent sound in the back of her throat. Her mind continued its brazen assault on her, flooding her with imaginings of Traevyn doing very wicked things to her in that grand bed of his.

She forced herself back to the present, confusion clouding her thoughts. Wait, why was he touching her this way? Kissing her? He had never been this way with her before. She far from minded, but it didn't make sense, and it frightened her because she knew she was falling so hard she feared she'd never be able to get back up. She reached up to touch his hair. "Traevyn?" she questioned softly.

He raised his head, logic returning to him. He looked

down into her confused eyes and knew he should be embarrassed at his forwardness, but he wasn't. He cupped her cheek in his palm and smiled down at her, feeling warm all over. There were no shadows at the moment. No evil, lurking demons. Just beautiful, blinding rays of light.

Evie's face lit up at the sight of his smile, and her eyes filled with so much warmth that it made his heart stutter for a moment. He wanted her lips, wanted them under his own. He wanted to taste that smile and that light.

"Hey! You guys all right down there?" Talis's voice called.

Traevyn blinked as sense came tearing back to him, and he sat up with a frown. "Yeah!" he called.

Evie sat up also, feeling bereft. She let out a soft sigh and tried to smooth her hair. She glanced at Traevyn, who looked rather puzzled. "Sorry I landed on you," she remarked.

He slid his eyes over to her and let out a dry chuckle. "I don't think I minded."

She blushed.

He looked down with a sudden shy smile and pointed to Evie's neck. "You have... You have a—" His face flushed and he touched her neck gently.

Her eyes widened and she covered her neck with her palm. "Did you give me a hickey?" she cried in horror.

His beautiful, always composed face turned an even deeper shade of red. "N—No," he stammered. "It's just a...bite mark."

She sighed in relief. "Oh. Well, I'll just tell the others I must have scraped myself."

He rubbed the bridge of his nose, obviously feeling very uncomfortable. "Well, yes, except that it looks undeniably like a...bite mark."

She bit her bottom lip. "Oh...well...we were only playing around." She knew she sounded unconvincing even as she said it.

He gave her a look. "This is my brother," he said flatly. "And *your* brother. You really think they'll buy that?"

She sighed. "Not a chance. I'll just stay here until it goes away."

"What are you two doing down there?" Draco shouted.

"We're just chilling!" Evie called back, grateful the whole previous scene had been out of everyone's line of sight. "I just totally took out Traevyn! I knocked the air out of myself and almost killed him! I need to rest! We'll be up in a bit!"

"Are you hurt?" Ash's voice came.

Traevyn visibly bristled.

Evie smiled. "No, I'm okay!" She glanced at Traevyn, who now looked awkward. She gave him a bashful smile. "I always knew you were a vampire," she teased.

He laughed, and her words seemed to ease some of his discomfort. He gave her a soft smile.

Suddenly, someone shouted. It was followed by a great tumbling sound. Seth appeared, skidding to a stop on his stomach in front of them. Evie arched her eyebrows.

Seth groaned and flipped over, breathing heavily and staring up at the sky. "Aw man," he grumbled. "I hate this stupid sport."

Evie giggled.

"I don't know," Traevyn remarked quietly. "I find it rather enjoyable."

Seth frowned and sat up. "What are you talking about? You've been sitting down here on your butt the entire time."

Traevyn and Evie exchanged a glance, and she looked down to hide a blush.

Seth rolled his eyes. "Dude, I don't even want to know." He stood and dusted himself off, heading back up to the top.

Evie touched her neck and smiled to herself. She could still feel his lips there. She sighed, wishing that was a regular occurrence. His affection was intoxicating and addicting. She looked up as she felt Traevyn's fingers on her hand. He pulled it to his lips and kissed it, then stood.

"Come on," he said. "Let's go before Seth starts spreading rumors."

She nodded and they both started back up the incline, their minds on anything but pine needle boarding.

# *Chapter Seventeen*

After a nice dinner in Flagstaff, everyone bade farewell to Draco and Leila and made their way back to Sedona, where it was unanimously decided that a dip in the pool would be refreshing. It was, after all, well into the triple digits, and after a long day of physical activity out in the sun, everyone was dirty and starting to stink.

Traevyn and Evie had remained relatively quiet with one another since their encounter, and Evie wondered what he was thinking. What had possessed him to do what he had done? Was it genuine desire, or was he just lonely? Had he been overcome by the feeling of a woman pressed against him when he hadn't been close to someone in so long? It was difficult to tell since Evie had long ago come to the conclusion that Traevyn didn't really communicate all that well.

Ash continued to be very attentive to Evie all day, drawing her into conversations about all sorts of things. He was very charming; she couldn't deny that, and it was nice to have someone making advances toward her instead of her typical gazing in adoration from afar.

She slipped into her swimsuit and headed outside to where everyone else was lounging by the pool. Talis and Traevyn were actually sitting in the hot tub, which she really couldn't understand, but she supposed that after bulldozing Traevyn earlier, he more than likely needed to soak his back. It was probably the same with Talis since he had spent about as much time eating dirt as Seth.

Ash and Seth were playfully racing one another in the pool, and Ash waved when he saw Evie step out into the yard. "Evie, come on over!" he urged.

She grinned and made her way to the pool, eager to feel the cool water against her skin.

\* \* \*

Traevyn watched Evie, and his heart beat out a strange rhythm at the sight of her. She was wearing a blue, two-piece swimsuit that showed off her ample curves very nicely. He swallowed uncomfortably and forced himself to turn his glance elsewhere. He was almost positive that the way his blood started to burn raised the temperature in the hot tub at least five degrees. "Something is happening to me, little brother," he said.

Talis grinned. "Congratulations, Traevyn, you're still a man."

Traevyn felt his face flush. "This is strange for me. Evie has been living at my home for two months. We've grown to be close friends. I can tell her things I can't tell anyone other than you and Julian. She understands me. I don't have to explain myself to her. She just blindly accepts me. She has from the beginning. I was an ogre, yet she never questioned me. She told me off several times, which I deserved, but never questioned my reasons." He shook his head. "Talis, I'm confused. My heart...it has been so guarded, but lately..." He didn't even know how to explain it. Nothing made sense to him anymore. What had happened between Evie and himself earlier really made no sense.

"Lately your heart seems to beat a little faster when Evie is around?" Talis questioned.

He met his eyes and nodded.

Talis gave Traevyn a gentle smile, obviously seeing the genuine terror lurking behind his eyes. Talis knew him even better than Julian did. He could read him like a book. Talis knew that the thought of Traevyn leaving himself open for another blow like the last petrified him. "Traevyn," he said, "would you change knowing and loving Amy if you had the chance?"

Traevyn frowned and looked down, wondering where that had come from. A twinge went through his heart at the mention of her name, and something deep inside told him to run as far away from this situation with Evie as possible and never look back. He forced the thought away, knowing it was a reaction due to fear. He thought of Amy and the unspoiled years he'd had with her. She had taught him many things about love. They had been happy together at one point. He had to force himself to think past the bitter poison that tainted his memories of her, but he remembered how his heart had felt so full and warm when he was in love. He loved the feeling of knowing he was completely devoted to one person, that she was his and he was hers. And then there was Leanna. He would never trade his years with his precious baby girl.

He sighed and shook his head. "No," he answered.

Talis nodded. "She hurt you, but your heart still beats, Traevyn. You're still alive. You survived. Don't let her ruin the life you have left by living in fear of what she did happening again. You've always known your heart. You've always known your path. Since we were kids."

Traevyn closed his eyes, feeling more lost than he ever had. "Talis, I lost my path when everything around me turned to blackness."

"Yes, but you have light now." He pointed to Evie, who was laughing with the others in the pool. "Don't just throw it away and return to your shadows because they're familiar and safe."

Traevyn fought a shiver at the thought of going back to that dark, desolate place inside himself. He looked over at Evie and Seth, who started to have a splash war with one another. He needed to spend some time with Evie away from everyone. He needed to be with her without distraction so he could properly decipher what he was feeling. He needed to know for sure before he drove himself mad. He stood. "I need some water," he announced. "Plus, I'm starting to stew over here. I'll be back."

Talis smiled and watched him go.

* * *

Evie watched Traevyn head into the house, thinking he looked strange in swim trunks. He was always so refined and sophisticated, and she'd always thought he seemed so much more like the old world knight trapped in the wrong time than a modern man. Seeing him in swim trunks just seemed weird somehow. Although, watching the play of muscles in his shoulders and back as he walked was a nice sight.

"Hey, Evie," Ash's voice came. "Can I talk to you for a second?"

She blinked, surprised by the sudden request, but she shrugged. "Sure." She got out of the pool and followed Ash around to the side of the house where it was private.

Ash turned to her with a shy smile and met her eyes. "Evie, I know I don't know you that well, but I've really had fun with you since you've been here."

She grinned. "Me too, Ash."

He scratched at the back of his head and took a deep breath. "I was wondering, I know tomorrow Talis wants to take us downtown, but tomorrow night I thought...maybe you'd like to go to a movie with me?"

She raised her eyebrows and opened her mouth to respond, but suddenly became very aware of a presence behind her. A silent presence she had grown accustomed to.

"Hello, Ashton," Traevyn's smooth voice interrupted.

Ash, who had been busy watching Evie's reaction, nearly jumped right up to the roof. "Holy crap!" he cried. "You scared me to death!"

Traevyn gave him a small, satisfied smile. "Evie already has plans tomorrow," he stated.

Evie frowned. "I do?"

"Yes," he emphasized. "You have plans with me."

She blinked up at him. "O—Oh..."

Traevyn stood protectively behind her, staring down at Ash with a calm, yet menacing look.

Ash seemed to shrink under Traevyn's stare, and he took a step back. "Oh, sorry," he said. "I didn't know." He gave Evie a dismal look. "Maybe some other time."

She tried to give him a reassuring smile and nodded, but he was retreating almost instantly. She frowned and turned to face Traevyn. "That was beyond rude," she spat.

He frowned. "Why was it rude? I was just stating a fact."

She folded her arms. "Stating a fact, were you? Well, I wasn't aware that we had plans tomorrow. It would have been nice if you'd asked." She snorted and rolled her eyes. "I swear, sometimes I think you crawled right out of the cave."

His dark eyebrows drew together in a scowl. "You mean you'd rather go off with him?"

She blinked in bewilderment. Where in the world was this coming from? "That's not the point. What's the matter with you? You can't just come up and inform me of what my plans are! At least he asked me like a gentleman! You were just rude! He was just trying to be nice!"

Traevyn stood up tall in the way he did when he was feeling backed into a corner. "Oh, I'm sure he'd like to do a lot more than be nice to you." His voice was more like a snarling hiss than anything else.

She stammered for a few incoherent seconds before she flung her arms up in the air in exasperation. "What the heck are you talking about?"

"It's only obvious to everyone here that he is interested in you."

Evie stood very still, feeling a molten rage replace the regular flow of her blood. How dare he! How dare he try and deter someone from liking her! It didn't happen very often! Actually, it never happened at all! "So what if he does?" she shouted. "Am I not allowed to have someone like me? Am I not worthy of that?"

Traevyn seemed slightly taken aback by her vehement response.

"I have the right to have a life! Who dubbed you my lord and master? Besides, even if he does like me, what does it matter to *you*?" She felt tears sting her eyes again. Hot, angry tears. What *did* it matter to him? Why did he even care? He'd said it himself. She was a special friend. *A friend*. So what did it matter if she went out with another guy?

Traevyn's face grew sober and dark. He walked up to her, trapping her against the wall and towering over her with his powerful presence. Evie gasped at his sudden nearness, and she looked up into his angry green eyes, her own fury rapidly dissipating.

He dipped his head so that his mouth was against her ear. "Perhaps I wanted you all to myself." His voice was still a snarl, but it carried a sensual, purring undertone that was devastating to her heart and breathing ability.

She shivered as his breath tickled her ear, and strange tingles ran down her spine. Then, just like that, he was gone, striding away and leaving her all alone. She let out a slow breath and looked down at her trembling hands, confused by that entire series of events.

"Evie!"

She jumped at her brother's sudden sharp remark and

frowned as Seth stood before her, scowling.

"What do you think you're doing?" he snapped.

She blinked rapidly in complete confusion.

"You've been flirting with Ash all day!" he supplied.

Her irritation quickly returned. "So what?" she cried. "Can't I flirt?"

"No!" he exclaimed. "You can't!"

She stepped back in surprise.

Seth shook his head and met her eyes with force, as if to drive home his point with his glare alone. "You are going to ruin everything. If you pulled your head out of your butt and started paying attention, you'd notice that Traevyn has been staring at you all friggin' day, not to mention whatever happened between you two in the mountains."

She looked down to hide a blush.

"You know how Traevyn was when we first met him," he continued. "Now he laughs and smiles and plays. That's because of you, idiot!"

She opened her mouth to reprimand him for calling her a name, but he took her firmly by the shoulders, cutting her off.

"You're being stupid, Evie," he stated. "That man does not open up to people. He opened up to you! That means something! And you're just going to let everything you want walk away because of your own stupid insecurity!" He snorted and let go of her. "Grow up." He turned and left her standing there.

Evie stared after Seth, feeling so overwhelmed she didn't know what to do with herself. She sat down where she was standing and put her head in her hands. She sighed and tried to sort out both Traevyn's reaction to the possibility of her going out with Ash and Seth's powerful words.

* * *

Talis gave Traevyn the once-over with his eyes as he entered the house. Traevyn pretended not to see as he continued to sit with an irritated frown on the sofa, but he saw well enough.

Talis sighed and sat next to him. "The next time you decide to scare the crap out of my roommate, do you think you could let me know first? That way I can start looking for a new one?"

Traevyn glanced at Talis dismally, but said nothing.

Talis rolled his eyes heavenward. "Traevyn, you look like a wet cat."

"Thanks ,Talis, but you're really not making me feel any better."

Talis chuckled. "Did she reject you?"

He frowned. "Not exactly... Unless her calling me a caveman counts."

"No, that was just stating the obvious."

Traevyn expelled a forceful breath. There were times when he really hated having brothers.

"Did she say she would go out with Ash?"

"No, but she wanted to," he snapped.

"Did she say that?"

Traevyn's sullen frown deepened.

Talis nodded. "I thought so. Next time, try communicating. It works better than dictatorship." He patted Traevyn on the shoulder and stood to leave.

"How do you know all of this anyway?" Traevyn questioned. "You weren't part of the conversation."

Talis fixed Traevyn with a look. "Please, the way you two were yelling...the entire neighborhood was part of the conversation."

Traevyn sighed in irritation at both himself and the entire situation. He knew he might not have behaved in a very dignified manner, but he couldn't help it. Something about the thought of Evie spending time alone with Ash... Not that there was anything wrong with Ash. He was actually rather nice. It was just that he had grown accustomed to having Evie to himself...

He rolled his eyes. Oh, come on. Who was he trying to fool? The truth was that the thought of Evie choosing Ash over him made him sick because Amy had chosen another man over him. He was terrified of being rejected, and his response to that was to act like a jerk. Yeah, that would definitely ensure him a place by her side.

He sighed again. Evie had no reason to feel guilty. She didn't owe anything to him. He had no claim on her. Had he just assumed that the beautiful light she emitted was solely for him? A sharp pain stabbed at his heart to think that it wasn't, to think of her showering her beauty on some other man. When had he come to cherish that? When had he come to want it all for himself? The same voice inside him, the one that kept seeming to point out the obvious, told him that the desire to have all of her beauty for himself meant something, meant more than he had been willing to admit. It terrified him. It invigorated him. It made him want to scream with the confusion of it all.

Just then, Evie entered the house, and his heart leapt into his throat, nearly choking him. "Evie," he croaked.

She stopped and gave him a measured stare. "Yes, Conan?"

His lips quirked at the corners and he averted his gaze. "Come here, please." It was not a command, just a quiet request.

She went to sit next to him, her arms folded.

Traevyn turned to face her. "There's this place by the airport called Airport Mesa. It's a lookout point where you can watch the sun set over the red rocks. I..." He looked down, hating how she always made him feel so vulnerable. He'd sworn he would never feel vulnerable again, but he knew, deep in his heart, that Evie had the ability to hurt him badly if she wanted to.

He thought back to when she had kissed him to stop his emotional tangent. He remembered how she had anchored him, led him to safety with her gentle, guiding light. How many times had he turned to her since then? How many times had he sought out her company to chase the shadows away? He had told her that she held a part of him, part of his soul. She held the one part of his soul that had not been poisoned, the one part that was still good and pure and hopeful. He had given it to her out of blind trust, something he would never have done for anyone else. She held the only good left in him and she could shatter it in a second if she wanted to. This realization hit him hard, and his hands started to tremble.

He cleared his throat and tried to focus. "I was hoping maybe you would go to dinner with me and then I could take you there, but..." He swallowed hard and closed his eyes, forcing himself to say what nearly killed him. "If you would be happier going to the movies with Ash, go... I have no right to claim anything on you or your life, and I'm sorry." He shivered, feeling very cold. She could slay him, slay him right now, and she didn't even know it. She didn't know it because he had never told her. He hadn't even told himself until now. He hadn't wanted to believe that he could care for her so much because it would make him weak. It would make him open and vulnerable. Love had always been his weakness, emotion his undoing. He supposed it came with the territory of being creative.

"Traevyn..."

Her soft voice sent waves of warmth through him. He felt her gentle fingers lightly close over his, and his heart lurched. He feared her words, feared her rejection, yet he held onto her soft touch.

"Hey, look at me," she coaxed.

Traevyn slowly turned his eyes up to meet Evie's. She gave him a soft smile. "I would rather go to dinner with you than go to a hundred movies with someone else," she murmured. "All you had to do was ask."

Several different emotions flashed through him right before his lips split into a grin. His fingers tightened on hers, and happiness surged to life inside of him.

She smiled and lifted her free hand to touch his cheek. Traevyn trapped her hand there with his own, leaning his cheek into her palm and feeling her touch in the very depths of his being. He needed Evie. It was suddenly clear to him. He needed Evie to live. She showed him how to breathe again. She made his heart remember how to beat.

He shook his head and let out a slow breath. "I'm sorry for how I treated you back there. It was rather barbaric of me. I actually imagine clubbing you over the head and dragging you by the hair might have had better results."

She giggled.

"It's just that—" He needed to tell her. He needed to tell her how much she meant to him. He met her gaze. "Evie, I—" The words got stuck in his throat, refused to emerge. He couldn't. Not yet. He couldn't face her possible rejection yet. It would destroy him if she turned him down.

The words he would have said dissolved and he forced a smile. "Never mind." He clasped both of her hands in his and gave her a great fake smile when everything inside of him was in turmoil. "Let's go back out and enjoy everyone's company," he suggested. "I promise not to be insane."

She grinned and rolled her eyes playfully. "You can't really get around that one."

She stood and kept her hand in his, guiding him back outside.

Traevyn tried to force his troubled thoughts out of his mind for the time being. He just wanted to have a good time without being so lost in his own mind that he looked like a brooding statue. He had already scared the wits out of Ash... A sadistic, satisfied smile twisted his lips. He was kind of happy about that. He couldn't deny it.

Evie led him to the pool and jumped in while he stood, trying to decide if he even wanted to get in. He was already almost dry and—

Suddenly, Seth and Talis crashed into him, and all three of them went flying into the water.

Evie shrieked as an enormous splash attacked her, and Traevyn emerged coughing and sputtering, his hair clinging to his face, as well as Seth's.

Seth swatted at the wet strands, trying to remove them. One was coiled around his throat and he snorted. "Dude, this is like a bad horror movie." He shoved Traevyn's hair aside and laughed, treading water nearby.

Traevyn pulled his hair out of his face and shook his head. He fixed a scowl on Talis and Seth, but couldn't maintain it for long. They were grinning like the devils they were and he chuckled. He pulled his arm back and sent a stream of water right at both of them.

Evie shrieked again as she got some of the attack. She frowned and advanced, sending a splash of her own as Talis and Seth retaliated. The three of them had backed Traevyn into a corner, and he lunged forward, hauling Seth out of the water and body slamming him back into it.

Evie laughed as her brother went flying. She saw Traevyn turn his attention to her next and she squealed, trying to turn and escape. He was too fast. His arm was around her waist and he pulled her up to hold in front of him as Talis continued to send little annoying splashes directly in his face.

Traevyn laughed. "Stop! I have a hostage!" he cried.

Talis ignored him and continued to splash.

Evie squeezed her eyes shut as she got most of it. "Quit it!" she sputtered. "You're going to drown me!"

Seth attacked from behind, grabbing Traevyn around the shoulders and pulling him backward to dunk him again. Evie

escaped and Traevyn emerged, shaking his head and sending water flying everywhere. "Come on, you guys," he com-
plained. "Three against one? Tell me how this is fair. Where's
Ash when you need him?"

"You scared him into the next century," Talis grumbled.

They all laughed and continued to play, all troublesome
thoughts momentarily forgotten.

# Chapter Eighteen

Evie was taking much longer to get ready than she rightly should and she felt stupid for it, but she was technically, kinda sorta, going on a date with Traevyn, and she wanted to look magnificent. She didn't know if she could really consider it a "date," but she figured it was close enough, and she was going to indulge herself. She huffed in frustration and yanked her shirt off. She threw it on Talis's bed, since she was using his room to change. Nothing was satisfying her. She wanted to look alluring and sexy, but everything she tried on made her feel short and frumpy.

The door opened without warning and she shrieked. Seth walked in, completely unabashed. "Seth!" Evie yelled. "What are you doing? Can't you see I'm in my bra?"

He shrugged. "Nothing I haven't seen before." He flopped down on the bed.

Evie rolled her eyes.

"Why aren't you ready yet?" he asked. "Traevyn's only been waiting for you for about a million years. He does have reservations, you know."

She scowled and tried on another shirt. "I can't decide what to wear. How does this look?" She turned to show Seth the bright yellow shirt she had donned.

He made a face. "You look like a giant banana."

She let out a frustrated growl and yanked the shirt off again. "It's hopeless!" she cried.

Seth sighed and laid back to stare up at the ceiling. "You're being dumb, Evie. Just put something on."

She rummaged through her suitcase until she found a V-neck, rose-colored shirt and a pair of black slacks. She put them on and turned to face Seth, still feeling rather boring. "Look, this is the last outfit I have and it's just as dull as all the others."

He blinked. "Well, that shirt gives you a nice cleavage shot."

She looked down at how much the V-neckline revealed and she blushed.

"Look, who cares?" Seth asked. "You don't want to act like a stupid middle-schooler. Besides, Traevyn's seen you in your pajamas and after you've cleaned his house. I don't think you really have to worry about impressing him." He stood up and went around behind her to give her a shove. "Just go."

"But—"

He placed his hands firmly on her back and started pushing her toward the door. "Go!"

Evie grumbled something incoherent as she stumbled out the door and into the living room. Traevyn waited patiently on the couch. He smiled when she came in.

"Ready?" he questioned.

She gave him a cheesy grin, which meant she was nowhere near ready, but no longer had a choice in the matter.

Traevyn chuckled. "I made reservations for us at this nice Italian restaurant. I hope you're not sick of Italian."

"Are you kidding?" she asked. "I could eat Italian food every night of my life."

He smiled and they headed out to Talis's car. They had spent a nice day wandering around downtown Sedona with Talis and Ash earlier. It was cute and touristy, and Evie had found several things to take home as souvenirs. They had found many beautiful art galleries, and Talis had taken them to a few nice scenic areas where Evie had exhausted her poor camera.

She didn't know if she'd just been reading too much into everything, but it seemed to her that Traevyn had been much more attentive to her than usual. It seemed that he'd been standing closer, and had gone out of his way to be near her. Her heart beat a little faster at the possibility of his earlier actions.

They were at the restaurant soon, and Evie was impressed with how gorgeous it was. It was high class and elegant with beautiful paintings and decorations, but even though it was apparent that she was in a very upscale place, the fine décor didn't compare to the way Traevyn had transformed his living room for her. That would always be the best as far as she was concerned.

Traevyn watched Evie quietly as they waited for their food. She was reading the wine list, but felt his eyes on her. Her heart skipped a beat as she felt his fingers brush against hers, and she looked up to see him smiling.

"Tell me, Evie," he said softly. "You have been my apprentice for two months now. Have you really even learned anything?" He chuckled.

"Of course I have! I've learned how to clean a gothic mansion, cook a different meal every night, and entertain a dark, brooding, beautiful man."

A faint flush touched his cheeks and he looked down at the table. "Beautiful, you say?"

She blushed at her own forwardness and nodded.

He smiled at her flattering words and he brought her fingers to his lips. "Well, that's all well and good," he said, "but have you learned anything about art?"

"Of course I have," she said with a smile. "I'm not intimidated to paint anymore. I've learned how to better choose colors to express my feelings, to use my heart and emotions to create more than logic and thought." She met his eyes. "You have always inspired me, Traevyn. You do more so now that I know you."

"Evie, you inspire me every day of my life," he murmured.

She swallowed hard and averted her gaze. Her heart felt like it was going to burst.

"How do you like Arizona so far?" he questioned.

"It's beautiful. At least what I've seen is." She frowned in thought. "Where does your other brother live?"

"Julian? He lives in South Lake Tahoe, California."

"But you were all born and raised in Portland, right?"
He nodded.

"How old are your brothers, and how did you end up in such different places?"

"What is this, an interview?" he asked with a chuckle.

Evie blushed. "Sorry, but there is no information about you on the Internet. I had to do a report on you and I'm surprised I even got a grade."

"Yes, I like to keep my private life private. How long did this report of yours have to be?"

"Five pages," she grumbled, "and three fourths of it was BS. Although it must have been good BS because I think it's what got me chosen as your apprentice."

"So you'd like me to fill in the blanks for you?" He grinned. "I would think you'd already know way too much information about me."

She held his gaze. "I think I could live my whole life and never know enough." It came out before she could stop it, and she wanted to kick herself. Stupid brain! Couldn't it ever sensor itself?

He caressed his thumb across the back of her hand and gave a soft sigh. "Well, Julian is twenty-three. He went to school in Portland, but moved to South Lake Tahoe when he got a job offer to be a veterinary assistant. Someone he went to school with hooked him up with the connection. He's finishing up school at UNR in Reno, Nevada, which is only an hour drive from where he lives. Talis is twenty."

Evie frowned. She was older than Talis? She never would have guessed that, but the Whitelaw brothers seemed to have a way of coming off more mature than their age would suggest. She could bet Julian was the same way.

"Talis has always been a free spirit," he continued. "He never went to college. A friend of his he knew in high school moved to Sedona after graduation and started his tattoo business. He asked Talis if he wanted to come out with him after he graduated, so he did. Just because he could. He's always been a good artist. He learned the trade, and that was that... And he's always loved medieval history. It's no surprise to me that he does what he does."

She shook her head. "I wish I could be free and spontaneous like that."

He smiled. "Do you think I am like my little brother?"

Evie thought for a moment. Talis and Traevyn had the same calm intensity, and they were both amazing artists. Talis's art was just displayed on human flesh instead of canvas. She glanced up at Traevyn's eyes. Talis's were a different color, but they held the same gentleness. And when Traevyn had been playing with all of them in the pool, the shadows had momentarily lifted and his eyes had sparkled like his brother's. She smiled. "A little."

Talis was beautiful like Traevyn, but more modern. Traevyn seemed more like a lord of old. That was ironic considering Talis was the one who made a living every summer by pretending he was in the middle ages.

Their food came and they both lapsed into the kind of small talk that generally accompanied stuffing one's face. After their meal, Evie was surprised when a crème brulee was put on their table with a candle in it and the waitress spread rose petals across their table. "Congratulations," she said with a grin.

Evie frowned, and Traevyn turned a confused glance up to the waitress. "I beg your pardon?"

"On your anniversary," she supplied. "The dessert is on us."

Evie's cheeks turned hot and she looked down.

Traevyn frowned. "I'm sorry, there must be some kind of misunderstanding. This is not our anniversary."

The waitress frowned. "Oh... Well, a young man just called here and told us that it was. He gave us your description and told us he was your brother."

Traevyn's eyes narrowed. "Mine or hers?"

The waitress shrugged helplessly. "He didn't specify."

"Matchmaking brats," he muttered. He gave the waitress a smile. "Thank you."

She nodded and left.

Evie glanced up at Traevyn. Her face was on fire, she was sure of it.

He chuckled. "Well, we may as well eat it," he said, indicating the rejected crème brulee. "It's free and all."

She gave him a withered smile and picked up the spoon. She ate her portion quickly and was silent as they drove to Airport Mesa. She was quite certain that she was going to murder Seth when they got back to Talis's. Although it had been very romantic, it was also very embarrassing considering she and Traevyn weren't even dating let alone married.

She sighed as she thought of being Traevyn's wife. How amazing would it be to wake up next to such a magnificent man every morning? She bet he was a really good lover. Everything about Traevyn was so intense. Her cheeks turned red at the thought of it. Had his ex-wife been absolutely out of her mind? Who would cheat on Traevyn? What a stupid, stupid woman.

She stole a sidelong glance at him. His hair was flowing over one shoulder, and she reached out impulsively to touch a strand of it. He looked over at her and smiled.

Her heart stuttered for a moment. She would do anything, give up anything, if it meant she could keep him smiling like that. She looked down and swallowed hard. Oh man, this was so much worse than Maxim had ever been.

Traevyn noticed that Evie had fallen silent since the restaurant. As they parked the car and made their way to the lookout point, he studied her. She was walking slightly in front of him so he could look his fill without her realizing it. He smiled to himself. She was so different from Amy. Amy had been tall, sultry, the kind of woman any man would have gone after. Her makeup had always been perfect, her clothing and hair perfect, every move looking like she had planned it to her advantage. She had been every man's fantasy come to life.

Evie was short with luscious curves. He had seen her in her pajamas with bed head. Pink, karate chopping monkey pajamas. Amy would never have been caught dead wearing something like that. She had always worn silk and satin negligees to bed. At the time, he had found it incredibly sexy, but there was something endearing about Evie's monkey PJs.

He had seen all sides of Evie. He'd seen her look casual. He'd seen her dressed nice. He'd seen her covered in paint smudges. He'd seen her in a baggy t-shirt and ripped jeans with bright yellow gloves on as she scrubbed his bathtub. She was low-maintenance, giving all of her time and attention to everyone else before herself.

They came to stand at the edge of the lookout point, gazing down at the city below and the red rocks towering around it. He lapsed back into thought as Evie took in the breathtaking scenery.

How was it that he could find himself so attracted to Evie when she was so different from anything he had loved about Amy? Evie was not fluid, not graceful. She was loud. She was opinionated. She summoned him to dinner by crashing a gong. She threw sandals at him. She called him a caveman directly to his face and told him just where he could go when he ticked her off. She was like a chaotic storm threatening anything that dare come in her path. But...when the storm was calm, it was paradise.

She listened to him. She understood him. Everything he loved, she shared a passion for. She knew what he was feeling and he didn't even have to say anything. She saw him. Since day one, she had seen him. She saw past the barriers, past the cold walls. She saw past all the strange symbolism in his paintings and could put her finger directly on the message of his soul. She could touch him when no one else could even get close. She had been the one person he felt he could confide in, let inside. He had given her the good part of his soul, trusting implicitly that she would not destroy it. And she hadn't. She carried it gently, protected it. Protected him.

He sighed as the setting sun kissed her hair, glinting golden off the blonde and turning the brown into a warm amber color. He remembered her hair looking the same way the night he had gone to the beach with her and Seth. That night... That had been the turning point, the moment where he had begun to feel life and light in his heart again. The night on the anniversary of Leanna's death. He should have felt guilty for it, but he didn't. Leanna had been all about life. She would have wanted him to be there. He knew that now. He had done nothing wrong. He would do far better to grace his daughter's memory by living every day instead of brooding in stoic silence. Evie had shown him that.

Evie glanced over her shoulder at him then, frowning slightly. "What are you doing back there? Are you alive? You bring me out here just to stand back there and brood?"

He smirked and watched as the sun began to sink down behind the mountains, making the red rocks glow in a blaze of orange and gold.

"This is so beautiful, Traevyn," she said as she gazed out at the breathtaking landscape. "I wish I could paint it."

Traevyn smiled and walked up behind her. He wrapped his arms around her shoulders and pulled her close to him, close to his heart. He heard her sharp intake of breath and knew he had surprised her. He felt her pulse pounding. He closed his eyes as he soaked in the warmth she emitted, the warmth that kept his soul alive.

He leaned his cheek against the top of Evie's head and let his senses fill with her. She felt right in his arms, soft and welcoming, like he had come home after a long and exhausting journey. She smelled clean and sweet, probably like her shampoo. She was not dripping in artificial, perfumy fragrance. She smelled real. She felt real.

He had never seen Amy as anything other than a goddess, and he had always felt unworthy because of the subtle arrogance such beauty had given her. The silent message that seemed to whisper, "I could have any man I want, but I chose you. Be grateful." Well, in the end, she had chosen another.

Amy had always seemed unreal to him, like a fantasy or a waking dream. Evie was real, complete, a real life fairy tale. He smiled and hugged her closer. "Evie," he whispered against her ear, "do you read fairy tales?"

"I did when I was little."

"Which one was your favorite?"

She thought for a moment. "*Beauty and the Beast*," she replied simply.

Traevyn smiled and closed his eyes. "Of course it was." He pressed a soft kiss to the base of her neck before returning his attention to the sunset.

Yes, Evie was real, and so were the feelings he held for her in his heart. More real, he'd say, than anything else he'd ever experienced. It was clear to him now.

# *Chapter Nineteen*

Evie was, to say the least, apprehensive as she got ready for the gallery opening. She was nervous because she'd never been to one before, was afraid she was going to look like a complete idiot, and Traevyn had been acting weird all day. She had wracked her brain all night trying to figure out why he had held her against him at Airport Mesa like he never wanted to let her go again. She knew Seth thought she was stupid for doubting the fact that Traevyn had feelings for her, but he had never said anything. What if he just liked being close to her because he had been alone for so long?

After they had returned from Airport Mesa and had lectured their siblings—both whom thought they were hilarious—Traevyn had spent a long time sketching on Talis's porch. When they'd gone to bed, he'd asked Evie if she believed fairy tales existed in real life. When she'd said yes, he'd asked if she thought he could ever have a happy ending. She'd told him that no one deserved to live happily ever after more than him and she was sure he would have his fairy tale ending. For some reason, this had prompted him to reach out and touch her face so delicately that she'd nearly passed out. Then he'd seized her hand, held it over his heart, and had fallen asleep like that. She was still trying to figure it out.

She had barely seen him all day. He'd all but locked himself inside Talis's bedroom and had been painting for hours. She was a little hurt by the fact that he apparently wanted to exclude her from his project, but she tried not to dwell on it.

She sighed as she applied the finishing touches to her makeup and made sure her hair was going to stay in the up-do she had put it in. When she was relatively satisfied with her appearance, she emerged from the bathroom to see Traevyn standing in the living room talking to Seth, Talis, and Ash while he waited. Evie drew her breath in sharply. He looked gorgeous dressed in a black suit with a black shirt and a dark burgundy tie. She had been expecting a tux, but she was glad he was wearing what he was. Seeing Traevyn in a tux would be almost as weird as seeing him in swim trunks.

She gathered her courage and made her way into the living room.

Traevyn glanced up to see Evie enter the room and all thought fled from his mind. The air slammed out of his lungs, and he was suddenly overwhelmed by such strong desire that he thought he would incinerate right there. She was radiant. Radiant beyond words.

Seth let out a slow whistle. "Dang, sis. You're a hottie."

Evie's cheeks turned pink and she rolled her eyes. "Shut up," she muttered.

"Actually," Traevyn said as he took both of her hands in his and kissed them, "I would have to agree with Seth on this one." He let his eyes feast on the glory that was all Evie. The gown fit her perfectly, and she had put matching smudges of turquoise eye shadow on. Her lashes stood out long and thick, and a faint blush accentuated her cheekbones. She was dazzling. "You're going to distract all my patrons. No one will look at my art because they will all be too busy looking at you."

She met his eyes and her heart melted at the gentleness they radiated. Two months ago, she never would have thought that Traevyn would gaze at her in such a way, or say such nice things to her. She smiled and averted her eyes.

Traevyn smiled and took one of her hands, lacing their fingers together. He turned to the others. "Goodnight," he said, eyeballing Seth and Talis. "Try not to get into too much trouble while we're gone."

Talis grinned. "Us?"

Seth nodded. "You two should get into lots of trouble." He gave a dramatic wink.

Traevyn chuckled and led Evie out to the car. She grew quiet and he seemed to notice because he stopped at her door and gave her hand an encouraging squeeze. "Are you all right?"

She nodded, but even she knew she looked unconvincing.

He smiled. "Don't be nervous, Evie. It's my art everyone will be staring at."

She rolled her eyes. "Traevyn, you're already established. The people at this thing will already know and love your art. I've never been to one of these before and I'm afraid I..." She sighed. "I'm afraid I won't fit in."

He frowned. "Won't fit in? Evie,"—he brought his mouth close to her ear, his breath tickling her— "you will be the finest piece of art there." He pressed a lingering kiss to the back of her jaw.

Evie's breath caught, then came out shaky. She instinctively pressed closer to him, wanting his strength, wanting his warmth, wanting his arms around her, wanting him so badly that it hurt. It was getting worse. Her feelings weren't diminishing. They were only growing stronger. His constant affection wasn't helping. If she survived the rest of the summer it would be a miracle.

Traevyn pulled her into his arms for a short, comforting hug, then looked down at her with a smile.

She forced a smile and got in the car after he opened her door. She had a cold, twisted knot in her stomach the entire way to the gallery that did not recede when they arrived.

Traevyn's gallery was small, like most of the privately owned galleries in Sedona, but it was fairly bursting with people. She clung to Traevyn's hand as he led her through the throng, mingling with some and introducing her to people she would never remember the next day. Everyone was dressed very fashionably and seemed so aristocratic. It was like a whole different world to her.

"Evie," Traevyn's voice came, "I have to speak with the gallery director for a moment. Please, look around. I know you know all of my art already, but..." He shrugged.

She grinned. "I never get tired of your art, Traevyn."

"I'll come and find you in a bit."

She wandered through the different rooms, studying each one of his magnificent paintings as if it was the first time she had ever seen it. She marveled over the fact that, several years ago, she had seen a painting of Traevyn's in a museum and it had inspired her. The painting done by a mysterious man she had never thought she would know, let alone be in love with. She sighed. It was frightening to admit that to herself, but it was pointless and stupid to deny it any longer. She loved Traevyn in a way she hadn't even known she could love, and it killed her to know that her paradise would end in a little less than a month.

She continued from painting to painting and lost track of time somewhere along the line. She heard a woman mention the large painting in the far back room and how it was exquisite, but not for sale, much to her dismay. Evie frowned, wondering what the painting was. Deciding to check it out, she headed toward the back, but was stopped by a copy of "Innerworkings of a Creative Soul." She turned toward it, unable to pass it by, and just stared. This painting... Traevyn's darkest moment. No light, no beauty. Just chaotic torment. It still beckoned her. She wanted to reach out and touch it, soothe the shadows away. She imagined she always would.

"Brilliant piece, isn't it?" a man's voice came from behind her.

She turned to see a young man in maybe his late twenties coming to stand next to her. She nodded with a smile and turned back to the painting.

"How amazing for someone to paint their creative soul in such a way. To use the colors to represent such passionate turbulence. It's so inspiring."

She blinked. Inspiring? Now that she knew what the painting really represented, she couldn't call it inspiring. It was painful. "It doesn't represent creation and passion," she found herself saying.

He frowned. "I beg your pardon?" He fixed her with an incredulous look.

"Well, look at the black shades and the darker colors. If you look closely, they swirl into the shape of a man screaming. It represents pain, torment, heart-wrenching sorrow."

The man's frown deepened. "You'll forgive me if I disagree with you. This painting is one of Traevyn Whitelaw's most famous. It is discussed in art classes across the nation. It's very clearly a representation of creative genius." His smile was smug. "You see, I'm a bit of a Traevyn Whitelaw historian. I did my final on him for my art history class."

She smirked. "Did you?"

He nodded.

"Yes, so did I. Fun, isn't it? Filling up pages with information that doesn't exist. Let me ask you something. Have you ever actually met Traevyn Whitelaw?"

"No," he replied, gazing back up at the painting. "I saw him here tonight, but I can't bring myself to speak with him. It would be like talking to DaVinci."

Evie grinned and shook her head. "He's just a man," she said, her eyes softening at the thought of him. "Imperfect as you and me, but with such a beautiful soul."

"I beg to differ."

She arched an eyebrow in amusement. "Do you?"

"Yes. I believe he would be very well-rounded and dynamic. I bet he sees beauty in everything."

Evie almost laughed aloud. "Just out of curiosity, what grade did you get on your final?"

He frowned in confusion.

She waved it away. "Never mind. Anyway, trust me when I say that Traevyn is not larger than life. He is human. He is real, and this painting does not represent his creative drive."

He folded his arms, looking irritated. "Who are you anyway?"

"Evie Austin," she replied. "I'm Mr. Whitelaw's apprentice."

He blinked.

"Evie, there you are," Traevyn said, striding up to her. "Where have you been?"

She glanced to the young gentleman, who was now considerably pale. She grinned. "Just having a friendly debate."

The man looked away rather hurriedly and scratched at the back of his head.

Evie arched an eyebrow and couldn't help herself. "He's a Traevyn Whitelaw historian."

The man glanced up in bewilderment, and his pale face flushed.

Traevyn regarded him. "Oh, well it's good to meet such an avid fan." He smiled and reached out to shake the man's hand.

The man stammered for a few seconds, his blush deepening. "Yes, Mr. Whitelaw," he finally got out, gripping Traevyn's hand. "I am a huge fan." He glanced at Evie. "Is this really your apprentice?"

"Yes, she is the most astute artist I have ever met. Why

do you ask?"

"We were arguing over your painting here," Evie supplied, indicating the canvas behind her.

Traevyn threw a look back at it, and his lips split into a grin. "Ah, I see," he said with a chuckle. "Yes, that one." He met the eyes of the man in front of him. "A word of advice, don't believe everything they teach you in school." He winked at him and turned back to Evie. "Come with me. I want to show you something." He took her hand and started to lead her out of the room when a tall, blonde woman and an equally tall man rounded the corner.

"Traevyn!" the woman called. "Oh how lovely to see you!"

Evie felt him bristle, and she looked over at the woman. Slender, elegant, gorgeous... Evie averted her eyes.

Traevyn's sigh sounded weary. "Hello, Jane," he greeted flatly.

"Well, I haven't seen you in ages. How have you been?"

"Just peachy," he grumbled.

She made a *tsk* noise. "Oh I can imagine the last few years must have been so hard on you. You poor thing."

Evie frowned at her patronizing tone.

Jane's eyes fell on Evie, and she made a face of disdain. "And who's this?" she asked with fake cheerfulness.

"Evie," Traevyn introduced, "this is Jane Meadows. Jane, Evie Austin, my apprentice."

"Apprentice?" Sne sniffed and appeared to regard Evie like she was appraising her worth.

"Yes, she is an art student from SOU staying with me for the summer to study."

Jane flashed the most nauseating smile Evie had ever seen and laughed shrilly. "Oh, I thought maybe she was your girlfriend!"

Evie blushed. "Oh, no," she said. Her voice sounded much too breathy and shy to suit her.

"Well, that's good," Jane continued. She turned her attention back to Traevyn. "I mean, not really your type, is she?" She gave another sickening giggle. "You usually go for such sophisticated ladies, not short, homely...little girls. I mean, she really wouldn't fit into your world, would she?" She laughed as though her evil words had been a fantastic joke.

Evie looked down and time stopped. Those words... The words she feared the most. They echoed through her mind. *She really wouldn't fit into your world, would she?* She bit her bottom lip and felt the familiar sting of tears. She forced herself to face Jane. She refused to cry in front of everyone and make a fool out of herself. She gave them both a wobbly smile. "Please excuse me for a moment," she murmured.

Traevyn watched as Evie all but fled, and he let out an exasperated sigh. Jane's lips were twisted into an arrogant, satisfied smile and it sickened him. "Good to see you haven't changed, Jane," he snarled. "Class was never something you were good at." He turned and strode out after Evie.

# Chapter Twenty

Traevyn's heart broke at the sight of Evie. She was sitting outside on a bench in between a bubbling fountain and a bronze statue of a fairy. The moonlight bathed her in silvery light and her face was in her hands. He could see her body shaking with sobs. It would have been a tragically beautiful sight if he didn't care for her so much. He sighed. Seeing her so hurt stabbed at his heart. Everything in his world disappeared except for the desire to make her stop crying. He approached her slowly. "Evie," he said in a soothing tone.

She looked up at him. "Oh," she said, trying in vain to wipe her tears away. "I was just, uh..." She shook her head as fresh tears coursed down her cheeks.

Traevyn knelt in front of her and ran his hands up her arms. "Shhh, Evie. Please, please stop crying," he breathed. "You're killing me inside." He reached up and cradled her face in his hands. "Don't listen to Jane. She hates me because she tried to date me at one point and I wouldn't go for it. Since then she's made it her sole purpose in life to make my existence miserable."

Evie shook her head. "It wouldn't hurt so badly if what she'd said hadn't been true," she sniffed. "I am short and I'm not pretty. I know this. I accepted it a long time ago, but I don't need it flung in my face. I know I'll never measure up to any of the beautiful women you've known in your life, but I'm still human! I still have feelings!" She let out another little sob.

Traevyn frowned. "Never measure up— Not pretty? Evie, who has told you such things?"

"Oh, only every guy I've ever liked!" she spat.

He sighed and gently wiped at her tears. "Evie," he said, "look at me please."

She struggled with it for a moment. He saw the hesitation flash across her face, but she eventually managed to look into his eyes.

He studied her face. He had rarely seen her without her glasses and, since she had taken them off to cry, he took the liberty of appraising the contours of her face. So gentle and soft, all feminine beauty. "Evie, you're right," he stated. "You're not pretty."

She flinched as if she'd been slapped.

He smiled and cupped her cheek in his palm. "You're gorgeous."

She stared at him in baffled silence. "Wh—What?"

"Even gorgeous is too weak a word. Everything about you is exquisite. Your lovely hair." He reached up to tuck back a wayward strand. "Your fantastic, curvaceous body."

A soft blush touched her cheeks.

"Your eyes that can see directly into my soul." He ran his fingers down her cheek. "Your soft skin..." His gaze fell on her lips and he suddenly found it difficult to breathe. "Your full, supple lips," he whispered, running his thumb along the bottom one. "Lips I ache to know..." He slowly pulled her toward him, needing to feel a real kiss from her, needing to show her the things he felt, but had trouble expressing.

She seemed shocked at first, stunned and timid. He felt her lips tremble as they touched his, and she drew in a shaky breath that made him fill with desire for her. She made him feel so much. Her awe and admiration for his work made him feel like an amazing artist. Her gentle prodding and subtle reformation of his character made him feel like a human. The way she reacted to his lips on hers made him feel like a man. He drew her small, shaky breath into his body, breathed it into himself, and felt everything within him come alive.

He caressed her mouth with his, and all the feelings he had buried deep inside him came to life with an intensity that would have frightened him at any other moment.

He held her face in his hands like he was holding a fragile object, and he ran his tongue in a slow caress along her bottom lip before pulling it into his mouth, asking for entrance, needing to sample all the beauty he knew she possessed. It had been so long since he'd felt passion. It engulfed him like a tidal wave, and he basked in it.

Evie's chest constricted as he gently sucked on her bottom lip. She couldn't breathe and her whole body tingled. Her blood burned through her veins and reality began to slip away. She opened her mouth for Traevyn, allowing his tongue to sweep over hers and claim her mouth. She clutched at his suit jacket, gripping the material as if afraid he might vanish at any moment.

For several heartbeats, he continued to kiss her, to pour his very essence into her just as he claimed hers. When he pulled away, she was shaking badly, and she reached up to touch her lips. She met his beautiful green eyes and he gave her a soft smile. It nearly killed her. Silent tears fell from her eyes. "You shouldn't have done that," she whispered.

His frown was quizzical. "Why?"

She looked down, the ache in her chest so acute she thought she would die. "Because I don't think I can live without those now."

He smiled and moved up to claim her lips again, taking his time, exploring until she was breathless and couldn't take it anymore. "Traevyn," she murmured, shaking her head. "I can't do this. I have to go home."

"All right. Just let me tell the gallery director."

She fought a sob that threatened to consume her and stood, putting some distance between them. "No, I mean I have to go home! Back to Oregon!"

He stared at her for a moment. "Why? You're still supposed to stay with me for another month."

She forced herself to meet his eyes, which was becoming increasingly hard to do. *"She wouldn't really fit into your world, would she?"* She winced and looked down. "Because if I stay, I'm going to get really hurt, and I just can't do it. I'm sorry."

He frowned and stood, going to her. "But, Evie, I need you—"

"And I'll always be here for you. Just not *here* for you." She couldn't do it. Not anymore. She loved him too much. She couldn't just be the person who made him feel. She couldn't be his companion. It was all or nothing. She needed him completely, not just shards of him.

Traevyn stared at Evie, his heart beating sluggishly in his chest. "Why?" he breathed. "Why are you saying this?" He felt the good part of his soul trembling in fear, in complete horror. It could shatter in one moment if she said the wrong word. In one second, she could shatter all he was.

"Because," she cried, "you heard what Jane said. She was right! I'll never fit into your world!"

He felt his eyes flash fire. "Never fit into my world? You *are* my world!"

He all but shouted it and Evie jumped. She stared at him in obvious confusion. "What?" she whispered, her voice shaking from pure emotion.

He grabbed her by the shoulders. "Without you I am nothing!" he cried. "I was nothing before you. A hopeless, pathetic shell of a half man who felt nothing but overwhelming sorrow. Would you send me back there, Evie? Would you send me back to that dark place?" He started to tremble, terrified of this entire situation. All she had made him, all she had given him, was threatening to disappear.

Evie shook her head, shrinking back at the raw, unadulterated despair he knew his eyes reflected. "No, Traevyn, I—"

"Do you know I have not slept worth anything since Amy left and Leanna died? Every night I was plagued, haunted by their faces. Since you came to me, I can sleep. Do you know why? Because, before I close my eyes at night, I think of you. I think of your smile and your laugh and your touch. Your smile lights up my whole universe. Your laugh is more beautiful than any music on the earth, and your touch..." He shook his head. "Your touch drives away every recess of darkness, every grasping demon. I think of those things and I sleep because I know that the sooner I sleep, the sooner I can experience the splendor of you all over again." He let it all out, every emotion and secret thought spilling out over the next. He risked it all, laid himself bare. He opened his arms wide and invited the last stab to his obliterated heart, the one that would surely kill him. If he couldn't have Evie, he didn't want to live.

"And when I sleep," he continued softly, "it is your face I see." He stared into her eyes, which were now wide with overwhelmed emotion. "Would you send me back there?" he whispered, a tear streaking down his cheek as his voice shook. "Would you banish me back to the darkness? Back to hell?" He turned away from her, unable to look at her any longer. It hurt too much. His heart, it was dissolving. Not breaking, dissolving. It was ceasing to be.

Evie stared at his broad-shouldered back, trying to pro-cess what he had just told her. In all her life, she had never expected that reaction. She reached out to him tentatively, but let her hand drop, unsure of how to proceed. "Traevyn," she murmured.

"I love you, Evie," he murmured.

Evie froze. Her heart stopped, then started to beat way too fast. "What?" she rasped, realizing she seemed to be saying that a lot. She couldn't have heard him right. Surely, that was just a trick of her deluded imagination.

He turned back to her, his shining hair glistening in the moonlight as it fell to frame his flawless face. "I love you," he repeated, fixing her with a forlorn expression. "I love you more than the sunlight, the moonlight, or the stars in the night sky. I love you more than the ocean, the fog, or even my art..." He held his arms out in a helpless gesture. "There. It's done. I said it. It doesn't even matter if I'm afraid. It doesn't matter if I get hurt. Nothing matters if I can't have you."

More tears began to fall from her eyes. Tears of joy. Tears of confusion. Tears of every emotion in the world.

Traevyn reached out to catch her tears with his fingers. "Evie, I love you more than I ever could have hoped to love Amy."

She shook her head violently. "Oh no," she sobbed. "Don't say it. Don't say it if you don't mean it." Loving any-one more than Amy was impossible. She had been his life, his goddess.

He took her face in both his hands and forced her to meet his eyes. "I never say anything I don't mean."

She stared at him for a millisecond of time before collaps-ing against him and sobbing into his shoulder. She clung to him with a ferocity she didn't even know she possessed. He loved her? This beautiful, perfect man loved her? Evie? Loud, abrasive, unrefined Evie? Her stupid brother had been right the entire time?

Traevyn's arms crept around Evie and he held her to him, his heart aching and heavy. "You...don't love me?" he whis-pered. It was as he feared. Why else would she be sobbing like that? She felt bad that she would have to hurt him. His world started to crumble as if he could see the pieces falling around him.

She pulled back and looked up at him. "Are you out of your mind?" she all but shouted. "I love you so much it makes me dizzy! I can't even breathe without you!"

The threatening shadows were incinerated by the inferno of love and passion that swept through him. He enfolded her in his arms and held her close, wanting to make her a part of him, wanting to be a part of her. "Then why do you cry like your heart is breaking?"

"Because I never thought—" She buried her face against his chest, relishing the feel of him. Strong, solid, unyielding.

"How could I not love you, Evie?" he said softly. "You brought me back to life."

She wrapped her arms around his waist and held on. She was still trembling. She couldn't help it. She felt as if her entire world had inverted, then exploded like a supernova. Seth... For some reason his smug face flashed before her eyes. She would never live this down. She closed her eyes as she felt Traevyn caress her back. More than Amy... He'd said he loved her more. She never would have even hoped to touch that one. She would have been content that he loved her at all. She never would have gone for the gold medal.

"Evie," he whispered. "Why are you trembling so badly?"

She pulled away and looked up into his concerned eyes. "I can't stop," she said with a small smile.

He wiped the remnants of her tears and gave her a gentle smile. "Please, never scare me like that again. In one moment, I saw my entire life ending. I can't let you go. You hold part of my soul, remember? If you leave, it goes with you."

"I have one year of college left," she stated.

He nodded and continued to trail his fingers across her cheek and down her neck. "I know that... And I will wait for you. I'll be holding my breath."

She smiled a little more genuinely, her shock abating to let her joy through. "You know when you're eighty, I'll only be seventy-one."

Traevyn grinned. "And all the old men next to me in the nursing home will be jealous of my hot, young woman."

She laughed.

He gazed at her with open adoration. "Never doubt your beauty," he said. "You are the most beautiful woman ever created."

Tremors worked their way through her body at his words. She looked up into his eyes and was drawn into their depths.

"I love you, Evie," he whispered over her lips before claiming them for his own once again.

She melted into him, fused her body to his as much as she could. His arms tightened around her and held her there even as she pulled away. "Say it again," she pleaded.

He smiled. "I love you." He punctuated it with another kiss.

She reeled with the satiny softness of his lips. "Again."

"You're greedy," he teased.

"Very," she agreed.

He grinned and dipped her dramatically, causing her to squeak in surprise. He pressed a lingering kiss to her throat. "I." He kissed her chin. "Love." He positioned himself over her lips again and gazed down into her eyes. "You," he finished, lowering his lips to hers. One of her hands came up to tangle in his hair as he took his time, relishing in the feel of her, the taste of her, everything that was her.

He sighed as he pulled her back up into a standing position. "Now, I really want to show you something," he said softly, "but we have to go back inside."

She cringed.

"Don't worry," he assured her. "No one had better ever insult you in front of me again."

She smiled, marveling over how Traevyn was so openly declaring his feelings for her. How long had he been feeling them in silence like she had? If she had known all it would take to get him to spill it was threatening to leave, she would have done it a long time ago.

He took her hand in his, leading her back into the gallery. They moved swiftly, not stopping to make conversation with anyone, until they reached the back room. Evie gasped as they entered. There was a large painting on the far wall. A painting she had never seen. In it was a man she could only assume was Traevyn, sitting on the ground, his eyes downcast and sad. A woman stood behind with her arms wrapped around him. She was surrounded by an aura of fire and she had great white wings hovering over Traevyn, sheltering and protecting him. She was wearing the same gown as Evie, and it was apparent that it *was* Evie.

"Oh my gosh!" she breathed, going to the painting. "When did you do this?"

"Last night and today. It's your portrait. You see, the fire represents your passion."

She turned to look at him. "And the wings?"

He swallowed and met her eyes. "Well, the wings are because... because you are my angel. My angel coming to rescue me... It's symbolic."

Evie felt tears again, although she didn't know how she could possibly have any left.

"Do you like it?" he asked softly. "It's for you."

"I love it. Traevyn, I—" She shook her head. "There are no words."

He smiled and came up close to her, resting his forehead against hers. He closed his eyes. "Love me," he whispered.

Evie couldn't mistake the ache in his voice, the pleading note that let her know how vulnerable he was at that moment. He was begging her not to hurt him, not to destroy what he had become. She wrapped her arms around him and closed her eyes, sighing. "For as long as you'll have me, I will love you," she promised. She knew it was true. Traevyn could very possibly be it for her. She had never felt for anyone the way she felt for him.

His lips found hers again and he kissed her slowly, deliberately, indulging himself. He had forgotten affection, forgotten how marvelous it felt to kiss someone, hold someone, lose himself in someone. He had forgotten how it felt to know his heart was beating. Evie had given him back his life, his soul, his very breath. She *was* his angel and she *had* rescued him. He would not take that for granted. He would hold onto her forever. He couldn't exist without her now. He wouldn't know how.

He wrapped her petite frame up in his arms and held her close to him. He felt so much. His heart seemed to sigh in contentment, as if he could finally rest after such a long time. He felt whole, completed. Because of her...Evie. His savior, his world. His home.

# Chapter Twenty-One

Everyone was asleep when Traevyn and Evie arrived back at Talis's house. They had remained at the gallery despite Evie's earlier requests to go home. She had figured it would be rude for Traevyn to leave the opening of his own gallery and, with him at her side all night, holding her hand and sneaking kisses at every opportunity, she no longer cared what anyone thought. She was invincible with the knowledge that he loved her. And, as if he hadn't surprised her enough for one evening, Jane Meadows had come in to view Traevyn's new painting when they were still in there. She had given Evie a gloating smirk before turning a critical eye to the portrait.

"Just your apprentice, is she?" she said as she looked at the painting. Her voice was witchy and full of malice.

Traevyn gave a smug smile and pulled Evie into his arms protectively. "I lied," he stated. "She's not just my apprentice."

"So this sad excuse for a little girl actually is your girlfriend?" she spat, looking very agitated.

Traevyn smiled down at Evie. "No," he murmured. "She's my life." He punctuated it with the kind of kiss that was sinful, and he continued to kiss her until Jane left the room in complete disgust.

They entered the house quietly so as not to wake anyone and, as soon as the front door closed, Traevyn backed Evie up against it with a devilish grin. He took her face in his hands and kissed her with sensual slowness. She sighed, melted against him, and it made him smile. He slipped an arm around her shoulders and pulled her up close, pressing his full body to hers. It almost set her on fire.

"So, I take it things went well?"

Evie jumped almost to the ceiling as Traevyn pulled his lips off of hers. Talis was standing in the living room, smirking. She had only ever seen Traevyn blush once, but the way he blushed now made up for all of the other times he hadn't.

Talis shook his head and chuckled. "Poor Ash," he muttered. "He never had a chance." He turned and headed back to his room.

Traevyn turned back to Evie and gave her a bashful smile that turned her heart to goo. She giggled.

"I'm going to go change," he stated.

She nodded.

He kissed her again before turning toward the bathroom.

Evie waited until he was gone before slumping back against the front door and sighing in bliss. She toyed with the fabric of her sleeve and glanced at Seth, who was fast asleep on the hide-a-bed. She grinned and ran toward it, jumping directly on top of him.

He groaned. "Bubbly tuna," he muttered.

She frowned, then shook her head and laughed as she bounced up and down on him. "Seth!" she exclaimed. "Wake up!"

Several unpleasant words came out of his mouth before he managed to throw her off and sit up. He blinked at her, disoriented and irritated. "What the crap are you doing?"

She grinned and sat up. "You don't have to worry about your video games," she stated.

His frown deepened. "What the heck are you talking about?"

"Remember our deal? You won."

He stared at her for a long time before recognition seemed to dawn on him. He raised his eyebrows. "Are you serious?" he breathed. "He made a move? The dude actually got off it and made a move?"

She grabbed Seth's hands and gripped them in excitement. "He told me he loved me." She whispered it like it was some great secret.

Seth reacted as if someone had just smacked him in the face. He jumped back in surprise and his eyes bulged. "Dude!" he shouted.

"Shhh!" She giggled softly. She looked up to see Talis

come back into the kitchen, a sly smile on his lips. He poured himself a glass of water, then walked over to Evie, where he bent and pressed a kiss to her forehead. She blinked in surprise.

"Evie," he said, "go to breakfast with me in the morning, would you?"

She frowned. "Just you and me?"

"If you don't mind."

She shrugged. "No, that's fine."

He nodded and winked at her before turning back to his room.

Evie frowned and looked at Seth. "Why does he want to take me to breakfast?"

"Probably to say thank you. We were talking the other night when you and Traevyn were at dinner. He was telling me how worried he's been about Traevyn, how he and his other brother thought he'd never come out of his depression."

Just then, Traevyn emerged from the bathroom, silencing their conversation. Seth grinned at Evie as she stood and grabbed her pajamas, making her way into the bathroom next.

Traevyn watched Evie pass and breathed a soft sigh. He bent to fix the pillows and covers on his side of the bed, deliberately avoiding eye contact with Seth. When Seth apparently got irritated at him not looking, he punched him in the arm. Traevyn rubbed at his shoulder, frowning. He looked up at Seth, who was grinning from ear to ear. Traevyn chuckled.

"Traevyn," Seth said, "you have redeemed yourself."

He frowned. "From what?"

"From being an idiot."

Traevyn rolled his eyes. "Would you shut up and just go back to sleep?" He smiled.

Seth lay down, stilling grinning, and turned on his side away from Traevyn.

Traevyn sat down, waiting for Evie. She finally came back out in her monkey pajamas, and he felt his heart swell. She met his eyes from across the room and flashed him a smile as she placed her gown in the garment bag and zipped it up.

He held his arms out to her as she approached, and she went into them willingly, closing her eyes as he pulled her up onto his lap and against his chest. She buried her face against his neck. "Your brother asked me to go to breakfast with him tomorrow," she said. "Don't freak out on me, okay?"

He smiled. "Talis is no competition for me," he said with arrogance.

Evie feigned irritation. "Whatever. I happen to love medieval tattooists."

He chuckled and cradled her close, drinking in her warmth. "Lie next to me," he whispered. "Please?"

She pulled back and frowned at him. "All three of us on this bed?"

"I'll just have to hold you extra close." He reached up and threaded his fingers through her hair. "It's been so long since I've been close to someone. Forgive me if I seem too attached."

She giggled and wrapped her arms around his neck, resting her forehead against his. "Do I look like I mind?"

He smiled.

She climbed down off of his lap and let him get in bed, her heart beating erratically as he pulled the covers back and motioned for her to climb in next to him. She had never slept next to a man. Only in her craziest daydreams. It made her want to tremble to think that she would be sleeping next to Traevyn, the most beautiful man ever created. He was her idol, her mentor, her inspiration... More than that, he was the only man she had ever really loved.

She managed to make her body not shiver as she slipped into bed next to him and felt his arm go around her waist, pulling her flush up against him. She closed her eyes, unable to believe that she was actually lying next to him with his arms around her, that he was holding her like she was something precious and desired. It made her want to cry all over again.

"Evie," he whispered.

His breath brushed against the back of her neck, tickling her and sending delicious shivers up her spine. "Yeah?"

"I love you." He nuzzled his nose against her neck and hugged her tighter.

She squeezed her eyes shut as tears threatened. "I love you too," she choked out.

"Aw, I love you guys too," Seth mocked suddenly.

Evie burst into giggles.

"Dude," he continued in warning, "if you guys even think about doing the dirty while I'm laying here you can just forget it right now."

Evie's face burned, but Traevyn's rumbling chuckle made her smile. She loved that he laughed more often. She sighed and thought back to the night they'd spent stranded in the fog. She had felt so right sleeping close to him, being near him. That night had changed everything for her.

She could feel Traevyn's heartbeat as she lay there, and it made her own heart sigh a little. His beautiful heart. It was still beating. It was still alive and, as long as she lived, she would make sure it never broke again. As long as he was willing to give her his heart, she would protect it always.

\* \* \*

Evie had to admit, she was a little nervous sitting across from Talis. While he was much more easygoing and light-hearted than Traevyn, he had the same nerve-wracking intensity when he was being serious. She folded her hands in front of her, waiting for whatever it was he wanted to say, as it was apparent he wanted to say something.

The waitress came by to refill their coffee and take their orders, and when she left, Talis turned his light blue eyes up to Evie and smiled.

"Evie," he began, "why do you love my brother?"

She blinked. "Excuse me?" What kind of a conversation starter was that? Talk about getting right to the point.

His smile broadened. "I mean Traevyn, in the state he was in when you met him, was not an easy man to love. He didn't really have a lot of redeeming qualities. I'm just curious as to how someone as vibrant as you managed to fall in love with him despite his obvious issues. Julian and I could barely stand him and we're his family. Our parents didn't even know who he was anymore."

She gave a small smile and played with one of the sugar packets. "Traevyn has always been beautiful to me," she said. "Granted, I thought he was a world class jerk when I met him, but that didn't change the fact that his art was fantastic, and I knew his art was a reflection of his soul. When he gave me a glimpse of that soul outside of his paintings, I could do nothing less than love it." She sighed. "Talis, no one's ever really understood me. No one ever made me feel beautiful or validated. Traevyn understands me. He understands my passion and my creativity. He's always made me feel validated in my thoughts, even when we were having conversations about nothing at all."

Talis smiled. "I remember when I was fifteen, I was pissed because Traevyn was getting married and I thought I'd never see him again. Me, Julian, and Traevyn were like the Three Musketeers our whole lives, but Traevyn always understood me in a way Julian couldn't. Julian is very smart, very kind, but not really that creative. Not in the ways Traevyn and I are. Traevyn's always made me feel validated, like you said." He paused for a moment and frowned down at the table. "How in the world did you get him to open up to you? None of us could do it, Evie. We thought he was going to kill himself one day. His sorrow was just eating him alive..."

Sudden tears filled his eyes and he stopped to clear his throat and compose himself. When he had his emotions under control, he looked back up at Evie. "He never got any better. He never worked through his grief. He just became more and more distant and cold. There was nothing we could do. Julian and I just had to sit back and watch as our brother and best friend slowly slipped away from us.

"When I saw him coming toward me in the airport, I didn't even know who I was looking at. He was a completely different person. He was the brother I remembered." He shook his head in wonder. "How? How did you do it? How did you bring him back when none of us could?"

Evie stared at him, her heart twisting at Talis's obvious display of emotion. She shrugged helplessly. "I don't even know, Talis. I just listened to him...and loved him. He was so easy to love. I never thought he'd love me back." She was actually still having trouble believing any of what had happened the night before. It seemed like such a surreal dream.

"My brother has never taken love lightly. It's not a casual thing to him. For him to tell you he loves you... Amy was a sorry excuse for a human. Maybe he can experience real love with you, Evie. The kind he deserves."

She smiled. "I hope so, Talis. I hope I can always be everything he needs. I know that sounds really sudden, but..."

He shook his head. "It doesn't sound sudden. If that's

how your heart feels, there doesn't need to be any set times. Just love him, Evie. Love him for real, the way he deserves. If you do, he'll be yours forever." He smiled. "Traevyn mates for life."

She grinned and felt a blush stain her cheeks. She knew she should be unsettled by the seriousness of the conversation when Traevyn had only told her he loved her the night before, but it didn't feel strange to her. She wanted to be with Traevyn. She wanted to love him forever. Talis's words did not make her uncomfortable.

"Evie."

She looked up and met Talis's gaze again.

"You are a unique and amazing person. Thank you for bringing my brother and best friend back to me. Julian will love you as well when you meet him, as will our parents. You brought light back into our family."

Evie bit her bottom lip and averted her gaze, feeling her eyes fill with tears. Blind acceptance was new to her. She thought back to the party at the deBoers, how she had watched everyone in envy, how she had wanted so much to have a close group of family and friends. Maybe she could have that with Traevyn and his family. It seemed attainable when she was talking to Talis. She sighed, thinking that Traevyn may just be the answer to all of her prayers. Perhaps they could both make one another's dreams come true.

# Chapter Twenty-Two

The day was clearer than normal with the sun shining joyfully down on the water as Evie sat on Traevyn's balcony. She was sketching, as usual. It had been a week since they'd left Sedona, and Evie had graduated to drawing on Traevyn's balcony as it had a better view. Plus, he didn't mind now that they were together. She spent more time in his room than anywhere else anyway, especially since he had that gigantic tub. She practically lived in that tub.

Her life had been nothing short of bliss since leaving Sedona. She and Traevyn spent almost all of their time together and were so affectionate that Seth's gag reflexes were working overtime. Half the time Evie didn't even know what to do with herself. She'd never had a real boyfriend, and every guy she'd liked had only thought of her as a sister. Maxim deBoer had been more in her league at least, even if he was married. Traevyn was one of those men she never would have even attempted to go for. He was like a celebrity. Unattainable, too beautiful and amazing for someone like her.

Her mind reeled every time he kissed her, making her feel breathless and lightheaded, and her blood burned every time he touched her. To her, Traevyn was like one of those steamy romance novel men who fulfilled every woman's most wicked desires.

A smile curled her lips as she added some shading to her drawing. She was drawing Traevyn again, as usual. He was her favorite subject. Suddenly, she felt a light touch on the back of her neck and her hair moved away from her shoulder. She smiled wider. He was always so silent, sneaking up on her without warning. She closed her eyes as she felt his lips touch her neck. Her heart skipped a beat, as it was accustomed to doing, and she let out a soft sigh. His hands rested on her shoulders and one of them crept up to hold her head while he continued to lavish her neck and jaw with intoxicating, tender kisses.

"What are you drawing?" he whispered, grazing his teeth along her skin.

She grinned. "The only thing I ever draw."

He smiled and rested his chin on her shoulder as he peered down at the sketch. There was no real structure to it. Just an absent sketch done as if she couldn't get him out of her mind. He hoped that was the case. In the past week, he had come to crave Evie. She was not only something he needed, but something he wanted desperately.

It was strange being in love, yet feeling so differently. With Amy, he had worshipped her, would have laid down and died for her if she'd asked. At the time, he'd been sure that was real love, but now he thought it felt more like slavery. While there was no doubt in his mind that his love for Amy had been nothing but genuine, Evie made him feel differently. She didn't make him feel like he needed to sacrifice anything to be with her. She didn't demand anything from him, except her usage of his tub, but he could overlook that. With Evie, he felt more like a complimentary part to something already beautiful. Like the right shading on a well-drawn picture. She made him feel like he was special just as he was. She had always made him feel that way. Even during his blackest days.

Amy's reasoning for cheating on him had been that she'd felt second to his painting. Evie understood his art. She was as passionate about it as he was. She would never ask him to give it up. It was essential to his survival, and she knew that. He was a whole person with Evie. She made him better; she made him good. And even though she felt plain, he thought she was magnificent. He had never seen her as plain. Even on that first day when she had come to his door, he had thought she was lovely, though he would never have admitted it at the time. He had long ago lost his taste for tall, figureless women with perfect hair, perfect makeup, and perfect skin. He would much rather have Evie with her fantastic curves, petite frame, and bright smile. She was more of a goddess to him than any woman on earth.

He heaved a sigh, dreading what he was going to say next. "Evie, I want to show you something."

She frowned and twisted in her chair so she could look at him. His voice had a serious note to it, and that troubled her. "What is it?"

He gave her a small smile and took her hand in his, helping her out of the chair and leading her into his room. He sat down on the edge of his bed and slid over two thick picture albums, pulling them onto his lap.

Evie's eyes widened as she recognized them. They were the ones Seth had knocked over, the ones Traevyn had gotten so upset about. She met his eyes and gave him a questioning frown.

He sighed again. "I want to share everything with you," he murmured. "This is my past, who I was to make me who I am. I need to show this to you, Evie."

She stared at him, amazed and touched that he trusted her so completely, that he wanted her to know all of him, even the parts that caused him pain. She sat down next to him, close so that their bodies were touching.

Traevyn closed his eyes, and she felt him ease almost instantly at her presence. She reached her hand up to cradle his cheek in her palm, and he smiled. "Traevyn, you don't have to do this," she assured him. "You don't owe me anything. I have never asked you to share your past with me, and I never will. If it hurts you to look at these—"

He shook his head, silencing her. "It does hurt me," he stated. He opened his eyes to look into hers. "But this was my life. Amy and Leanna were real. They happened. I can't pretend they didn't. And it's not fair for me to ask you to pretend they didn't either. You shouldn't have to wonder about the secrets I hold inside. I don't want to keep anything from you. Ever." He sighed. "I need to heal, and I can't do it if I keep all of my problems up on a shelf where I run from them every time I glance their direction. I need to look at these even if it hurts me. I have to do it. I have to remember so I can move on. I can't look at them alone. I need you here with me, Evie. You make me strong."

She nodded and reached down to take his hand in hers. "Whatever you need, Traevyn."

His eyes filled with tenderness. "I remember you saying that to me before." He shook his head and touched her face.

"You have always been so willing to give me whatever I've needed."

She smiled, knowing in her heart that there would never be anything he could ask of her that would be too much. She would do anything for him. He'd had her under his spell from the moment he'd opened his door.

"I will show you the pictures of my wedding first," he said. "Then I will share with you the joy of my baby girl."

She squeezed his hand in reassurance and waited.

Traevyn swallowed, took a deep breath, and opened the wedding album he had sworn he would never look at again. The first picture was their main wedding picture. He and Amy standing in a beautiful garden. He was in a double-breasted tux, and his hair was pulled back and braided. Amy was in a cream-colored dress with spaghetti straps and a large skirt with a long train. He drew in a shaky breath as he looked at her face. He remembered her laugh, remembered the feel of her hand as he slipped the ring on her finger...

"Traevyn, we don't have to look at these, really," Evie said, obviously seeing how difficult it was for him.

Her voice anchored him. She was a light banishing the threatening darkness. He shook his head, dispersing the painful memories. "It's not Amy that it pains me to remember," he said. "It's the betrayal, but I'm fine."

Evie looked down at the wedding picture and wrinkled her nose.

Traevyn caught the expression and frowned thoughtfully. "What's wrong?"

She shook her head. "You look funny in a tux, out of place. If I was marrying you, I wouldn't want you in a tux, and I would want your beautiful hair flowing free." She suddenly seemed to realize what she was saying and clamped her mouth shut, a furious blush staining her cheeks.

He smiled and lifted her chin with his finger. He gazed down into her eyes and kissed her with gentleness. When he pulled away, he touched her cheek, then turned back to the photo album and began the journey through his past.

It was strange to revisit his storybook wedding. It seemed like so long ago...in another lifetime, really. He supposed that's what it was. A page in history and nothing more. There had been times, right after the divorce, when he'd stared at the pictures for hours, recalling every detail so as to never forget the way she felt, the way she smelled. Now, they were only fleeting memories. It was painful to remember, but no longer devastating. It was a dull ache brought about by the memory of such a bitter betrayal and heartbreak, but it was not her that he missed.

When Traevyn turned the last page, he felt a sense of relief come over him. He'd made it through. He still lived. It seemed less painful somehow. Maybe it was because he had confronted his demons. Maybe it was because Evie was there, still holding his hand. For whatever reason, he felt a little freer than he had before. He closed the book and ran his hand over the back cover, saying a silent goodbye to the life he once knew.

He sighed. "So, what did you think?"

"You had a lovely wedding, Traevyn," she replied, her tone flat.

He smiled. She sounded very unconvincing. He was sure that looking at pictures of him and his ex-wife was about as fun for her as it was for him. He reached out to absently play with her hair. "How would you want your wedding?" he asked. "Have you thought about it before?"

"Thought about it?" She giggled, some of the tension in her voice dissipating. "I've fantasized until my brain hurt."

His smile turned into a grin. "Tell me."

"I always wanted to get married at night."

He raised his eyebrows. "At night?"

She nodded. "Outside somewhere with lots of torches and Japanese paper lanterns. I don't know. Something about the soft glow seems so romantic. All the tables lit by candles..."

"That sounds beautiful, Evie." He didn't tell her that he had secretly always wanted a nighttime wedding as well. Amy would never have gone for that. She was very traditional. She would have thought he'd lost his mind.

With dread, he got back to the task at hand. He set the wedding album aside, exposing Leanna's baby book. He stared at it for a moment, and his fingers trembled as he opened the cover. He was blasted by a picture of her as a newborn, and a dried wildflower slipped out of the fold and down the page. The air slammed out of his lungs as the memory assaulted him. She had picked him that flower. The three of them had been walking and she'd run ahead. She'd given it to him along with a huge hug...

He squeezed his eyes shut, feeling sick to his stomach. Images of her barraged him, followed by the terrible scene of her little body falling under the wheels of that truck. He started to shake uncontrollably. "I can't do this," he rasped.

Evie took the book off of his lap and set it aside. She stood to wrap her arms around him and cradled his head to her chest. "You need to let it out, Traevyn," she soothed. "It's okay. I'm with you. You're not alone. It's okay to miss her. It's okay to cry."

His body shook as he fought for control. He had cried in front of Evie before, but he had never completely lost it in front of anyone. He hadn't cried at her funeral. For a solid two weeks, he had remained in bed afterward, his tears a never-ending flood, but he had always been by himself. He hadn't cried in front of his brothers. Not like he wanted to now. Not the body-wracking sobs that were threatening to choke him.

"Traevyn."

Her voice was so soft, so loving. He forced himself to meet her eyes. She caressed her fingers across his face, tracing the lines. "Trust me," she pleaded. "Trust me enough to let me see your grief. Trust me with the burden you have always carried alone. Trust me enough to let me in the darkest shadow of your heart. If you don't, you will never be whole. You'll never heal. You'll always be broken."

He stared at her for a moment before grabbing the book and turning it to the back page where a picture of Leanna right before she had died resided. One of her smiling as her golden hair curled around her face to make her look like a cherub. "This was my little girl," he choked out. "This was my life. My heart doesn't beat like it used to anymore. The sunlight is dulled. I ache inside every day of my life and I fear it will never go away." He clutched the book to his chest as a sob was torn from his throat. He hung his head and let himself cry. He opened the last recess of his soul for her, let her see the ugly, black pain that he carried within him. The sorrow, the guilt, the emptiness.

He let it out as he let her in and, as she held him to her, running her fingers softly through his hair, a kind of calm overcame him. It came with knowing he did not bear the weight of his burden alone. He had someone to lean on, rely on. Trust. He had someone he could trust with the darkest part of him. That was something he'd never thought he would have.

As the worst of the sobs abated, he let out a shuddering breath. "I miss her so much, Evie," he whispered.

She pulled back and smoothed his hair, wiped his tears. "Tell me about her," she coaxed. "What was she like?"

A pained smile twisted his lips as he began to tell Evie about Leanna. He spoke about her love for life, her laugh, how she loved to dance, her favorite color, favorite animal, favorite food. He found pictures in the book to coincide with his stories. He laughed, he cried, but most importantly, he remembered. He remembered Leanna for what she was. He remembered her life and not just her death. For hours, he spilled his memories of her, not running from the pain they brought, not fearing tears. He let the emotions come and flow through him, accepted them, and continued on.

At the end of it all, he was exhausted, but strangely at peace. He turned the last page of the baby book, realizing he'd made it through. He expelled an enormous sigh and closed it. He felt Evie's hand rubbing his back in consolation, and he gave a meager smile. The ever-present ache in his heart was still there. It always would be, but it didn't feel like a piercing knife anymore. He hadn't realized that half the reason he'd hurt so much was because he'd never talked to anyone, never shared himself. He'd held everything inside and let it eat at him like a cancer for years.

"Are you all right?"

He closed his eyes. Her soft voice again. His anchor. His light. He nodded slowly and turned his head to look at her. "I might need to have more talks about this in the future."

She gave him a gentle smile and caressed his face. "That's fine, Traevyn. You can talk to me whenever you want. That's how we heal."

He bent to rest his forehead against hers and sighed. "My little apprentice," he said. "She is so wise. You came here so I could teach you about art, but you have taught me about life. I am the real student."

She took his face in her hands and kissed his forehead. "When it comes to life, we are all students."

He met her eyes, then lowered his lips to hers in a slow, tender kiss. He relished the feel of her supple lips. A knock on the door interrupted them, and they pulled away from one another. Traevyn's eyes lingered on Evie's, saying a hundred different things.

"Uh...guys?" Seth's voice came. "I don't mean to interrupt whatever it is you're doing, but...I'm starving!" He wailed the last part.

Evie laughed and rolled her eyes. "Heaven forbid he make something for himself."

Traevyn shook his head. "Unthinkable."

She stood. "I'd better go make something."

He followed as she started for the door and took her hand. "I'll help you."

She grinned and they headed downstairs together. As they reached the kitchen, Evie started to pull things out and hummed softly to herself. Traevyn went to her and enfolded her in his arms, holding her tight.

She blinked in surprise and tried to give him a questioning look when he pulled away, but she didn't get a chance. His lips met hers with blinding passion and he kissed her deep and thorough, pressing her to him and tangling his fingers in her hair. She clutched at the front of his shirt as he continued to dominate her mouth, and her legs started to feel wobbly. This was the kind of kiss she had only ever dreamed about, the kind of kiss she'd never thought she would be on the receiving end of. She felt like he was trying to devour her very soul.

One of his hands cupped her cheek and the other one snaked around her back. He explored her mouth to his heart's content, running his hand along the luscious curve of her hip. He backed her up against the island in the kitchen and turned his attention to her neck.

Any kind of coherent thought that might have been hanging on in Evie's mind fled. She couldn't focus on anything save Traevyn's lips and heated kisses. She sighed in pleasure and leaned back, offering him free rein to do and go wherever he wanted. She couldn't have stopped him if she'd wanted to... And she definitely didn't want to.

Her elbow hit the edge of a plate and sent it crashing to the floor. Neither of them paid it any attention. She slipped her hands underneath his shirt and ran her fingers lightly up his sides, then back down, grazing his skin with her fingernails. He drew in a sharp breath and moved his lips back to her mouth.

"Evie, are you all right?" Seth called from the living room. "I heard something—holy crap!" He spun away from the doorway as soon as he entered. "I'm blind!"

Traevyn managed to separate himself from Evie for a moment to shoot Seth's retreating form an amused look.

Evie put her hand over her heart, as if doing so might still the pounding. "Seth," she breathed. She cleared her throat. "We were just...uh...making dinner."

Seth made a strangled sound and threw his arms in the air wildly. "La, la, la la!" he shouted as he all but fled back into the living room.

Traevyn chuckled and met Evie's eyes with a devilish twinkle in his own.

Evie arched an eyebrow. "I think I'd better make dinner alone."

He gave her a playful pout. "You don't want to do that." He slipped his arm around her waist again and pulled her up against his body. "Do you?" He pressed his hips suggestively against her.

Evie's throat went dry and her head swam. No, she didn't want to make dinner alone. She didn't want to make dinner at all. She wanted to go back upstairs and make something else. His eyes seemed to hold all sorts of hidden promises and she desperately wanted to explore all of them.

He ran his hand down the length of her hair and his face grew serious. "Thank you for making me feel alive again, Evie. All you have done..." He shook his head. "Words don't exist to express my gratitude."

She sighed, resting her head against his chest. Suddenly, a great reverberating ring filled the house, and Evie lifted her head with a frown as Traevyn clenched his teeth.

Seth came into the kitchen carrying the gong mallet. "Star—va—tion," he stated.

Evie rolled her eyes and pulled away from Traevyn. "You know what?" she muttered. She opened the refrigerator door and pulled out a carrot. She handed it to Seth. "Enjoy." She took Traevyn's hand and started to lead him out. "Come on, we're going *out* to dinner."

Seth stared forlornly at the carrot. He looked up at Evie. "No way, come on! Traevyn did the exact same thing to me with a banana!"

She grinned and couldn't help herself. "I really don't need to know what you did with Traevyn's banana, Seth." He made that same strangled noise and Traevyn shoved her lightly with a halfhearted scowl. She giggled.

"Come on, guys!" Seth cried.

She grabbed her keys and a light jacket and headed for the front door. "See ya later." They both disappeared out the door, leaving Seth standing there in dismay with his produce.

# Chapter Twenty-Three

Traevyn awoke as if something had startled him, but he didn't know what. He frowned as he stared up at the ceiling, letting his eyes adjust to the darkness. He heard the waves in the distance, pounding out their soothing rhythm, but they refused to calm him tonight for reasons that he couldn't place. He tried to remember if he had been dreaming, and he immediately thought that it had to have been about Leanna or Amy. Why else would he have awoken so suddenly with a fine sheen of perspiration across his skin?

A vision of Evie flashed before his eyes and he blinked. Evie... Had he been dreaming about her? The memory of their passionate kisses in the kitchen invaded his thoughts. His heart started to pound at the recollection of her soft lips against his, her beautiful body beneath his hands...

He swallowed painfully and sat up, shaking his head. His hair fell over his shoulder in a half-braided mess and he frowned. What had happened to his hair tie? He raked his fingers through it in irritation and flung it back behind him, contemplating hacking it all off for a moment. It was too heavy and too hot.

No, he couldn't do that. He loved his long hair, and so did Evie. He thought of how she tangled her fingers in it when they kissed, how gently she brushed and braided it...

With a frustrated growl, Traevyn stood and paced for a few restless moments. She was plaguing him. He couldn't get her out of his mind. It had to have been in the low forties and his body felt like it was on fire. He felt like he was back in Arizona. He sighed. He needed a glass of water. That would help.

Turning abruptly, he headed for the door, pulling off his black silk pajama shirt and flinging it to the floor. It was just too bloody hot.

* * *

Evie flicked on her bedside light and squinted at the clock. Good lord, it was two A.M. She sat up and sighed in frustration. She had been tossing and turning for the past two hours and had only managed to doze for about twenty minutes. What was her problem? All she could think about was Traevyn. Her mind kept replaying the way he had kissed her. Reality was so much better than her fantasies, but man, she needed her sleep too.

She grasped for her glasses and shoved them on, then sighed again and flung the covers back. Maybe if she wandered around and drank some water or something...

She yawned as she headed down the hallway, the wooden floorboards cold on her bare feet. She stretched as she approached the staircase, then jumped and let out a startled squeak as she saw Traevyn standing at the end of his corridor, shrouded in shadow with his raven black hair falling around his bare shoulders in a wild mess. "Traevyn," she whispered, drawing in a shaky breath. "What are you doing?"

"I couldn't sleep." His eyes focused on her, taking her in. He wanted to groan aloud. She was so perfect it hurt. Desire inflamed him. He was sure he would incinerate.

"Me either," she said. She swallowed and her eyes roamed up his torso. "I...uh...was going to get some water. I just keep tossing and turning." She met his eyes. "Why, um...why can't you sleep?"

"Too hot," he rasped. He couldn't tear his eyes from her. He just wanted to be near her. His hands ached to touch her and, at that precise moment, he did not want any part of her body unkissed.

She frowned, feeling flushed under his gaze. His eyes held that promise again. That promise of all those secret and wicked things she wanted to explore. Her heart picked up its pace as he stepped closer to her, his tall frame towering over her and exuding raw sensuality. "Too hot?" she repeated.

He nodded. "Oh yes." Without warning, he bent and scooped her up into his arms, carrying her back down the hallway.

Evie wrapped her arms around his neck and snuggled close to him, stunned and dazed, but far from unwilling. He carried her effortlessly all the way to his room and set her down on his bed, leaning in to give her a hungry kiss before she even had a chance to formulate a thought. It was a savage kind of kiss, and her world spun as his tongue plundered her mouth. Her hands slid up his shoulders as she twined her arms around his neck, and he gently pushed her back so that she was lying against several soft pillows.

He broke the kiss and came up to lie beside her before wrapping his arm around her waist and pulling her full up against him, seeking her mouth once more. As soon as her body touched his, all her blood was set aflame. She trailed her fingers down his spine, relishing the feel of his smooth skin and the way his muscles moved and played beneath it.

Traevyn brought one hand up to cradle Evie's cheek and threaded his fingers through her hair. He softened his kisses, making them sensual and seductive, taking her breath away until she thought she would die.

"You're so beautiful," he whispered, trailing his lips down to her neck and throat.

She shivered as his fingers slipped deftly beneath her shirt to caress up her side and across her stomach, and she gasped as he ever so slightly brushed his hand along the underside of her breasts. He kissed down the column of her throat and ran his tongue in an agonizingly slow stroke across her collarbone. She was having trouble catching her breath. Her mind was spinning out of control, making it impossible for her to focus on anything other than his touch and his kiss.

He painstakingly pulled the strap of her tank top down over her shoulder and kissed her there. He nuzzled her neck, grazing her skin with his teeth. "I love you," he purred. "I want you." He left her neck to press kisses along her exposed stomach, pulling down the waistband of her pants so that he could access her hipbone as well. He spent a few seconds there before his hands deftly removed her pajama pants altogether.

Evie squeezed her eyes shut and, somewhere within the waves of passion that were crashing over her, a shred of rational thought crept in. She tangled her fingers in his hair and frowned, trying to come back to reality, even though she really didn't want to. Traevyn ran his hand slowly up her leg and nibbled on her hip again, teasing the edge of her panties with his teeth. Holy cow, she *really* didn't want him to stop.

She sighed in bliss and attempted to make her mind go blank, but when she felt his fingers begin to take her panties down the same path as her discarded pants, she grabbed his hand to stop him. "Oh my gosh," she breathed, trying to bring her wildly spinning mind to some kind of halt. "Traevyn, we have to stop." She *hated* saying those words.

He pulled away and came back up to look into her eyes. "Too fast?" he murmured.

She shook her head. "No." She frowned. "Yes. I mean..." She sighed. "Kind of."

He gave her a gentle smile and touched her face, even though it killed him to just lie there when everything inside of him was screaming for him to peel all of her clothes from her body and get drunk off of her. "What is it, Evie?"

"It's just... I always wanted to wait." She frowned, embarrassed. She felt way too prudish all of a sudden. He would probably think she was completely stupid.

"You're a virgin?"

She swallowed and met his eyes. She nodded uneasily.

He gave her a very soft smile and leaned in to press a tender kiss to her lips. "That's wonderful, Evie."

She blinked. "It is?"

He nodded, caressing his hand down her shoulder and arm.

Her cheeks turned pink. "I just always had these crazy fantasies of a romantic wedding night when I'd get to experience everything with my husband. I never liked the thought of comparing my husband with someone else. I know it sounds old fashioned, but I want to marry the man I give my heart to and I think that, if I love him enough to be with him forever, he should be the only one to ever have all of me. It's like a gift, you know?"

His fingers ran a torturously slow course down her side again, and Evie thought that his eyes seemed to hold a soft light.

"I have never dated casually," he said. "Whenever I date someone, it is because I feel I may have a future with that person. I am a one woman man. I do not say 'I love you' unless I am sure that I speak truth." He met her eyes. "Evie, I would not be with you unless I had intentions to one day marry you."

Evie's heart stuttered and she felt the color drain from her face, but from surprise more than anything else.

"I hope that doesn't make you uncomfortable," he said. "I don't, of course, mean right now."

She shook her head numbly. "It doesn't make me feel uncomfortable," she whispered. Her throat felt like sandpaper. The thought of being married to Traevyn was like heaven.

He ran his fingers across her jaw and down her neck, breathing a soft sigh. "I will wait for the divine bliss that is you," he said. "It may kill me, but I will." He smiled.

She bit her bottom lip.

He nuzzled his nose against her neck again. "I just wish that I could give you the same gift, Evie."

She smiled and her heart melted. She wrapped her arms around him and held him close to her. "The gift of your heart is enough for me," she murmured. "It's the only gift that matters."

He tightened his arm around her, needing to feel her pressed against him. He still felt like he was smoldering inside, but he tried to tame his savage impulses. He admired and respected Evie for her decision and would not try to manipulate her into changing her mind just because his body was screaming at him. And it was screaming. He had been celibate far too long.

He forced his carnal thoughts away and contented himself just to hold her. Maybe he would start taking a routine dip in the ocean every morning. That sounded like an appealing option. "Will you stay with me?" he asked. "I need to feel you next to me, Evie. I can't stand being away from you." His hand drifted back to her stomach where he idly caressed his palm over it. Her skin was as soft as rose petals.

"Of course I will," she whispered. Part of her was kicking herself for telling him to stop. It was Traevyn Whitelaw for crying out loud! How many people got *that* opportunity? There was no way to tell this early in their relationship if they would last. What if they didn't and she had passed up intimacy with him? She would regret it forever.

She sighed. But what if they did make it? She would only

ever know Traevyn. Traevyn's touch, Traevyn's kiss, Traevyn's body. She was much more willing to take the chance and wait. The reward would be so much greater in the end. She wanted all of Traevyn forever. She wanted a lifetime with him, not just several moments of passion. Although, sleeping with a famous artist did make for good back-to-school gossip. That would get Barrett deBoer off her back for sure. She giggled at the thought.

Traevyn raised his head and frowned. "What's so funny?"

She met his gaze. "I was just thinking about Barrett deBoer."

He cocked an eyebrow and propped his head up on his elbow. "I try to make love to you and you're thinking about the married man you have a crush on?"

"No, that's Maxim. Barrett is his brother, and he's been trying to date me for years."

Traevyn arched both of his eyebrows this time. "That's even worse!" he exclaimed. He put his hand over his heart. "You're wounding me, Evie," he teased.

She giggled again. "Don't worry, he's a jerk. I was just thinking of the look on his face if I were to tell him I'd slept with you."

Traevyn blinked and feigned shock. "So now I'm a conquest? You're breaking my heart!" He fell onto his back dramatically.

Evie laughed and wrapped her arm around his waist, resting her head on his shoulder. "Didn't you know that was my plan all along? I rigged it so that I could come on this trip and seduce you."

"And yet, you refuse to let me have you, and instead, decide to drive me crazy with your perfection and your adorable little froggy panties."

She looked down at her panties and her face flamed. Yup, sure enough. Little frogs hopping onto lily pads. She groaned and put her hands over her face. How sexy was that, really? She needed a makeover.

He chuckled. "Don't be embarrassed. I love them. Your perfect body and everything about you drives me wild."

Having someone like Traevyn tell her that she made him sexually frustrated with her perfection was not the kind of comment she was used to hearing. She turned her face into his shoulder as if to hide it and smiled shyly. Having him say he loved her stupid bikini briefs was even worse. She felt his hand come up to stroke her hair, and she snuggled closer to him. "I love you, Traevyn," she whispered.

He turned over on his side and cupped her cheek in his palm, gazing directly into her eyes. "You are quickly becoming everything to me."

She sighed as his lips came to claim hers once again. Every color on an artist's pallet flashed through her mind when he kissed her, every beautiful image that had ever inspired her. He was a masterpiece in every way.

\* \* \*

When Traevyn awoke, he realized he felt something strange, foreign. He frowned as he tried to place what it was. Gradually, he became aware of Evie's presence beside him, and he turned his head to see her curled on her side away from him, still sleeping soundly. He smiled to himself and caressed her arm, then pressed a kiss to her shoulder and pulled the cover up over her. He sat up and swung his legs out of bed with a sigh.

That was it. He felt complete.

He stood and opened the French doors, stepping out onto the balcony and closing his eyes as the morning mist attacked his bare skin. He took a deep breath and grinned. For the first time in so long, every single part of him felt alive.

He turned and went back inside, not wanting to make Evie cold. He slipped a robe on and quietly made his way out of the room. He stopped in the doorway and looked back at her, loving how right she looked in his bed, in his room...in his world.

She belonged. She always had. She was the missing piece. He smiled and walked down to the office where he rummaged through his things until he located a leather journal not unlike the poetry book he had given Evie to read. The only difference was that this one had a Celtic knot pattern embossed on the front.

He smiled and sat down at his desk, running through all the many songs and poems he had locked away in his mind. After a moment, he began to write.

# Chapter Twenty-Four

As Evie loaded the last of her luggage into the trunk of her car, a horrible, painful lump rose in her throat, matching the horrible, painful pressure around her heart. She turned slowly toward the mansion that had been her home for the past three months, and the breeze blew her hair gently as it rustled the eucalyptus leaves. She tried to fix the scene in her memory, tried to take in every gothic detail.

Her eyes strayed to the front door as Seth emerged, followed by Traevyn. Her heart twisted and she wanted to bawl like a baby. He'd told her that he would come see her on winter break, that he wanted to see her home and her life, but that was at least three months away. What had gone by so quickly while she was living in Big Sur suddenly seemed like an eternity. She folded her arms and looked down at the ground, fighting her tears.

Traevyn sighed as he saw Evie. Seth looked up at him and gave him an understanding smile. "Traevyn," he said, "I can honestly say it has been a pleasure."

Traevyn looked down at Seth, his heart warming at the boy's words. "Seth Austin," he said, "I owe you more than I could ever express."

A knowing look passed between them and Seth smirked, nodding a little. "You're a good man, Traevyn," he said, embracing him.

Traevyn smiled and returned the embrace. "I'm very happy I got the chance to know you," he said.

Seth frowned and pulled away. "Come on, don't act like you'll never see me again. We're going to be a family, after all." He winked and flashed a mischievous grin.

Traevyn chuckled and followed Seth toward the car, toward Evie. She went into his arms without hesitation, hiding her face against his chest and wrapping her arms fiercely around his waist. He twisted his lips into a sad smile and sighed. He could tell she was crying. He touched her hair. "Walk with me for a moment?" he queried.

She nodded and he led her down the path she had used many mornings. He kept his arm around her as they walked, kept her close to his body. His heart felt like it was ripping in half, but he knew he needed to be strong for her. She had done so much for him. The least he could do was let her go off to her last year of school without making her feel guilty for his being sad.

He stopped once they were far enough away to feel isolated under a large eucalyptus tree. The fog swirled around them and he turned her to face him. "Evie," he murmured, "I don't want you to be sad."

She snorted and looked up at him like he had just lost his mind.

He tucked her hair behind her ear. "For thirty years I have waited for you. I can handle one more year."

She looked down and shook her head. "I don't know if I can."

"You can," he assured her. "I will come and see you on winter break."

"And you'll call?"

He smiled. She sounded so small and sad. His heart twisted. "Every day," he whispered. "Darling, I have something for you." He had been holding the leather journal with the Celtic knot on it and he opened it. "I wrote you something."

She looked up at him, waiting, her heart aching in her chest. She felt like she had found paradise only to have it ripped from her. She couldn't bear it.

"Wandering fields, following wisps," Traevyn began,
"Of faces once remembered.
Holding on to that which
I no longer see.
It has such a hold on me.
Internal grip, cold,
Woven eternal,
My heart, scarred,

Thick with callous
Yet still, it bleeds,
Pieces missing, scattered.
Somewhere in the wake of my
Unlettered existence
You found me, lost in myself,
Showed me designs of a better person,
Soothed the pains of my damaged past.
Reluctant, hesitant, unbelieving in the
Perfection of you, I gathered myself.
Slowly, you tug at the roots
That bind my heart in the past,
Cauterize the pain that I may feel it no more.
Patiently, you wait for me.
I love you with an appreciation
I find hard to express.
I may be doubled over in pain,
As you excise my demons,
But these wounds heal.
The pain excruciating, but temporary.
You dress the wounds with your tears of joy,
Your smile covers over the
Discomfort and your kiss dulls the pain.
I live because of you.
I love because you do.
Within you, I find all the pieces
That have been lost to me.
Together, we put them back in place.
Together, I become a part of you,
As you do me.
One heart, two souls,
One love."

He finished and looked at her, his eyes filled with emotion that he couldn't hide. Tears were streaking down her cheeks and he reached gentle fingers out to wipe them.

Evie shook her head. "I changed my mind. I don't need a bachelor's degree. Or, wait," her eyes brightened, "I'll just transfer! Cal Poly's in San Luis Obispo!"

He arched an eyebrow. "You planning to commute six hours a day? That's more trouble than it's worth. Besides, you already registered for this semester."

She frowned. "It would be worth it if I could stay with you," she murmured. She felt stupid for acting so needy, but she was terrified that if she left, he would find someone better than her. She hated herself for her insecurity, but she'd never felt beautiful and had never been able to attract the attention of any man she'd liked. The men she'd liked in the past had been normal guys. Traevyn was extraordinary. She had a hard time believing that a bunch of normal guys had looked over her, but the most amazing man ever created wanted her.

"Have some faith in me, Evie," he said, bringing his mouth close to her ear. "There is no one but you."

Her eyes widened. Geez, was she that transparent? She sighed in defeat and leaned her forehead against his shoulder. She closed her eyes as his arms came around her, enveloping her in warmth.

"I want you to take this journal," he said. "I made it for you. There is one poem or song for every week you are away from me. Read one every Monday; start your week off with love from me." He pulled back and arched an eyebrow. "Do not cheat and read ahead."

She smiled at him.

He held the book just out of her reach. "I want your word on that. I'll know if you cheat."

She put her hands on her hips. "How will you know?" she challenged.

"Because I can read your thoughts." He grinned and slipped his arm around her waist.

"Oh yeah?"

He nodded and brought his lips to hover over hers, close enough to taunt her with his breath. "For instance, you desperately want to kiss me right now," he whispered. He slowly ran his tongue along her bottom lip, causing her to draw in a shaky breath. He smirked. "Don't you?"

She grabbed the front of his shirt and pulled him to her, fastening her lips to his. His arms went around her, pulling her up against his body, and she went plaint in his embrace. He kissed her until she was dizzy, until her senses were filled with only him.

"Traevyn," she gasped in between kisses, "I'm beginning to rethink this whole making love to you thing."

He pulled away with a curious frown. "You mean right

here in broad daylight against a tree with your brother up the road?"

She laughed at the picture he painted. "Not a good place for firsts?" she teased.

He wrinkled his nose and shook his head. He stepped back, handing her the journal. "Take this," he said. "Don't cheat."

She grinned.

"I will be with you every day. I will call you every night." He stepped close to her again in the sensual way that made her heart race. "And every dream you have will be haunted by me." He kissed her again, slowly, languidly, as if trying to memorize the feel and taste of her. "Know I love you. Believe I love you. We will be together again soon."

She nodded and clutched the journal close to her heart.

Traevyn smiled softly and put his arm around her shoulders. "Come on, angel," he murmured. "You need to go."

She sighed and followed him back up to the car, dragging her feet the entire way.

Seth was waiting patiently. He approached Evie with an understanding smile. "Hey, sis, let me drive, okay?"

Evie nodded and handed him the car keys, knowing she would be in no condition to drive once they pulled away.

Seth took the keys and got in the car, giving Traevyn and Evie as much privacy as he could.

Traevyn kissed Evie one more time, then broke away, his emotion apparent as he drew in a shaky breath. "Get in the car, Evie," he whispered. "Just go before I make you stay. This is killing me slowly."

She looked up into his mezmerising green eyes and whispered, "I love you."

He took her face in his hands and stared intently into her eyes as if trying to drive home his point. "And I love you. Please call me when you get home. Let me know you're safe."

"I will."

He pulled her to him, gave her a quick kiss, then turned away. "Go," he rasped.

Evie bit her bottom lip and forced herself to get in the car. She hated the way the door slammed with a note of finality. She hated the way the engine started and, most of all, she hated watching Traevyn as he stood in the doorway, watching as they drove away, the wind tugging at his hair. Alone and stoic, the way she had found him...

She burst into tears and sobbed like a baby all the way back to the main road. She felt ridiculous, but she didn't care. Her heart hurt. That was the only thing she knew for sure. Her heart hurt so badly she thought she would die.

Seth reached out and began to rub Evie's neck gently. "Evie, you need to breathe," he said. "You're going to make yourself sick."

She glanced over at him, briefly wondering who he was and what he had done with her brother. What pod person had replaced Seth Austin over the summer?

"Traevyn loves you," he continued. "You guys will be fine. December's not that far away."

"But we just left him there all alone!" she cried. "And what if—"

"What if what?" he interrupted. "Don't be stupid, Evie. He loves you. He'll be fine. Traevyn was a lot worse off before you found him and he managed to survive. I'm sure he'll survive now, and I really don't think he's the shopping around type of guy." He gave her a pointed look. "He barely had contact with the outside world for three years. You think he's going to go out and find a girl because he's lonely? You, of all people, know him better than that."

She sniffed. "I know. It's just..." She sighed. "I'm just sad, Seth. I guess I'm trying to find reasons to justify it, but I'm just sad."

He smiled a little. "Then be sad. You're leaving the man you love. You don't need a reason. That's reason enough. Here." He turned the radio to a soft rock station. "We'll even listen to sappy love songs so you can wallow properly."

She laughed, then sighed and leaned over to rest her head on Seth's shoulder. Right about then, he felt like a pretty good support beam, much to her amazement.

His smile broadened. "Thanks, Evie," he said.

"For what?"

"For the best summer of my life."

* * *

Evie was not in the mood to go to class, as was evident by her appearance. She was in a pair of plaid pajama pants and a black tank top, and she'd shoved a black beanie on over her pigtails. She'd somehow managed to force her way through Sociology and Italian, and now she was on her way to Advanced Art. She gave a dismal sigh, moping all the way down the hall.

The first day of a new semester was always the worst. It was the day reality hit with blinding force and she realized that summer really was over. The only good part of her day had been the song of the week she'd read that morning in Traevyn's journal. It had been "Kiss from a Rose" by Seal, and the words had warmed her heart. For a moment, it had almost been as good as having him there with her.

With a yawn, Evie trudged into class and flopped into a seat. Her book bag was already near to bursting with all the junk her professors had given her. Syllabuses and supply lists. All of the stuff she hated. Man, graduation couldn't come fast enough to suit her.

People filed in, and soon Professor Roth entered, looking way too perky for the first Monday of the semester.

"Hello everyone!" he greeted. "It's good to see you all again! Hopefully your summers went well."

Evie sighed again, this one even more dismal than the first.

"I have something exciting to share with you all," he said. "Over the summer, Evie got to be an apprentice for Traevyn Whitelaw at his home in Big Sur."

Evie arched an eyebrow as everyone seemed to stare at her. Great. She smiled tremulously.

"No way!" someone shouted.

"What's he like?" someone else asked.

"Hold on, hold on," Professor Roth interrupted with a chuckle. "We'll get there. As I was saying, Evie was able to spend her summer with Mr. Whitelaw, and he has sent a letter for me to read to the class, along with a painting he'd like for me to display."

Dread started to work its way through her. Something about all of this did not feel good to her.

"'To all art students,'" Professor Roth began after unfolding a piece of paper. "'I am writing this so that you may know that you have genius among you. I recently had the great pleasure of taking Miss Evelina Austin as my apprentice. Not only is she a brilliant artist, but she is a great inspiration, as I am sure many of you may already know. Her work is fresh and raw, portraying human emotion and depth excellently. I am honored to have had the opportunity to work with her, and I know she will go very far. I say this without bias and speak only from a professional standpoint.'" Professor Roth paused for a moment to shoot a proud grin Evie's direction. "'I have sent this painting because my life has been changed by Miss Austin's radiant light and I wish to show you what she has inspired. She is truly an extraordinary person and a unique talent.

'Please, if you would, take down that hideous monstrosity in the foyer and replace it with this painting. I don't care how famous 'Innerworkings of a Creative Soul' is. None of you really have a clue what it's about and it is outdated.'" Professor Roth seemed flustered for a moment at Traveyn's blunt statement debunking what every art professor thought they knew about that painting. He cleared his throat and continued. "'Replace it with this painting, for it is a much more current reflection of me. Sincerely, Traevyn Whitelaw.'"

Evie tried not to grin, but it was practically impossible.

"Show us the painting!" someone shouted.

Professor Roth chuckled and went to the canvas on an easel toward the far wall. He pulled the cover off to reveal the painting Traevyn had done before the gallery opening in Sedona.

Evie's heart stopped and the entire room went silent. She fought a groan and put her head in her hand.

"Is that... Is that *you*, Evie?" a girl sitting next to her asked.

"Is that *him*?" someone else asked. "Is that what he looks like? Holy crap, he's gorgeous!"

Evie covered her face with both of her hands and sank lower into her chair, trying to disappear. Wasn't there a hole somewhere that she could crawl into?

"Professor Roth, there's something on the back of the letter," someone pointed out.

Professor Roth frowned and turned the paper over. "Oh, there's a p.s." He cleared his throat. "'And to all the men in the room who never bothered to glance Evie's direction, what is the matter with you? She is gorgeous! You are the ones who miss out. She is a fantastic kisser.'"

Evie's face burned and she squeezed her eyes shut. She

could see him in her mind. She could see him writing that horrible letter, grinning like a devil. Ohhhh, she was going to kill him. She was going to kill him twice.

Whistles and laughter sounded around the room, along with several crude remarks. Even Professor Roth looked flushed.

Evie shook her head. Yeah, he was dead. Definitely. He was evil. Evil with a capital E. However, in the deepest part of her, under the layers of extreme humiliation she was currently feeling, her heart smiled.

# Chapter Twenty-Five

*May*

All was chaos at Jeff deBoer's as Evie and Meg walked in decked out in cap and gown. Somebody cued "Pomp and Circumstance" to play as they walked in the door, and everyone cheered. Evie's family was there right along with everyone else, and she laughed joyfully.

She hadn't been given a choice as to how to spend her graduation. Jeff had taken over and had informed both Evie and her family that they would be present at the gigantic party he was throwing for Meg and Evie at his house. Evie felt good to be included like she was part of the family. It meant more to her than she could express.

She could hardly believe that she was a college graduate. She was more than positive that the only reason she had survived the year was because of Traevyn. They had talked every night for hours, and she had read his beautiful lyrics and poems every week, as instructed. They had really gotten her through all the stress. He'd given her the lyrics to many love songs that he thought applied to them or how he felt for her, but he had figured perfectly when her mid-terms and finals would be and had given her poems of encouragement, or something humorous to lighten her mood. There were excerpts from *Wuthering Heights*, *Great Expectations*, *The Phantom of the Opera*, Shakespeare, all of their favorites. There were poems from contemporary poets as well as the greats, and some more of his own thrown in the mix.

Evie hadn't cheated, hadn't read ahead. She'd kept true to her word, but she had almost worn the cover off by going back and re-reading all of the passages she had gone through already.

The original plan had been for Traevyn to come and see her on winter break, but by that time, Evie had been so sick of school and life that she'd needed a vacation. So, she had gone to see him and they'd visited Talis in Sedona again. They spent some time in Phoenix as well, touring some of the better art museums and experiencing the culture. It had been a wonderful trip full of love, laughter, and heated kissing sessions. If possible, it had left Evie feeling even closer to Traevyn than she already did.

He had come to visit her for several days on her spring break, but her family had been out of town. Meg had been as well, so he remained a mystery to everyone but Seth. Her parents constantly teased and nagged her about the strange artist who had managed to steal their daughter's heart. She knew they didn't completely understand why she couldn't go for someone "normal," but Evie didn't need to explain herself to them. They'd never really understood her creativity, so she didn't expect them to understand Traevyn's either. Only Seth understood. Which was one of the biggest surprises.

Seth... He had been accepted to Cal Poly, much to everyone's surprise since he hadn't even told anyone that he'd taken the SAT's. He would graduate high school in a few weeks, and Evie was planning a huge party. They had remained close after their summer of bonding in Traevyn's gothic mansion, and they hung out at least three days out of the week. Evie was happy that they had grown to be such good friends. She no longer viewed him as her delinquent little brother. She cherished his friendship and had come to realize that he was a lot smarter than she had ever given him credit for.

As she made her way around to everyone, giving out hugs and thanks, she marveled over how her life seemed to have come full circle. One year ago, she had been here, at Maxim's party, aching and lonely. Now, here she was, back at Jeff's with the same people, and she had everything she'd ever wanted. A beautiful man to love her, a close group of family and friends, and now a degree in art. She could think of nothing that would dampen her spirits.

"Congratulations, Evelina."

Except maybe that. Her elation came to a screeching halt

and she came down off of her high very quickly. Barrett. She grimaced. Fantastic. She turned to see him standing behind her, smirking.

"Barrett, so help me!" Alyx deBoer's voice came. "If you piss her off again, I will not think twice about kicking you in the balls!"

Maxim nodded at his brother in warning. "She'll do it too."

Evie grinned, touched at the fact that they were sticking up for her.

Barrett ignored them and took Evie's elbow, guiding her away from a group of Meg's friends who were all laughing loudly. "So, where's your famous boyfriend?" he mocked.

"He's coming tomorrow. He had a show he had to be at."

He folded his arms, looking unconvinced. "Right. Kind of strange how I've never seen him."

She frowned. "That's not my problem. Last time I checked, I didn't need you to give me clearance before I dated someone."

He tapped his finger against his chin. "Come to think of it, has *anybody* seen him? Meg hasn't."

She rolled her eyes. "Meg's seen pictures. Besides, Seth's seen him."

He rolled his eyes. "Evie, please. You expect me to believe that some famous artist would go after you when you couldn't even get a boyfriend in your own town?"

She stared at him for a moment, wondering if being a jerk was just in his DNA. "Barrett, what are you suggesting?"

He smirked, as if he had a secret he desperately wanted to tell. "I don't think he exists."

She shook her head. "Dude, get over yourself. You need to back off right now."

"Yes, I agree," a silky voice came from behind her.

Evie's heart tripped over itself about seven times, and she whirled. Her dancing heart stopped for a few beats as her eyes fell upon Traevyn's radiant visage. He smiled down at her.

Throwing any kind of refinement she may have possessed to the wind, she squealed and jumped into his arms, wrapping her legs around his waist. She heard the fabric of her gown tear, but she didn't care. It wasn't like she was ever going to wear it again.

Traevyn chuckled and held her up as he kissed her. "How I have missed that perfect mouth," he whispered.

Her face grew warm and she grinned. "You said you weren't coming till tomorrow!"

"I lied," he laughed. "I wanted to surprise you."

She tangled her fingers in his hair and studied his gorgeous face with a contented sigh. She leaned in to claim his lips again, and he made a slow, deliberate exploration of her mouth, both of them not caring about the snickers and stares they were receiving.

"Dude! Get a room!" Seth finally shouted.

Evie blushed and climbed down off of Traevyn, remembering that her parents were watching. She glanced at them to see them both shaking their heads, but smiling. Seth was grinning. Meg, her friends, and even Alyx seemed to be staring at Traevyn in a dazed awe. Barrett just looked unamused.

Evie grinned and took Traevyn's hand. "Barrett, meet Traevyn."

Traevyn fixed Barrett with a piercing stare.

Barrett lowered his eyes and walked away, saying nothing.

Traevyn grinned and wrapped his arm around Evie's shoulders. "So, where is this famous Maxim?" he queried.

Evie giggled and pointed to where Maxim and Jeff were laughing in the kitchen.

"That guy?" He snorted arrogantly. "I'm much better looking than him."

Evie rolled her eyes and elbowed him playfully in the side. "Come on, I want you to meet everyone," she said. "That way no one else thinks I made you up."

He smiled and followed her as they made the ceremonial trip around the room.

Traevyn was more than willing to meet all of the people Evie had spoken so much about, but after awhile, he began to hate the fact that there were so many people he had to make small talk with when all he wanted was Evie. He had missed her so much. His home seemed so cold and empty without her, as did his heart.

Before Evie, he had relished his dismal, empty house. It had resembled his dismal, empty heart. He had enjoyed the solitude, the quiet sounds of the sea, and the wind in the trees. But Evie and Seth had changed all that. They'd brought life and light back into his home, and he swore that his house seemed more like a tomb without them there.

"Evie?"

She looked up at him just as they'd finished talking to Alyx and her brother.

"Can we go outside for a moment?" he asked. "I want to give you your present now."

She smiled shyly and nodded, leading him out to Jeff's backyard.

Traevyn took a deep breath and sighed as she closed the sliding glass door, shutting out the festivities inside. Peace and quiet filled the air, and the late afternoon sun made everything seem tranquil in the spacious, lush yard. "Oh yes, this is much better," he said.

She grinned as they both sat down on the porch swing located on the deck. "You can take the man out of his reclusiveness, but you can't take the recluse out of the man." She giggled and leaned her head against his shoulder. He slipped his arm around her and she snuggled close, relishing the warmth of his body.

"So how does it feel to be a college graduate?" he asked.

She smiled. "Liberating."

"What are your plans now?"

"I have no idea. Just try and sell my work, I guess."

"Well, I have a theory."

She arched an eyebrow. "Oh yeah?"

He nodded. "I think all artists, upon their graduation, should go on a trip to the place that inspires them the most."

She giggled. "Sounds good to me."

He grinned and reached inside the folds of the jacket he was wearing, pulling out an envelope. "In that case..." He handed it to her. "Your present."

She frowned and peeked inside the envelope. "Is this a gift certificate?" she asked. "This had so better be a gift certificate."

Traevyn smiled and waited.

Evie pulled the paper out and blinked at it for a moment, trying to figure out what it was. Her eyes widened as recognition dawned on her. It was a plane ticket...with her name on it...to Italy. She couldn't breathe. "Oh my gosh," she whispered. "Traevyn..." She couldn't speak. She just stared at it. Her eyes roamed over the date. The reservations were six months away and... Her eyes bulged. "A month!" she cried. "Traevyn, I can't be out of the country for a month! I don't have the money! I'd have to quit my job! I'd lose my apartment! The only reason I was able to stay the summer with you was because of my parents. My cat! I have a cat! What about my cat? Meg took care of him while I was with you, but now she's going to be busy and—"

He smiled. "Don't worry about it, Evie. We'll sort it all out. Although, you do have a decision to make."

She looked up at him in confusion.

"I have another ticket," he stated. "You may take whoever you choose. Remember when you said you had no man to take on a romantic adventure with you? Well, I want you to have that. Maybe take that charming Barrett fellow."

She all but gagged.

He chuckled. "Or, if you'd like, you could take me. I may not be a deBoer, but I think I might be a decent Plan B. Besides, I've always wanted to go to Italy for a honeymoon."

She grinned as her mind filled with fantastic images of being in Italy with Traevyn. Wine tasting and the gorgeous countryside and—she frowned suddenly. "Wait, what? Honeymoon?" She pulled her eyes away from the ticket and looked up at him only to find herself staring straight at a black box with the most beautiful hunk of diamond she had ever seen. She screamed. She couldn't help it.

Traevyn retreated slightly at the volume of her scream and chuckled.

Evie started to shake, and she put her face in her hands. The tears were coming. She could feel them already. "Traevyn," she murmured. "Oh my gosh."

"You are my soul mate, Evie," he whispered. "I was deceived once, but I know better now. I was supposed to wait for you. This last year has been torture. I can't be without you. You are everything to me. You are my greatest inspiration and my greatest gift. I want to give you everything. A nighttime wedding with candles and Japanese lanterns, a tour of Italy, a home, a life...my heart, body, and soul. Please, spend your life with me, Evie. Be my wife."

*Wife.* The word lingered in her mind. The sound of it on his lips...

She looked into his eyes and she knew she would love

him for all eternity. She had been waiting for him too. "Yes," she whispered. "Please, yes."

He smiled and pulled the ring out of the box, slipping it gently onto her finger. He pressed a delicate kiss to her jaw. "My fiancée," he murmured.

Her heart flipped as she stared down at the ring on her finger. Tremendous joy welled up inside of her, pushing out the shock she was feeling. She grinned and squealed again, unable to contain her happiness. She flung her arms around him and kissed him passionately. "I love you."

"I love you too, angel," he whispered.

She pulled away with a quizzical frown. "Seth knows, doesn't he?"

Traevyn nodded with a chuckle.

Evie rolled her eyes. "He has been smiling like an idiot at me all day. You two are bad for each other."

He grinned and tucked her hair behind her ear. She had taken her cap off a little while ago and he now had free rein.

"No tux," she stated.

He shook his head.

"And your hair needs to be down."

He met her eyes. "Yes, sir."

She wrapped her arms around his neck and pulled herself up onto his lap. "And wherever we go for our wedding night, you had better make love to me until I can't walk."

His eyes smoldered as he held her, his hands caressing her back. "Oh I plan on it," he purred.

Delicious shivers worked through her body at his sensual voice, and she leaned in to kiss him. Her blood burned, and she ached to touch his skin, to explore every part of him. It had been agony to wait all this time. She couldn't count how many times she had cursed her virginity. She was amazed at her own self-control. "I think we should get married as soon as possible," she murmured.

He held her face in one hand as he kissed along her jaw line. "I can change the plane reservations."

She grinned. "I'm liking this plan."

He pulled away to look at her. "Whatever you want, love."

She slipped her hands inside his jacket and ran them up his chest. "I want you."

"I wonder how long the Justice of the Peace is open," he

teased.

She giggled.

He sighed. "We should go inside. Your friends will want to hear the news." He flashed her a devious grin.

She smiled and shook her head. "My parents are gonna flip. Barrett will crap his pants."

He smirked. "Good."

They stood and headed back inside, their fingers entwined in the same way their hearts were.

# Chapter Twenty-Six

*Crater Lake Lodge, two months later*

Evie awoke slowly, sore and exhausted, but happier than she'd been in her whole life. She felt Traevyn's body against hers and she opened her eyes. His back was toward her and she snuggled against it, pushing his hair aside so that she could feel his warm skin against hers. She sighed and let her mind replay the last twenty-four hours, savoring every fantastic detail.

They had been married at Lithia Park in Ashland, at dusk. Everybody, and she did mean everybody, had shown up. Traevyn had asked Seth to be his best man, much to the dismay of his own brothers. Traevyn claimed that he had Seth to thank for opening his eyes and thought it was only fair that he should stand at his side on his wedding day. This, of course, made Seth feel very important.

Evie had met Traevyn's parents and his brother Julian earlier in the week. She had been absolutely awestruck with how much Traevyn resembled his Native American father. She figured, if Traevyn looked that good when he got to be his father's age, she certainly wasn't going to complain.

Julian had been gentle and soft-spoken, but just as beautiful as Traevyn and Talis, only with golden blond hair instead of black. He had the same dignified, refined air that both of his brothers possessed, and she had enjoyed his company. He had been extremely helpful and mannerly.

Traevyn had worn all black with a black jacket that still made Evie drool to think about. The long sleeves had come down to his knuckles and had several silver buttons up the cuffs. In slight diagonal rows across the front were eight strips of narrow, black velvet with three lines of small, silver buttons in downward rows. It had been tailored to hug his lean body perfectly, and it had looked better than any tux. His hair had been down, flowing free, and his gorgeous eyes had held hers the entire time she'd walked down the aisle, shining with more love than she'd ever thought someone would show her.

Her dress had been of a Renaissance style, off white and simple with belled sleeves and a panel of cream-colored crushed velvet down the front. A wreath of white flowers had adorned her head rather than a veil.

Evie looked down at her ring finger as she absently caressed Traevyn's shoulders. She grinned. She loved the way the diamond sparkled in her engagement ring. More than that, she loved the way her wedding band looked right next to it. Her husband... Traevyn was her husband. Traevyn Whitelaw. It still seemed surreal to her.

She sighed. The wedding had been everything she had ever dreamed of and more. She was pretty sure that they had taken up most of the park with their massive party, and she was actually a little surprised that they all hadn't been carted away for disturbing the peace.

The reception had been an all out free-for-all with lots of laughter and dancing. They had stayed late into the night, and the party had still been in full swing when they'd left. Evie had no doubt in her mind that most of their friends and family members were nursing hangovers.

Traevyn had booked them two nights at the Crater Lake Lodge, a historical hotel that offered them an amazing view of the lake, which was the most brilliant shade of azure blue Evie had ever seen. She thought it was ridiculous that she had lived in Oregon her entire life and claimed to be an artist, but had never seen Crater Lake. It was a beautiful work of art created by nature, and she was happy that Traevyn had thought of staying there.

They were leaving for Italy in two days and they could spend the time up till then relaxing, enjoying one another, and admiring Nature's art.

Evie ran her hand along Traevyn's side and hip, loving the texture of his skin and deciding that she would never be able to touch him enough. She sighed and closed her eyes as she relived their first night together.

He had been so gentle with her and had nearly driven her to the point of insanity with his unhurried exploration of her body. She'd been a little nervous at first, but burning, molten desire had quickly replaced her jitters as soon as he put his hands on her.

The sun had been rising when they'd finally made love, and when they'd become one, Traevyn wept, whispering emotion-laden words to her before sweeping them both away in a tidal wave of passion. Evie had come to the conclusion that she had been correct in her original assumption—Traevyn *was* a fantastic lover. At least, that's what she imagined. She had never been with any other man, but generally, she thought seeing stars was a good sign.

Traevyn turned over and fixed his eyes on Evie's, smiling softly. "Good morning, my gorgeous bride," he murmured.

She yawned and stretched. "More like good afternoon."

He smiled and leaned over to kiss her neck, running his hand down the length of her body as he did so.

Evie sighed, luxuriating in his touch on her bare skin.

"I had a fantastic dream," he whispered.

"Oh yeah?"

He nodded and kissed along her collarbone. "I dreamed a beautiful angel came to me and took me to heaven." He pulled her into his arms and held her close.

She snuggled against his chest and listened to his heartbeat. "I had a dream too," she said.

"What's that?"

"I dreamed I found a man in a painting, a man in pain, in the darkest of places. I braved a journey into that dark place and found a masterpiece."

He pulled back a little and gazed down at her, framing her face with his hand. His eyes were soft, but serious. "A lifetime is not long enough to show you the magnitude of my love," he whispered.

She smiled and wrapped one leg around his waist. She rolled on top of him and sat up so she was straddling his hips. "Well, you'll just have to try," she said with a wicked gleam in her eye. "And you can start by refreshing my memory on all those things we did last night. My recollection of them is a little hazy."

He arched an eyebrow and smirked. "Oh really?"

She nodded. "Yes, I definitely think I need a refresher course."

He reached up and placed his hands on her hips. "Well, whatever my apprentice needs..." He squeezed her sides, causing her to squeal with laughter. He rolled her over onto her back and settled himself against her, his lips inches from hers, his hair falling around them like a silk curtain. "She most certainly will receive," he whispered, his voice a sinful caress against her skin.

Evie looked up into his eyes. The eyes of her husband, her soul mate, her world. She saw her whole life in those eyes, and she loved how life looked. She welcomed his kiss and wrapped her arms around him, her body catching fire to match the love that already burned like an inferno in her heart.

# *Epilogue*

*Three years later*

It was late when Traevyn returned from his trip to San Jose. He had gone for two days to meet with a dealer who had been interested in some of his paintings, and he was now far beyond exhausted. Home had never looked so good.

He opened the door and entered quietly, knowing that Evie and Julia would be asleep. He spotted Seth sitting on the couch, eating some concoction and watching television.

"Hey, welcome home," Seth said, barely looking away from the TV.

Traevyn grinned and set his keys and bag down. Seth had come to live with them while he was at college, and he was actually being very responsible about the whole thing. He lived in the dorms on campus during the week, but was with them on the weekends and during breaks. He paid rent during the summer, helped with the chores, and had been a lifesaver when it came to babysitting. Traevyn had watched him slowly morph into a man, and it made him proud to see the person he was turning in to.

"What are you doing up so late?" Traevyn questioned.

Seth sighed. "I have a gigantic mid-term in psychology on Monday. I was attempting to study." He rolled his eyes. "That's not working out so well. Studying was never my strong suit."

Traevyn chuckled and sat down next to him.

"How was your trip?" Seth asked.

He shrugged. "Boring mostly. I just wanted to come home. You know how I hate being away from your sister."

Seth nodded. "We were all wishing you'd come home soon too since you're the only one who can get Jules to sleep before two A.M."

Traevyn grinned and looked around at his living room. It was still basically the same, but it had Evie's touch all over it. Above the fireplace hung the painting he had done for her, and he had hung several of her paintings that he liked as well. She had taken one whole wall and decorated it with pictures of their family and friends, which he particularly liked. It made his home seem like life had come back to it after it had been so cold for so long.

Seth had taken over the basement, which he had turned into some kind of rock music lair, and one which Traevyn usually tried to avoid at all costs. There was always various music equipment strewn everywhere and it tended to smell like feet and bologna ninety-five percent of the time. He generally didn't mind. His house was enormous. He could sacrifice one small piece of it if it meant having Seth around.

"Well, I'm going to bed," he announced. "I'm barely awake as it is. Good luck with your studying."

Seth wrinkled his nose and grunted.

Traevyn started up the stairs. At the top of the staircase was another wall that Evie had claimed for her own. She had taken it over, forming it into a collage of pictures of just the two of them. Most of them were wedding pictures and shots from their trip to Italy, and he adored it. He stopped to admire it as he always did, and smiled.

Quietly, he moved down the corridor that had once been inhabited by his wife and her brother. He swung open the door that had been Evie's and his heart sighed in warm contentment. There, looking dwarfed in her pink bed, slept his daughter, Julia. Evie's greatest gift to him. He noticed she was wearing her pink and purple pointed princess hat they had gotten her at Disneyland. With a chuckle, he went to remove it.

"Seth put it on her," Evie's soft voice came from the doorway. "I told him she was too young to appreciate it, but he didn't care. He thought it was cute."

Traevyn smiled and took the hat off, then smoothed back his daughter's dark hair before pressing a kiss to her forehead. He studied her for a moment, marveling over her perfection. She looked just like Evie. He glanced over at his wife, standing in the doorway wearing a flannel shirt and baggy pajama pants. He grinned and went to her, wrapping his arms around her and pulling her close. "What are you doing up?" he murmured. "It's late."

Evie closed her eyes and rested her head against his chest. "You know I can't sleep when you're gone."

He tightened his arms around her and sighed. "The whole time I was gone, I just wanted to be home with you." He guided them out of the room and closed the door softly before giving Evie the kind of kiss he'd been dreaming of giving her since he'd left.

Evie moaned into the kiss and wrapped her arms around him. "I missed you," she whispered. "So did Julia."

He smiled, his heart feeling so full he thought it would burst. It had been Evie's idea to have children only a year into their marriage. Actually, she hadn't even told him she'd gone off of her birth control pills. She had just surprised him one day by telling him that he was going to be a father. He'd been apprehensive at first, right after Julia was born, still plagued by guilt that would not release its grip on him. Evie had patiently seen him through it, as she always had, and he could honestly say that he was all right now. He was whole again. All because of Evie. He owed his entire life to her.

She had given him everything he'd ever wanted and more. She'd given him a love greater than anything he could have imagined. She'd given him Seth, who he viewed as a brother and confidante. She'd given him Julia, who he loved in a way he hadn't thought he could love again. She'd given him a home and a family and a life. She had given him his life back. He was alive because of Evie.

"I love you, Evelina Whitelaw," he whispered.

Evie grinned. "How is it that I never get tired of hearing that?"

He smiled. "It's because *you* love *me* so much."

She gave a soft laugh. "I think you might be right." She raised herself on her toes to kiss him, then took his hand and began to pull him down the hallway. "Come on," she yawned. "Come to bed."

He snorted. "You're not tired, are you?" he teased. "That is not an option." He bent and lifted her into his arms, drawing a startled shriek from her.

"Traevyn!" she hissed, covering her mouth. "If you wake

her up, I'll never forgive you!" She smacked him half-heartedly on the shoulder.

He grinned devilishly and continued to carry her toward their bedroom.

"You're going to throw your back out," she grumbled.

He slid his gaze over to meet her eyes. "No one ever threw their back out from carrying a midget," he retorted.

Evie's eyes widened and she stared at him in shock. "I cannot believe you just said that. Forget your welcome home present."

He cocked an eyebrow. "You have a present for me?"

"Not anymore," she huffed.

His eyes narrowed. "Oh, you'll give me my present."

"No way!" she cried.

He let out a snarl and attacked her neck with his lips, causing her to dissolve into giggles. He carried her inside their bedroom and kicked the door shut. From inside the room, her laughter echoed throughout the house, bringing light and joy everywhere it touched.

# About the Author

If someone were to ask me what I am, it could be summed up in one, simple word: Dreamer. Ever since I was a small child my imagination has run wild. I have been telling stories for as long as I can remember, creating grand worlds in my head and going on adventures that were invisible to others around me. Am I eccentric? Yes. Am I proud of that? Absolutely.

I write about the things that inspire me, both in this world and in realms only seen with the imagination. My heroines are sassy and strong. My heroes are sometimes shy. I have an obsession with music (and musicians) and a fascination with wings. I believe true love does exist, and sometimes it is found in the strangest, most unexpected places. I also believe that family and close friends are the glue that hold people together.

Above all things, I believe in being true to yourself and seizing the day. Life is an amazing gift. Make your experience as beautiful as you possibly can.

www.ingramcontent.com/pod-product-compliance
Lightning Source LLC
Chambersburg PA
CBHW030141180626
46812CB00002B/799